# SHATTERED VOWS

P. RAYNE

## About Shattered Vows

Once upon a time, I thought I'd found my happy ever after. Until she ruined it all.

I'd been on the hunt for four long years, and I finally found her.

I planned the perfect revenge. Kidnapping Rapsody on the day she was set to marry another man and forcing her to face my wrath while trapped in the confines of my family's gothic manor.

Despite my desire to punish her, there is still an undeniable pull between us. But as the walls of the manor close in around us, we both have to confront the truth. Can we trust each other, or will my dark past consume us both?

# SHATTERED VOWS

## P. RAYNE

# Author's Note

Trigger warnings can be found on our website if you want to check them out.

PLEASE NOTE:
These warnings contain major spoilers.

https://piperrayne.com/p-rayne

# Playlist

Here's a list of songs that inspired us while we were writing the Midnight Manor series. You can follow the playlist (and us) on Spotify using the QR code below.

# I



*RAPSODY*

This is not how I imagined my wedding.

I thought I'd be marrying a man I loved. I would look at my reflection in the mirror, tearing up as I placed my veil on because it was the happiest day of my life. I wouldn't hold any frayed nerves that needed calming because I was certain of my choice and ready to take the leap of faith to my happily ever after.

Instead, I'm completely alone in a dingy room in the church, staring at my reflection, struggling to pin my veil into place. It took me long enough to secure my long blond hair into an updo. I'm not undoing all that hard work.

Alistair may not be my soulmate, but I do love him as a person and a friend. Even if I'm not madly *in* love with him, he represents something I value more than love—freedom.

When he asked me to marry him, I was honest and told him that I wasn't head over heels for him, but he insisted that was okay. He said that in time, I'd grow to love him, and I possessed qualities he wanted in a wife—respectful, supportive, and devoted.

If he knew the truth—that attending church was a way to force my mom to let me out of the apartment and have some semblance of a life—I'm not sure he'd feel that way. And if he ever knew the thoughts that race through my head late at night when I'm alone in bed, he definitely wouldn't feel that way.

Which is why I might throw up all over the ordinary white gown. What if I'm not what he wants after we're married? What if trying to conform to what he wants is more stifling than living under my mother's oppressive reign?

I squeeze my eyes shut. I'm a terrible daughter for having these thoughts after everything she gave up for me. Sucking in a deep breath, I open my eyes.

No. I can't think like that. It's normal to be scared on your wedding day. Everyone talks about cold feet. It's just that, what others experience before committing themselves to someone for the rest of their life.

Then why don't I feel scared...

Nope.

That too is something I can't think about. Not if I want to make it through today.

Today I'm going to marry an honest and righteous man who will never hurt me. Who will never lie to me. The life he'll give me is more than I ever hoped for, and I should be grateful.

"Let me do it."

I startle, glancing up through the mirror. My mother is at the door.

I turn to face her. The moment I do, the same guilt plagues me since I said yes to Alistair's proposal.

Her dark-brown eyes gaze at me with reproach and a hint of disdain.

"Thank you," I whisper, holding the veil out to her. I turn so my back is to her, watching in the mirror as she secures it in my hair.

"There's still time to change your mind," she says.

My shoulders slump. Not this again.

"Mom..." I face her and take her hands.

Tears build in her eyes as she looks at me with desperation.

"Alistair will be good to me. He's a good man."

Her sadness transforms into irritation, and she rolls her eyes. "You don't have any idea what men are capable of. Look at what—"

"I don't want to talk about that. Not today." I'm quick to cut her off, a rarity for me.

"Of course you don't. Because then you'd have to consider that you don't know everything and that you've put yourself in danger before."

"Alistair is different. He's—"

My mom arches an eyebrow. "A God-fearing man? Don't you know that some of the worst predators hide behind the façade of religion? The world is a dangerous place, Rap—Lillian. In ways you can't imagine. All I've ever done is try to protect you from the cruelty of this world. And what do I get for looking out for you?"

My chest tightens, and my throat closes up.

*No, no, no. Not now.*

I draw in a deep breath and hold it for a few seconds before I let the air stream out of my mouth slowly, then repeat the process several more times.

"Look at you, sweetheart. The stress of this wedding is clearly getting to you. How are you going to handle a marriage? Even in the happiest relationships, there are difficulties and stress." She squeezes my hands and places her cool palm on my cheek.

"I'm fine. I'll be okay."

"There's nothing I wouldn't do for you, you know that, right?"

I nod. My mother has given up so much for me through the years. For her to even bring me into the world was an emotional sacrifice I'll always be thankful for.

I'll never forget when I was younger, pouring over our photo albums. I asked her why there weren't any pictures of her when she was pregnant with me. She divulged that I had been the product of a sexual assault. The man who raped her was never caught, and when she found out she was pregnant, she wasn't sure what to do. She told me that something inside her told her I was special, so she continued with the pregnancy.

She always insists that the moment she saw me, she fell in love with me, regardless of how I came into being. But there's still a small part of me hidden in a box in a dark corner of my mind that I only take the lid off to examine every once in a while that wonders how true her words are. Every time I open that box, shame and guilt and disgust leap out at me, and I have to fight to put the lid back on. If only so I can carry on.

So yes, I know the sacrifices my mom has made for me over the years, including upending her life and moving across the country because of my screw-up four years ago. She may be entirely too overprotective, but how can I blame her after what happened to her? I always feel ungrateful and selfish when I have negative thoughts about her, so I push them away the best I can.

"I know, Mom." I place my hand over hers where it rests on my cheek.

She slips her hand out from under mine. "You're just going to marry Alistair and forget all about me." Her eyes water, and she gives me her back.

"I would never do that." I frown, unsure how to make her see that just because I'm getting married doesn't mean I'm abandoning her. "Alistair doesn't want me to work, so I'll be home all the time, the same way I am now.

You can come over whenever you want, and I'll come see you."

I have to get my driver's license, though, otherwise I'll be reliant on Seattle's bus system. That makes me a little nervous since I've never used it.

She sniffles and lets her chin fall to her chest. "It's not the same."

Sobs rack her small frame, and I rush to stand in front of her, hands on her shoulders. My chest cracks in two. "Mom... what can I do?"

I knew today would be hard, for a plethora of reasons, but watching the woman who's always looked out for me, and protected me, falling apart shreds me.

She lifts her chin, and her watery gaze meets mine, a glimmer of hope inside her dark-brown eyes. "Maybe you could talk to Alistair about having me move in with you two. That way I can look out for you when he's at work, and when you have children, I can help you."

Something in me withers at her suggestion —probably the hope that I could forge my own life somewhat separate from her. But then I feel like the worst person imaginable as I look at her, envisioning how hard she worked to raise me on her own, how the only thing she's ever wanted is what's best for me, and I can't deny her.

I nod. "Of course," I say in a hoarse voice. "I'll discuss it with him tonight after the wedding."

A pleased look crosses her face, and her tears dry up. "Wonderful. I know you'll make him see that it's best for everyone." She places a quick kiss on my cheek. "I'm going to go freshen up. All this crying you've made me do probably made my face all puffy."

She brushes past me and out the door, closing it behind her.

I sigh and walk back to the mirror. My nerves are replaced with disappointment.

No. I'm not going to ruin my wedding day.

Smoothing my hand down the front of my dress, I raise my chin, pushing away all the negativity. Even if my mother does move in with us, I'll still have more freedom, more of a life than I ever did when I lived alone with her. This is still an improvement. Plus, I get to spend the rest of my life with Alistair, an honest, dependable, predictable man. Everything will be okay. Everything will work out.

The door creaks open again. I look into the mirror, ready to greet my mom, but the smile dies on my lips. It's not her.

It's him.

The man who, despite my best efforts, never leaves my mind.

The man who is as dangerous as the lion sleeve tattoo inked on his left arm hidden under his expensive suit.

The man who is looking at me as if he's ready to murder me.

I open my mouth, but he closes the distance before I can scream. His warm, smooth palm slides over my lips. I thrash in his arms, but it's useless. He's too big, too strong.

His lips come to my ear. "Hello, Rapsody. Or should I say, Lillian?"

I haven't heard his gravelly voice in four long years. My green eyes meet his caramel ones in the mirror, and I still at the hatred resting in them.

"I've finally found you." His lips curl into a cunning smile.

The day has come.

My past has caught up to me.

Today of all days.

# 2

*KOL*

*TWO WEEKS EARLIER...*

**M**y heart jackhammers as I stare at the image on my phone.

*It's her.*

Over the years, there have been too many false alarms, so when my new private investigator, referred to me by Mr. Smith, texted me saying that he'd found Rapsody, I didn't hold out a lot of hope. Figured it was another false identification.

But there's no denying this is her. The long blond hair and emerald eyes that live in my nightmares. She still has the same innocent, almost childlike expression, as though everything in the world is shiny and new.

I run my thumb along the screen over her face. It's been a long three years of searching. It took a year for me to cave and try to track her down to seek my revenge. A year where I fell further and further into the depths of my depravity. Hunting her gave me something to do, somewhere to put my pent-up energy to appease the part of me bent on making her pay.

Once I've recovered from my shock, I glance across the dining room table at my brother Sid. He'd sit beside me if my three brothers were here, but Nero and his fiancée, Maude, are still in bed. My eldest brother, Asher, and Anabelle aren't returning from their honeymoon until tonight, so it'd be weird to sit next to Sid when it's just the two of us.

I punch out a message back.

> Give me an address where she's living.

THE RESPONSE COMES BACK IMMEDIATELY. Seattle.

> What else?

> She's going by the name Lillian Harris now.

I scowl.

"Did it personally offend you?" Sid asks from the other side of the table.

My head whips up, and I meet his gaze. "It's nothing." I set the phone face-down on the table and resume eating breakfast.

But Sid is no fool. "You going to tell me what was in that message, or do I have to fight you for that phone?"

"I'd like to see you try." I shove a piece of fruit in my mouth, narrowing my eyes.

We both know that with my special ops training, I'd have him on the floor and underneath me in seconds. But I'd be stupid to underestimate Sid. He might be the most charming of us Voss brothers, but there's more to him than the veneer he shows the world. He might be the most dangerous brother of all because he's so good at hiding his true self. The wolf tattoo peeking above the collar of his perfectly white pressed dress shirt is the only indication that there's more than meets the eye to the put-together-attorney persona he adopts.

He shrugs. "Didn't say I'd be successful. But I'd be a shit brother if I didn't try."

"It's nothing for you to worry about." I take a sip of my coffee, keeping my expression blank.

"I think you're lying. I haven't seen you with that look in your eye since—"

When he stops speaking, I look at him.

His nearly black eyes are wide. "Holy fuck, really?"

I have no interest in talking to him about Rapsody. The chair falls back toward the floor when I push away from the table, but I steady it with my hand and stalk from the room.

"You found her?" Sid calls.

Sid's footsteps echo in the wide hallway as I head from the communal part of the house toward the north wing, my private area.

"Where is she?"

"Leave it alone." I don't ease my pace or bother to look over my shoulder.

"Kol." He grips my elbow to try to pull me to a stop.

In seconds, I have him pressed up against the wall with my arm pushed against his neck. If he wasn't my brother, I'd be squeezing the life out of him. "I said leave it alone."

He glowers, eyes narrow, assessing. "At least tell me your plans."

"I don't know." I'm telling him the truth. I'm still processing that I found her.

Part of me wants to run off half-cocked, but my military training taught me not to act on emotion without a plan.

Sid studies me for a beat then nods, I guess believing me. "Do you need my help?"

I let my forearm drop, and he takes a couple deep breaths. "No."

"If you do, you'll tell me?" He meets my stare, and I nod.

Growing up, Sid was the closest to me out of my three brothers. Asher was the oldest and always trying to protect the rest of us from the wrath of our father—before attending boarding school in his teen years. I don't blame him for leaving. I did the same thing when I joined the military at eighteen, although my father had been dead for two years at that point.

And Nero was always the baby of the family, which left Sid and me to bond, stuck in the middle between the oldest and the youngest.

"Good luck." Without another word, Sid makes his way back to the dining room.

I stalk through the dim mansion to go to my wing to pack a bag, texting the pilot of my private jet that I want wheels up within the hour. I'll figure out my plan in the air.

WHEN I LAND IN SEATTLE, I purchase a run-of-the-mill minivan for cash from some guy in the outskirts of the city. A vehicle that blends in and screams suburban soccer dad of four, not billionaire ready to seek revenge.

Mr. Smith's guy sent me all the information he could find on Lillian Harris and her mother, Virginia Harris, whose name is on the lease of the crappy two-bedroom apartment they're renting.

Even without seeing Virginia, I know it's Rapsody's mother and not some aunt, cousin, or sister. My quick background check on Rapsody after we first met four years ago didn't bring up any other living relatives, and Rapsody told me it was just her and her mother.

I'm parked outside the apartment and seeing her again knocks the wind out of me as if I've been punched in the gut. It irritates me to admit that she's as beautiful as ever. Her long blonde hair hangs to her waist. It's styled in waves and swishes side to side as she walks toward a vehicle parked on the curb.

I clocked the guy when he pulled up—light-brown hair, neatly trimmed, mid to late twenties. As soon as he had his sedan in park, he picked up his phone off the console. He didn't garner much interest at first, but now that Rapsody is walking toward him, he has my full attention.

I type his license plate into my notes app. She smiles when she sees him and opens the passenger door. What kind of man doesn't get out of the car and go up to a woman's door, or at the very least get his ass out of the car and open the door for her?

Rapsody is dressed in a pair of baggy black dress pants and a light purple button-up blouse with no sleeves. Though nothing about her outfit is revealing, my cock jerks, noticing the swell of her breasts under the thin fabric. My hand tightens around my phone, annoyance with myself swelling along with my cock.

When she leans across the console and gives him a chaste kiss, my hand goes to the door handle to get out of this shitty vehicle and drag him out and introduce him to the heel of my boot.

Instead, I let them drive away and follow at a distance that won't raise suspicion. When they pull into the parking lot of a church, I bypass the entrance and circle back a few minutes later as they walk inside.

What the hell is she doing at a church?

I park in the far corner of the lot, away from their car, and wait a couple minutes to be sure they won't come back out right away. When there's no sign of them, I put on the baseball cap from the passenger seat, slide on my sunglasses, and exit the minivan.

I walk into the church, closing the doors behind me so they don't make noise. A few people are scattered through the pews, but none of them are Rapsody or the mystery guy. I figure the next logical place for them to be is meeting with someone or a group. Quiet enough not to draw attention to myself, I leave the nave of the church to seek them out.

I turn to my left first, but there are only a few locked doors and some bathrooms, so I head back in the other direction. A door behind me creaks, and I duck into a narrow hallway that leads to a storage closet. I slide into the shadows, careful not to make any noise as the sound of clicking heels grows closer and closer.

Rapsody passes the hallway not bothering to glance my way. She adjusts the waistband of her pants and presses her lips together as though she's nervous.

Once the clicking of her shoes has almost faded, I peek around the corner and see her walk into another doorway near the end of the hall. The door doesn't close fully behind her, so I cautiously make my way in that direction.

Voices murmur between two males and Rapsody. The heavy wood door restricts me from hearing, even through the crack. The odd word makes its way to me—all set, ceremony, excited.

A lull in the conversation occurs, and I hurry back to the hallway I hid in before. A couple of minutes later, Rapsody and the mystery man pass by, along with a man I assume is the pastor. I wait five minutes to be sure, then walk back to the room they were in.

The door swings open. After a quick glance around, I step inside. It's the pastor's office, filled with old tomes on the bookshelves that line each wall, and a pair of chairs sit dutifully across from the desk.

I thought I'd have to crack into the computer system. But the absence of a computer tells me either this guy is against modern technology or someone else in the church handles those affairs. Stepping over to the desk while not letting myself get too distracted to listen for footsteps, I see it all on the desk—the reason Rapsody is here with the mystery man. A marriage license.

The oxygen leaves my lungs, and I wheeze, trying to draw in more air. My eyes narrow, and my hands fist at my sides. Rage boils in my belly like a cauldron.

My gaze flicks to the leather date book on the corner of the desk. I reach for it, sure that Rapsody's big day will be in here given that there's no computer on his desk and the calendar is marked full of appointments.

There it is. The woman who disappeared on our wedding day without explanation is marrying another man.

Two weeks from today.

A Saturday.

Get ready, Rapsody, it's time you pay for your sins.

# 3

*RAPSODY*

*CURRENT DAY*

"I've finally found you."

A shiver runs up my spine at the sound of Kol's voice. A cry similar to a wounded animal erupts from my throat.

"This is how it's going to play out. You're not getting married today. You're leaving with me."

My eyes meet his in the mirror, widening in shock, and his delighted eyes shine at my distress. The vibrations from his chuckle thump on my back.

"Did you think I wouldn't find you?"

Yes. No. I tried not to think about it. About any of it.

I'm not sure what answer he wants or how I'm supposed to answer him with his hand over my mouth. My answer might piss him off, and he'll snap my neck. There's no doubt that he could do it with one easy twist of his hands.

"We're going to leave out the back way without incident. If you scream or fight me in any way, I won't hesitate to knock you out, understand?"

My heart beats like a bass drum pounding against my rib cage, and my breathing increases. I nod, tears welling in my eyes.

This time, he shows zero reaction to my distress. His burnished copper eyes hold immense resentment and fury, making my stomach curdle. What is he going to do to me once we leave the church? With a man like Kol, it won't be anything good.

"Do not scream when I remove my hand. Understood?"

I nod as much as I can with his hand covering half my face. I could risk it and scream, but who knows what he'll do if I defy him? I don't want to find out.

He slowly removes his hand and steps back. I spin to face him, my limbs trembling.

I'm sucked into a time warp, getting a full look at him instead of his reflection. His hair is still almost shaved off, his jaw sculpted to perfection. The only difference is rather than being dressed in fatigues, he wears a tailored deep blue suit that highlights his broad shoulders. He looks even more lethal in the polished attire.

After four years, my body still purrs at the sight of him, which is beyond messed up since I'm supposed to be marrying another man. And this man wants to harm me.

His gaze roams my body quickly, and his lips furrow into a frown. He yanks me by my wrist, dragging me toward the door. "Let's go."

My feet barely hit the floor as we move through the door to the hallway that runs along the side of the sanctuary, then out the side door of the church. He knows the church too well, speaking to his training.

When I realize he's taking me out of the church, I unsuccessfully try to dig my heels into the tiles.

He doesn't let up and looks over his shoulder, his eyes brimming with irritation. "Don't test me, Rapsody."

It's as if he's not talking to me. No one's called me Rapsody for years.

I stop fussing. Maybe I can escape once we reach the door or call for help when we're outside the church. I struggle to keep up. He opens the side door and leads us across the grass to a beat-up minivan backed into a parking spot.

Movement from my right draws my attention across the road. I open my mouth, but his hand lands on my neck, squeezing.

"Fuck," he mutters.

My vision blurs before I can strangle out any words. My limbs grow heavy, and my body goes limp. I think about the first time I met this man and how different I thought he was then.

*My mom had developed complications from a MRSA infection, and her doctor told me that she'd likely be hospitalized for at least two weeks.*

*It was on the second day of my mother's hospital stay that I first saw him in the cafeteria.*

*I was tired, emotionally drained, and overwhelmed. I sat quietly crying into a tissue at one of the tables in the cafeteria. She was all I'd ever known. Until she came home with me, healthy and back to her old self, there was no way I'd sleep through the night.*

*Kol walked in, and I sat up, taking notice. He was in a T-shirt with army cargo pants and boots, dark hair shorn short, and he commanded attention as though it was owed to him. A God-given right.*

*I was eighteen and sheltered—homeschooled. My mom had never allowed me to have a job or leave the house without her, and even then, it was a rarity. In the couple of days I'd been left alone, it was overwhelming. I shrank back from anyone I encountered, anxiety washing over me.*

*I wasn't the only one who noticed Kol. Everyone's head turned in his direction, but most diverted their eyes right away from his intimidating presence. Not me, though. I couldn't take my eyes off the man.*

*He ordered and sat on his own, eating farther down the same row as me.*

*He turned in my direction, and I swung my gaze down to my food, cheeks heated.*

*After almost getting caught staring, I forced myself not to look in his direction again. There was no point. Once my mother felt better, she would never allow me to date anyone, let alone him. He was clearly older than me by at least a decade. My mother would never approve of me spending time with him. She didn't even allow me to walk to the corner store on my own.*

*I was used to my mother's overprotectiveness. She was always going on about the dangers of the world and how you can't trust anyone. After seeing the nightly news at the age of ten, I knew she was right. School shootings, homelessness, mental health issues, political corruption, endless wars—the world overflowed with evil.*

*Usually, my lack of freedom didn't bother me, but for the past year, I'd felt antsy, as if there was more for me out there than staying within the walls of our two-bedroom apartment.*

*While the past two days on my own had been overwhelming and downright scary, the simple freedom of calling a taxi and taking it on my own to the hospital, heck, even just going down to the cafeteria, felt like a small victory. But those thoughts left me feeling guilty because the only reason I was experiencing a little bit of freedom was because my mom was ill.*

*Maybe once my mom was better, we could discuss the possibility of giving me some more independence. That's if she got better...*

*Tears pooled in my eyes as I worried again about the possibility that she might not improve. The doctor had made it clear that her recovery wasn't a given at this point. I judged myself for thinking about my own life while my mother's hung on a thread. She had to get better. She just had to.*

*I stood, grabbing the tray to dispose of the garbage. My vision concentrated on my tray as I passed Kol's table, and I silently repeated to myself not to look at him. But an urge came over me as I approached, and I just had to take one last look. But in doing so, I didn't see the doctor cutting through the aisle in the opposite direction. It was too late to prepare for when he passed in front of me, causing me to come to a sudden stop. The empty water bottle resting on my tray tipped over and rolled off.*

*Right over to the base of Kol's table.*

*Having no choice, I swallowed and met his gaze. Rushing over, I bent to pick up the piece of plastic.*

*"Sorry." My voice was hardly audible, and I felt my face heat, knowing how beet red I most likely was.*

*I set the water bottle on my tray, and the damn thing tipped over a second time, rolling off. His hand caught it right before it hit the floor.*

*I straightened up and locked eyes with him. He held the water bottle out to me, and at that moment, I knew. I knew that this man's face would be etched into my memory forever. That this moment would play over and over in my head.*

*What I didn't know at the time was that our chance meeting would go from us chatting for a few minutes, to him inviting me to sit down, to the two of us meeting again the next day when I came down to the cafeteria. Soon when I told my mom I was going home for the evening, I was really spending my nights with Kol, traipsing around Atlanta and falling in love with him. The biggest surprise was him asking me to marry him before he left for his final deployment.*

*It happened fast and felt like a whirlwind, a magical sign of fate.*

*But just as my mother had taught me, the world was filled with cruel individuals.*

*It was all a lie.*

The mechanical hum of something is the first sound my mind registers when I wake up. The second is the slight jostling of the world underneath me.

Am I in a vehicle? Where am I?

My eyes blink open, and it takes a moment to register the softness under me. I'm on a bed in some strange room, based on the pattern of the blanket my cheek is plastered to and the small nightstand to my left.

Something pulls on my hair, and I reach back and feel rough fabric. I pull out my veil. and the nightmare of what happened rushes back to my mind.

I startle and roll over, bolting into a sitting position.

"Good, you're awake."

My head whips in the direction of Kol's voice. He sits in a chair in the corner of the room.

I don't know how long I've been out, but my mother must be freaking out. I can't imagine her panic when she returned to the room I was in, only to find it empty.

And what about Alistair? He's going to think I'm some runaway bride.

"Where are we?"

"Probably thirty-five thousand feet above Idaho."

"What?" I shriek, looking right and left.

My chest tightens, restricting my airflow.

*No, no, no.*

I force myself to inhale a deep, steadying breath and hold it for a moment before releasing the air through my nose. I do it again a few more times, trying to calm myself.

"I've never flown before." Why am I even bothering to tell him that? He just kidnapped me. He definitely doesn't care that I feel uneasy being airborne.

He frowns, and a line creases on his forehead as if I'm lying. "How'd you move from Atlanta to outside Seattle?"

"We drove. My mom won't fly." I don't want to discuss that move and why we had to do it in the first place.

I shuffle to the edge of the bed and glance out the small plane window. Seeing the clouds below us makes my stomach swoop as if I jumped from the plane.

Kol remains quiet, but I feel his eyes on me.

I shut my eyes to calm my nerves and get my emotions under control. It's unbelievable I'm in this confined space with Kol. How many times did I daydream about being with him again? How many times did I wonder what he thought when I didn't show up at city hall to marry him? And now he's here.

I have no idea how he's going to punish me.

"Where are we going?" I ask, not turning around.

"You'll see." I can hear the smirk in his voice.

He's enjoying making me off-kilter. He wants to scare me.

If I give him what he wants and cower to his needs, maybe he'll let me go? No, probably not. He'll probably relish his revenge even more.

Maybe I'm best to not show him how deeply afraid I am but rather to act unaffected. Maybe if he doesn't get the reaction he desires, he'll tire of me.

My eyes snap open and stare at the clouds again, but this time I don't balk. I turn and meet his gaze. "Great, tell me when we get there. I'm going to take a nap."

I step over to the bed, pull back the covers, and slide under the blankets, wedding dress and all. I purposely turn my back on him. But I don't fall asleep. I lie with my eyes closed and even out my breathing to pretend. After a while, I hear him rise from the chair and walk out of the room. It's only then that I can take a full breath.

Rolling over, I stare at the ceiling of the plane. How am I ever going to get away from this man?

# 4



We land somewhere in the south. I recognize the early June heat and the first hints of humidity from when I lived in Georgia. The road signs are in English as Kol speeds his sports car down the road, so we're not in Mexico. The ever-present summer humidity is something I didn't miss when we moved to the Pacific Northwest.

I don't bother asking where we are or where we're going. One, he'll never tell me. And two, Kol will think I care, and I'm doing my best to make him think I *don't* care. Even though the questions are pressed against the back of my lips and dying to be released.

Eventually, he turns off the highway onto a country road, then through a cute small town with shops and cafés. He takes a winding road up a hill, slowing his speed in front of two iron gates.

I swallow hard. It's not like I had a vision of where we were headed, but these gates make me fear that wherever we are, it's going to be harder to escape than just sneaking out the fire escape of a building.

Kol presses a code into the pad key on his side, and the gates creak open.

Damn it. I should've paid attention to the code he used.

He eases the car through the gates, and we continue on a winding road lined with tall trees that must have been here for decades if not centuries.

"Welcome to Midnight Manor," Kol says.

The name sounds ominous. As the trees clear, a massive, sprawling mansion comes into view, and Midnight Manor seems aptly named. There is nothing bright and sunshiny about this place. It's dark and intimidating. And huge—so huge.

I don't know anything about architecture, but I'd bet my safety that this place is a Gothic manor. Even the dark gray stone sucks up the sunlight as though no light is welcome here. At each end of the house is a spire that rises up, up, up.

Kol parks in the circular drive and climbs out, rounding the front of his car to my side. My nerves hit me full force now that we've arrived where he intends to keep me hidden, and my bravado falters. Questions race through my mind. What are we doing here? Is this his home? Why did he bring me here? I work to calm my breathing as he wrenches the car door open and yanks me out with his hand on my upper arm. In seconds, he's leading me toward the massive front door, never taking his hand off me.

I glance up to find stone gargoyles perched along the top of the manor. I wish this was some movie where I could call to them for help, and they would fly me out of here so I don't have to endure what Kol has planned for me. My vision quickly shifts with so much of the mansion to see. The stained-glass window over the towering door draws me in, and I admire the beauty of the piece mixed into the dark menacing monstrosity. If only I could sit in front of it, painting the intricate work of art. But Kol pushes open the door, leading me inside, and that thought withers and dies.

The place seems even more massive now that we're inside. My eyes are unable to focus on one thing, continuously drawn to ornate pieces of furniture. It resembles what I imagine European palaces that are hundreds of years old look like. Kol doesn't say anything as he drags me through room after room. How can he so easily dismiss this radiance?

We don't come upon anyone, and even if we did, I'm unsure I'd ask them for help anyway. From how well he's navigating the sheer size of the manor, this must be where Kol lives. We're moving so fast that if I was able to escape, I'm not sure I'd find my way out.

Every room is dimly lit as though the early evening sun isn't shining brightly outside. The hallways are wide, and the wall sconces flicker with minimal light that does nothing to hide the shadows littering the walls, the ceiling, and the stone floor.

Eventually we arrive at a long hallway with a high, pointed-arch ceiling, and on the left are large archways with stained glass in them, just as alluring as the window that adorned the front door. Most of the glass art depicts landscapes or an array of colorful shapes. The center arch is different. It's a massive lion, facing forward with an intense stare. I divert my eyes, tensing as if its eyes are on me. Kol doesn't stop, and it feels as if the lion is watching, a predator lying in the fields until it's time to pounce.

"This is my wing," Kol says, drawing my attention away from the captivating stained glass. "There's no point in screaming for help. No one will hear you. And if by chance you do see a member of the staff, know that they are loyal to the Voss family."

I grit my teeth, feeling stifled and suffocated. I'm never escaping Kol.

"What do you plan to do to me?" I ask when we reach the end of the lengthy hallway and he stops us in front of a closed door.

"Whatever I want." His words are sinister.

A shiver runs up my spine, but I'm unsure if it's because of the dark promise in his voice or from fear. Hopefully the latter, otherwise there is something very, very wrong with the way my body reacts to him.

Kol pushes a hand into his pocket and produces an old skeleton key, which he puts into the keyhole of the door. The audible click of the lock echoes down the hallway as he twists the key, unlocking the door. The sound seems to signify death... my death.

He swings the door open and pushes me inside. "Walk."

A set of stairs spirals up, and panic makes my heartbeat race as I consider where it leads.

"Go." Kol's voice is at my back.

I lift the skirt of my wedding gown at the front, taking the first step with his breath at my neck. My dress slips out of my grasp, and I stumble over the hem a few times, but Kol doesn't offer any assistance. Why would he? He loathes me and is hell-bent on paying me back for embarrassing him at the altar years ago. The yearning for my mom and Alistair hits me hard, and I stifle a sob.

The muscles in my thighs burn by the time I reach the top. I'm greeted by another thick wooden door with ornate carvings on it. Without a word, Kol brushes past me and inserts the same key into the lock before pushing the door open. We're at the top of one of the spires I spied from outside.

He waves me forward, and I swallow hard while my chest grows even tighter, as though someone keeps tightening and tightening a band around it.

Slowly, I step inside and look around. It's a circular room with a bed on one wall be-tween two of the arched windows and the usual bedroom dresser and furnishings scattered throughout. A large ornate carpet rests under the bed, and a small sofa and two chairs sit in front of a large, open fireplace. On the wall to the right of the bed is a set of doors that appears to lead out to a balcony.

Kol motions to a door on the left that is on the only wall built into the room. "Bathroom."

He says it as though there are no other bathrooms in this monstrous house for me to use. My stomach drops at the realization that this is where he plans to keep me. I've traded one prison for another, only this one will be worse than living with an overprotective mother because I have a feeling I'm to stay here by myself.

I whip around to face him. "You're going to keep me up here like a prisoner?" My throat closes.

"Only until I decide what to do with you."

I try to suck oxygen into my lungs, but my mouth dries, and I gasp from the squeezing of my chest. My heart races as though it's building up into a crescendo and soon will stop completely. I clutch at the fabric at the front of my dress, as if that will signal to my body and my racing thoughts to let me get air into my lungs.

I try again, but it's just another wheeze.

My eyes water as Kol glares. "What the hell is wrong with you?"

I crumple to my knees, hitting the hardwood, bent over, hands splayed on the floor, my back arching as my chest heaves, feeling strangled from the air. I do my best to calm my racing heart, my fear and anxiety rising about being trapped like one of those fairy-tale princesses until he decides to let me go or I free myself. Kol crouches beside me. For a moment, I take his reaction for kindness.

"Is this some kind of ploy to get me to let down my guard? If so, it's a waste of time."

I ignore his comment, trying to get my breathing under control as the air wheezes in and out of my lungs, but it's not working. More panic flares inside me, and my lungs constrict further. My eyesight blurs, and I clutch at my throat with one hand.

I'm going to die. In a dress I planned to wed another man in with the man I originally wanted to marry right by my side.

Kol's large hand falls to my back. "Breathe. Just calm down and breathe."

Heat from his paw-like hand seeps through my dress, and my body starts to calm. For the first time in minutes, a small amount of air fills my lungs, and my mind clears from the sheer panic. I concentrate on the feel of his hand rubbing up and down my back and use it as a distraction to even my breathing and allow my heart rate to slow.

After a minute or two, I sit back on my heels, my breathing near normal. I scrub at the tears and black marks on my hands tell me mascara has streaked down my face.

Kol shifts to rest in front of me. If I didn't know better, I'd think the expression on his face was of concern. "Does that happen often?"

He doesn't bother to ask what exactly happened. He's clearly figured out I had a panic attack.

"Sometimes." I push up off the floor to stand.

His hand wraps around my arm, and I rip it out of his hold. He doesn't need to know that I never had a panic attack until after our supposed wedding day. I straighten and meet his scowl.

"I'll go get you something to change into." He turns and walks toward the door, closing it behind him.

Just as I think he's being nice, the click of the lock falling into place reminds me that I'm not here because he was desperate to have me.

Once alone, I spring into action. There has to be a way to get out of here besides that door. First, I check the bathroom—which is beautiful with a large tub and separate walk-in shower—but sadly, no exit. I check the rest of the room for any breaks in the stone on the walls or the floor that might signify a secret passage.

This place is clearly old, and aren't secret bookshelves that take you to a hidden hallway a thing in old mansions like this one?

My shoulders sink, not finding any way to secretly escape. Then my eyes land on the set of double doors. I hurry over and push them open.

I was right about a balcony. It wraps around the entire spire. I step up to the edge and stand on the bottom of the thick stone railing to look for a way down, but I'm stunned by the gorgeous view of the expansive surroundings that must belong to the manor. Green grass covers the rolling landscape, and the edge of what appears to be a large pond sits way off in the distance.

I walk to both ends of the balcony, but there are no stairs or anything else that might allow me to free myself, and we're way too high for me to jump to safety. I stomp my heel like a frustrated child, but the impact with the stone reverberates up my leg, and I cringe from the pain sprawling from my foot to my hip. Never do that again.

I make my way back into the room, and Kol stands in the middle of the room with a crooked smirk. As if it's humorous to him that I'm trying to find a way out, away from him.

"You're wasting your time." He tosses a folded set of clothes onto the bed. "I brought you some of Anabelle's clothes. You look like you're probably about the same size, so they should fit. Get out of that fucking dress. It's ugly as shit."

He says it as if he doesn't think I picked this dress. But how does he know that my mother refused to allow me to go around to all the wedding shops, trying on gowns, and instead ordered me one off the internet?

"I'll get you clothes tomorrow." He rubs his palm over his shaved head.

Who is this Anabelle? I hate the way my stomach turns with jealousy at the thought because I have bigger things to worry about. Is she his girlfriend or, God forbid, his wife? Is that why I'm being sequestered up here? To hide me like some secret mistress?

"Why do I need my own set of clothes? How

long do you plan to keep me here?" I bite my bottom lip.

He scoffs, his face void of emotion except for maybe annoyance. "For as long as I like." Then he turns and heads toward the door. "I'll bring you some food in a bit."

He walks out the door, the lock clicking behind him. Leaving me alone in this godforsaken tower where I'll be kept from the world until he sees fit to either release me or kill me. My throat closes, my nose tickles, and tears spring up again. The world I knew might have been a small one, but it was bigger than one measly room.

# 5

I trudge down the steps of the tower and enter my bedroom across the hallway.

It's not lost on me that I put Rapsody exactly where I did so that she'd be close to me.

"Fuck!" I shout, wishing I had longer hair so I could run my hands through it.

For an ex-military man who took the time to have a perfect plan, I sure am fucked. Because now that she's here, I don't know what to do with Rapsody. I hadn't really thought that far ahead. All I saw was red when I found out she was marrying another man. I wanted to punish her, and the best way to do that was to stop her from marrying the man she chose over me. She left me high and dry on the day we were to be wed, but she was dressed in her gown, waiting to walk down the aisle to a man who would never satisfy her.

I shake my head. Looking back, all those years ago, I don't understand what the hell made me ask her to marry me so quickly. I knew it was my last deployment, and that after, I'd be back on US soil. I was leaving the military to return to Midnight Manor and take my place within the family business at Voss Enterprises. I'd bailed on my family and enlisted the minute I turned eighteen in an effort to leave my past behind me, not realizing that once pain has its claws in you, it follows you anywhere and everywhere.

Asking Rapsody to marry me in the first place was a mistake. I'm unable to have a normal relationship. Not only am I fucked in the head from my upbringing, but I don't deserve to have happiness after the things I've done over my lifetime.

Pacing, I rub my palm over my shaved head, trying to clear my head of emotions and think strategically like my training taught me.

The fact I wanted to marry her so quickly has no bearing now. She's the one who did me wrong. She made a vow and didn't live up to it. She made me feel like a fool for allowing myself to think for even one moment that a woman like her could love someone like me. I know what and who I am, and she pretended to be someone she isn't. She deserves to be punished for her bait-and-switch move.

So I'll punish her by keeping her from her fiancé long enough that he moves on, and she loses the best thing to come into her life. Just like I did.

SWEAT FALLS off my skin and onto the wooden floor, my biceps burning from the last of my push-ups, when there's a knock on the door. I drag myself off the floor and move steadily toward the door.

My body feels as if I'm hungover because I slept like shit last night. Rapsody refused to eat the meal I brought to her, saying she didn't trust me not to have poisoned it.

I whip open my door, and Sid stands on the other side. He pushes past me, his shoulder brushing mine, without waiting for an invitation to enter my room.

"What the fuck were you thinking?" he says in a deceptively calm voice.

I turn to face him and blow out a breath, hands on my hips. "What are you talking about?" Since I am about done with my workout, I walk to the en suite bathroom.

He follows me. "Who came back with you yesterday?"

I push down my athletic shorts until they fall on the floor and turn on the water in the shower. "I don't know what you're talking about."

My brother doesn't even blink at my nakedness. "Security said you came through the gates with someone."

I look over my shoulder at him. "You keeping tabs on me, little brother?" Reaching in, I find the water is hot and step inside the large walk-in shower. "Am I not allowed guests in my own home?"

Sid's hands fist at his sides. "I saw the tapes. The woman was Rapsody."

I shrug, grabbing the bar of soap. "Maybe I have one of those fascinations with fucking women who look like her?"

"We both know you don't do that. And she was in a fucking wedding dress!" His voice grows louder.

I'm taken aback, because Obsidian doesn't often lose his cool. It doesn't go with the calm, cool, collected lawyer thing he portrays, always hiding what's really lying beneath his suit.

I knew my brothers would find out I'd kidnapped Rapsody and brought her here. We have security everywhere. But I hoped I could keep it from them longer.

"She was supposed to get married yesterday." I don't allow any emotion to creep into my voice as I rub the bar of soap over my body, lest he know how much it gets under my skin to think of her marrying another man.

"Supposed to?"

I look through the glass while I wash my cock, and he lifts a brow.

"She didn't make it to the ceremony." I shrug, acting unaffected and continuing to wash my body.

Sid steps closer to the glass barrier that separates us. "Did she leave the church of her own free will?"

I wonder if our parents knew how well the name Obsidian would suit him. His eyes are as black as coal, but beyond that, a darkness shines through them when he allows it.

"Depends on your definition of free will. Do

you mean did she walk out of that church on her own two feet? Then yes."

His dark eyes widen, and he laces his fingers together on top of his head and stares at me. "Are you fucking crazy? I knew what went down fucked you up, but I thought you had more sense than this."

"I know what I'm doing."

*I don't know what the fuck I'm doing.*

I set down the bar of soap and step under the spray to rinse off the bubbles. By the time I'm done, Sid is gone.

Whatever. I have bigger issues to deal with than what one of my brothers thinks. I have to figure out what I'm going to do with Rapsody. I can't keep her here forever, but my pride demands that she pay for so callously toying with my emotions. I allowed myself to be vulnerable with her, and she took a knife to my kidneys the first chance she got. I'll never make that mistake twice.

Once I'm dressed, I instruct our house manager, Marcel, to bring me two dishes for breakfast since I've already missed breakfast in the dining room with my brothers. He doesn't inquire as to why I need two servings because he's smart enough not to want to know the answer.

When he drops them off, I instruct him to order women's clothing to be delivered. I give him an idea of what items I'm looking for, and her sizing, and tell him I want it all here by tonight. Marcel's brows crinkle, but he doesn't ask any questions.

I shovel down my breakfast in a couple of minutes. More than a decade in the armed forces means I usually don't linger over my meals unless I'm seated at a table with other people. When I'm finished, I bring Rapsody's breakfast to the top of the tower.

After a quick knock, I use the key and unlock the door to the bedroom. Rapsody is lying on her side in bed, her back facing me. She doesn't speak, doesn't move. I walk over to her side of the bed. She's staring aimlessly at the wall and the arched window.

I set the tray on the night table next to her. "Eat your breakfast."

She mumbles a word, barely blinking as her eyes stare straight ahead. Her eyes are red-rimmed, bloodshot, and puffy with gray bags underneath. I give her a withering glare, but she doesn't see it because she doesn't bother to even flick her gaze in my direction.

"We're not playing the game from yesterday. Eat, Rapsody." I set my hands on my hips, waiting for something, anything from her. I'll take her fighting me.

But she gives me nothing.

"Fine. Fucking starve!" I wrench the tray up, causing everything on it to clatter and slosh.

I prowl out of the room, steadying the tray on my hand to lock the door behind me. My mind is too filled with the shit position I put myself in as I head from the north wing to the communal part of the house in the middle that connects all four wings—one for each of us Voss brothers—and make my way to the kitchen. I'm not going back to my bedroom. I want no reminders of Rapsody and her fucking stubbornness.

Mrs. Potter is in the kitchen, along with the chef and sous chef, when I walk in, and I drop the tray, allowing it to crash onto the marble countertop. "See to it that this gets disposed of."

I circle on my heels and storm out of the room in case they want to ask me any questions as to why I wanted two plates this morning. I satisfy my sexual appetite in other places, so I'm sure they were all surprised I had a guest here. Though Mrs. Potter probably sensed my obvious mood and wouldn't pry.

I'm heading down the long hallway adjacent to the dining room when my eldest brother, Asher, walks toward me. I guess he and his new wife, Anabelle, have returned from their honeymoon. I would've thought he'd still be floating in apparent wedded bliss, but he wears his normal scowl and his hands are fisted at his sides. Some of his curls have fallen over his forehead, which makes him appear unkempt. Not like him at all. That, coupled with the athletic pants and white T-shirt, makes him appear nothing like the man who sits at the helm of our family company, Voss Enterprises.

"Wait! What is going on?" Anabelle says, trailing behind my brother.

If it were my youngest brother Nero's fiancée, Maude, it would have felt like cat claws scratching down the inside of my brain.

"Asher! Wait! Why did you rush out of the bedroom?" Anabelle finally reaches him, placing her hand on his forearm.

I stop walking toward Asher and heave out a sigh because his eyes are locked on me. I'm a smart man, so I figure I know why he crawled out of bed and left his new wife.

Sid is a fucking snitch.

Asher stops inches from me, his hand with the bear tattoo clenched into a fist, and he launches it forward, punching me in the stomach. "What the actual fuck, Kol?"

Anabelle yelps, and her hands fly up to her mouth.

I let him get in his shot because we both know I could snap his neck in two seconds if

I really wanted to. But I've brought trouble to his doorstep, so I'll allow one punch.

"What were you thinking?" Asher growls.

That's the question, isn't it? I wish I knew the answer.

"Ash, what's going on?" Anabella asks, stepping between us and glancing back and forth.

Asher ignores her, which is a testament to how pissed he is. Anabelle has softened my brother... well, toward her. No one else has been on the receiving end of the new Asher. "You kidnapped Rapsody and brought her here?"

Anabelle's eyes widen, and her head snaps up to look at me. "You kidnapped someone?"

When I don't answer, her gaze shoots to Asher.

He holds his hands up in front of himself. "Don't ask me." He pins me with his big-brother stare.

He wants answers as to my plans for Rapsody, and I have no idea how to answer. But I need to figure it out. And soon.

"You need to release her. Immediately," Asher demands, his voice bouncing off the walls.

"Not happening."

He swallows, but his anger doesn't lessen like he wants.

"Kol, you can't keep a woman captive. Surely you know that." Anabelle's blue eyes are filled with concern. Whether for me or Rapsody, who knows?

My vision falls to Anabelle's, and I arch an eyebrow. "Is it that different from what Asher did with you?"

Her face reddens, and her gaze falls to the floor.

Asher puffs out his chest and steps toward me. "Careful the way you talk to my wife, asshole." Then he squeezes Anabelle's shoulder. "Why don't you go back to our bedroom? I'll be right behind you."

She nods and glances at me for a beat with unsure eyes. Fuck, I hate the way that makes my guilt rise to the surface. Everything is so much easier when you just don't give a shit.

Asher waits until she's a distance away, watching her over his shoulder, like a bear protecting its cub. Once she disappears from view, he whips his head back toward me with the lethal gaze I'm familiar with. "You will apologize to Anabelle the next time you see her."

I nod begrudgingly. Begrudging not because I didn't already plan to apologize, but because Asher thinks I'm doing it because of his directive.

"You've been looking for years, so I'm not surprised you finally tracked her down, but I assumed it was so you could have it out with her and get answers to why she didn't show up to your wedding, not so you could kidnap her."

"I thought the same until I saw her ready to marry another man. Then..."

His lips purse, and his arms cross as if it's not a good enough excuse for what I did.

"Are you telling me that if Anabelle ditched you, and you found out she was marrying someone else, you wouldn't take matters into your own hands?" I ask.

He doesn't bother answering, but the way his mouth tightens, it's clear that I've struck a nerve. His tough alpha exterior slightly lessens. "What is your plan for Rapsody?"

"I don't know."

He inches closer. "Well, you better figure it out and fucking soon, because if I had to guess, her picture is going to be all over the fucking news and internet, if it's not already. You know how the media loves when a young, beautiful blonde girl is missing."

He's right, of course. Asher's one of those rare breeds with the ability to think before he acts. Even if it doesn't make national news, her disappearance will make the rounds in the Seattle area.

"I'll take care of it."

"You better. Otherwise, I will." He pokes me in the chest with his finger, and I tamp down the urge to grab it and break it.

Then he turns on his heel and heads back to his bedroom and his pretty little wife.

What a nice fucking life for him.

# 6



Two days pass, and all I've done is lie in bed and mourn the life I've lost, wondering whether I'll ever be allowed to return to it. I was finally going to be able to see more of the world by marrying Alistair. Sure, it would never be a fast-paced, exciting life, but I wouldn't be stuck in a tower.

God, Alistair. What must he be thinking? That I just ran off on him, that's what.

He's the second man I've left at the altar, and for some reason, picturing Alistair waiting there, unknowing and innocent as to why I wasn't showing, feels less like a punch to the gut compared to the agony I felt when it was Kol I pictured.

No part of me wants to explore what fucked-up reason explains that. All I know is that with Kol, I mourned for months—years really. Alistair has only been a brief thought when I'm not worrying about how long Kol plans to keep me sequestered here or what he might ultimately do to me.

The faint sound of footsteps on the stairs registers before a key is inserted into the lock. The door swings open, and like every time he's visited me, I don't face him. Instead, I keep gazing out the glass doors that lead to the outside and freedom. Freedom I'll never get during my lifetime.

Kol probably thinks I'm being difficult just to piss him off, and maybe a part of it is payback for leaving me here, but it pains me to look at him. He reminds me of what I thought I'd found once upon a time, only to find out it was all a lie—something that's been made even more clear to me since he kidnapped me from my own wedding.

Any romanticized version of him that still lingered in my head has been destroyed.

I don't know this man. I never did.

Kol's strong legs clad in jeans come into view when he comes to stand beside the bed. "Get up."

I don't blink, just stare blankly ahead.

"Get up, Rapsody. You need to shower and get dressed and then eat."

Again, I ignore him.

A growl rips out his throat. I really shouldn't enjoy making him angry, but he's leaving me here with too many unknowns. "Rapsody, either you get up on your own, or I will drag you into the bathroom myself, strip you, wash you, and force-feed you. The choice is yours."

I glance at him for a second then back at the window.

Kol grabs the edge of the blanket, tearing it off me. He bends and lifts me up and over his shoulder like a fireman saving a victim.

"Put me down!" I kick my legs and pound my closed fists against his back, but his stride doesn't break.

Even though I'm unsuccessful, it feels good to fight back for once. My entire life, I've done what my mother asked of me even if I didn't want to. I've quietly shoved down my wants and needs. Even with Alistair, I always went along with whatever he wanted, no questions asked—the dutiful girlfriend and then fiancée.

For all of my effort, Kol doesn't react. He sets me down, my feet landing on the tile floor.

He reaches for the hem of my shirt, and I smack his hand. "I'll do it myself."

"Then do it." A predatory light gleams in his eyes.

"Get out. I'll shower."

He studies me for a moment as though he's deciding whether or not he can believe me.

I'm serious, though. No man has ever seen me naked. The most Alistair and I did was share some chaste kisses, and while things went further with Kol, we never went far enough to be naked in front of each other. Because we were getting married so quickly, we decided to wait until our wedding night —a night that never came.

"Fine. I'm going to get you something to eat. When I get back, you better be showered and dressed."

I narrow my eyes, and he shows zero reaction before he leaves the bathroom. As soon as he's over the threshold, I slam the door shut and flip the lock on the door. It's not as if that puny door lock could keep Kol out, but it's the only peace of mind I can get at the moment.

I undress and step into the shower, the hot water feeling heavenly against my body. It's been days since I showered, so I take my time. When I finish, I feel less defeated for some reason. I towel off and realize I don't have any clean clothes in the bathroom, so I wrap the towel around myself, securing it as tightly as possible, and unlock and open the door to the bedroom, peeking out to make sure Kol hasn't returned.

Kol brought me a bunch of clothes the other day and put them in the dresser and the armoire. I never bothered to look if they're even my size.

I open the drawers, revealing underwear, socks, bras, T-shirts, leggings, shorts, and pajamas. A few pairs of jeans are snug in another drawer. I walk over to the armoire and swing open the doors to find casual dresses, summer blouses, and dress pants.

Between the dresser and the armoire, there's a consistent color—purple. My favorite color and something I shared with Kol four years ago. There's no way it's a coincidence, but it spurs me to worry why he's being so kind?

I slide a few of the hangers to look at every item. Everything is expensive and designer. Well above anything my mom and I could ever afford. The fabrics feel luxurious, and honestly, I'm surprised he'd even bother spending this kind of money on me, though money is not a factor for him.

I hear the key in the lock, and my head whips in that direction. Fear plagues me as I whirl around clad only in a towel. Kol stands on the threshold holding a tray of food. His gaze quickly skates up and down my body. As if his eyes alone could ramp up my body temperature, I grow hotter and hotter as he drinks me in.

The towel doesn't reveal much, but it's more than any man, including him, has ever seen. I imagined that the first time a man saw me near-naked, there would be love or at the very least lust in his eyes. But Kol's eyes narrow as if I'm tricking him by standing here with terry cloth wrapped around me.

"I didn't have any clothes in the bathroom." My voice is weak.

When he doesn't say anything, I walk back to the dresser and quickly grab socks, underwear, and a bra. Not wanting to bend over, I squat to the lower drawers to get a pair of leggings and a T-shirt. I stand and make my way into the bathroom, but when I go to close the door, Kol is still watching me, only this time there's a hint of something else in his gaze. Something that makes my blood heat along with my skin.

I slam the door and rest my back against the wood until I catch my breath.

There's no way I saw what I thought I did in Kol's gaze. He hates me. He kidnapped me. But what I saw was a glimpse of the military man I met at the hospital, not the asshole billionaire who ruined my wedding to Alistair.

But I know better than anyone how good Kol is at hiding the truth. This is probably just another one of his games. And I refuse to fall for it.

～

AFTER I DRESS, I eat the breakfast Kol brought to the room and set on the small round table in the living room section for me. I'm so famished I finish every little morsel. Kol sits across from me, relaxed on the sofa, his ankle resting on his knee, watching me eat and not speaking a word. Suits me fine, but I can't help but wonder what's going through his head.

He doesn't wait long to tell me what he's thinking. After I set my cutlery down on the tray, he leans forward and pushes the tray to the other side of the table. "You need to call your mother."

I sit up straight in my chair. "Really?" My eyes widen as hope blooms in my chest. He's going to let me go?

"You'll tell her you chose to leave and that you're safe. That you're tired of her controlling you. That you had second thoughts about marrying the prick. And that you ran away."

I slump down in my chair, frowning because he snuffed out all my hope. I cross my arms. "Why would I do that?"

"If you don't, they become my problem. And I don't like problems. I tend to make them disappear." He spears me with his whiskey eyes.

My frown indents further because he's not joking, and a ripple of fear traces up my spine like a million red ants crawling along my skin. "I'm sure either she or Alistair has already called the police."

His lips tighten when I mention Alistair by name. "Neither have. There are no reports about you missing."

My forehead creases. Why wouldn't my mother have called the police by now? I disappeared from my own wedding, for God's sake. And Alistair? Does he assume I left on my own?

Kol reaches into the pocket of his jeans and pulls out a small black phone, tossing it on the table. A burner phone, if I had to guess. It's not as though I've ever seen one in real life, but I've watched enough TV. I've never even had my own cell phone. Didn't need one. There was no one to call, and I barely left the house.

"Make it believable. If I catch you trying to use code words or slip her a message, you aren't going to like what happens."

My hands tremble picking up the phone. "What if I can't do it? What if she doesn't believe me?"

"Figure it out."

Anger rises in my belly until I'm almost choking. "It's not that easy. She's going to be upset."

He tsks and tilts his head, a cruel smile tilting his full lips. "We both know you have no problem lying, no problem hurting someone you profess to care about. Do it."

I press my lips together to stop them from trembling and swallow hard, then I open the phone and dial my mother's number. Tears build in my eyes as I bring the phone to my ear.

It rings only once before she picks it up.

"Hello?" Her voice sounds worried and stressed. She's always been an anxious person. I assumed her anxiety came from what happened to her.

"Mom, it's me." My voice comes out garbled, and I swallow back my tears.

"Rapsody! Oh, thank God. Where are you? Are you okay?"

"I...I can't tell you where I am. But I'm fine." The words rush out of my mouth before I'm inclined to let the truth spill from my lips.

"What do you mean you can't tell me? You disappeared from your own wedding! I've been worried sick. Now tell me where you are." Her tone turns more rigid and demanding.

"I'm not going to tell you. I had to get away for a bit. I...I didn't want to marry Alistair." I squeeze my eyes shut. "I didn't know what to do, so I took off. I just need to be on my own for a while." A single tear slips down my cheek.

"Rapsody, you can't be out there in the world on your own! It's dangerous!"

I glance at Kol. She has no idea the danger I'm in, and truthfully, neither do I. "I'll be okay."

"No, you won't. Now stop with this right now, and tell me where you are so I can come get you."

I shake my head, though she can't see me. "No, Mom. I can't."

She pauses, and my anxiety ramps up with her angry on the phone and Kol angry right in front of me. "Can't or won't?"

I look away from Kol. "Won't. I'm tired of being controlled and being sheltered by you. I want to live my own life, one of my own choosing. And if I make mistakes, then so be it, but they'll be my mistakes, and I'll own them. I'm sorry I couldn't find another way to tell you before making a mess of things, but this is how it has to be for now. Please tell Alistair I'm sorry for dragging him into all of this. I didn't mean to hurt him."

The words spill from my lips so easily, and it's as if someone lifted fifty pounds off my shoulders. My words are all truths that I've been holding inside me, pushing down for years—practically most of my life—but I've never been brave enough to say them until Kol forced my hand.

"I've only ever loved you. You're my daughter, my everything!" Her words come out strangled on a cry.

"I just need some space. I'll be in touch soon." I don't know whether that's true or not, but I flip the phone closed and set it on the table, staring at it.

I think she believed me. She sounded like she did. Whether Alistair will believe her when she relays my message is another question, but I don't think either of them will be calling the police to report me missing. Maybe that was a given since it hadn't been done already.

There's only silence in the room for a moment.

"Good." Kol holds his palm out in front of me. "Now give me your engagement ring. You don't need it."

I raise my head and meet Kol's stare head-on. I never would've guessed that the man I met and fell for could be this cruel of a bastard. But it's obvious he enjoys inflicting emotional turmoil on me.

I slide my ring off my finger and push it into his waiting hand. He looks at it with disgust before shoving it in his pocket.

"I'll be back with your lunch later."

He leaves, and I'm alone again, as always. You'd think I'd be comfortable by myself by now.

# 7



"You look like the eggs said something to piss you off."

I glance beside me at Sid. He's enjoying his fruit, as always, at breakfast.

"Fuck off." I dig my fork into the eggs and shovel a heap into my mouth.

"It's not the eggs. It's Rapsody's fiancé. He had me look into him yesterday," Nero says from the other side of the table.

He's right. I did some digging on Rapsody's

fiancé. In actuality, my youngest brother and computer nerd, Nero, did some digging.

Seems Alistair Lewis is a church-going man who got good grades throughout high school and college and now works as an accountant. He has no criminal history, not even a speeding ticket. He volunteers every week at the local food bank and donates ten percent of his annual salary to the church and various non-profits.

No wonder Rapsody wanted to marry him—he's a fucking saint.

"You don't say." Sid leans back in his seat and studies me in my peripheral vision.

Asher and Anabelle didn't grace us with their presence at breakfast this morning. They're likely still in bed fucking each other's brains out like the nymphos they are now.

"Do tell?" Sid asks Nero.

I block them out while Nero fills him in. I don't want to think about Rapsody's fiancé. Don't want to think about how she abandoned me the day of our wedding and yet seemed ready to marry some other guy.

Don't want to think about how Alistair is the kind of guy who deserves someone like Rapsody, even if she is a deceitful liar.

After Nero finishes, Sid settles his gaze on me. "What's your plan then?"

He's right, of course. It's been days, and though I'm usually always the one with a plan—hell, I usually have a plan, a contingency plan, and then a back-up plan in case all else fails—I'm no closer to deciding what to do with her than I was yesterday.

Stealing her from her wedding proved to be less fulfilling than I expected. I don't know why. I should be relishing the fact that she's miserable and crying up in that tower, but I'm not.

A flash of her legs in that tiny towel she wore after her shower flits through my brain. I'd be a liar if I tried to deny the punch of lust that hit my gut when I opened that door, but I quickly shut it down. There's not a chance in hell I'm going to allow her to have that power over me ever again. There's no chance my feelings never waned. I've spent the past four years cursing the fact that she was ever born.

Maybe I'm unsatisfied because I haven't dug in deep enough. Maybe I have to wholly ruin her, make her feel what I did before. Then it will feel like enough.

"Well? What are you going to do?" Sid prods.

It's then that an idea hits me with complete clarity. And I know what I have to do.

"I'm going to go all in."

Nero's forehead wrinkles. "What the hell does that mean?"

A slow smirk spreads across my face. "Not for you two to worry about."

I'm going to make sure she falls in love with me. I'm going to ruin her. Then I'm going to toss her aside and out of my life.

Sid chuckles beside me. "Good luck."

After I assemble a breakfast plate for Rapsody, I head back to the north wing and tower. As always when I enter, Rapsody is in her bed, facing the glass doors. She doesn't react to the sound of me moving through the room.

After I place the breakfast tray on the only table in the room, I stride over to the bed and haul back the covers. Her head whips in my direction, eyes narrowed, but she says nothing.

"C'mon, you have to eat." I nod toward the table in front of the fireplace. "And we have to talk."

A faint glimmer of hope lights her eyes. Perfect. I barely have to do anything.

If she had no hope, I'd have nothing to destroy, but if I water that hope and let it grow, I'll have the sweetest pleasure of ripping it all away in one fell swoop. Then I'll stare down at the devastation left in the aftermath.

I force my voice to soften. "Let's go, Rapsody. You can't just waste away."

She dramatically shifts into a seated position and crawls out of bed. I step back and sit in the same spot I did yesterday.

"Why are you being... nice?" she asks, removing the metal dome from over the plate and setting it aside.

It's clear nice wasn't the adjective she wanted to use but chose it anyway. She's right to be wary. I'm going to have to move slowly so as not to raise her suspicions.

I blow out a breath. "I'm not being nice. I'm being practical. I can't keep you here forever, despite what you might fear."

She looks at me cautiously. "Why are you keeping me here at all?"

There's a plea in her voice that makes my chest tighten, but I shut that shit down and answer her question honestly. "Because we were supposed to be married, and you left me on our wedding day without an explanation, and you disappeared. You made me think that you loved me and wanted to spend your life with me." I let some of the anger and betrayal seep into my voice.

Her gaze falls to the plate of food, but she says nothing.

I remember the first time I saw her in that hospital cafeteria. She was like a beaming ray of sunshine. It was as if the world knew that, because the light coming through the window glistened against her long blonde hair. She glowed from the inside out, so when that empty water bottle rolled my way, it was the opening I needed.

I didn't woo women. When I was enlisted, I got laid as the opportunity arose, but I've never been drawn to anyone like I was with Rapsody. After only a few minutes of conversation, it was obvious how sweet and sheltered she was. Something about her innocence drew me in, and not because I wanted to destroy it, but because I wanted to preserve it. But she'd played me for the fool. And now she'll end up as the fool.

"Why did you do it, Rapsody?"

She says nothing, staring at her plate.

Anger boils inside me. After all these years, she doesn't even deem me worthy enough to know the truth about why she ran out on me?

"Why?" I slam my hand on the table, and she flinches. "Was it just a ploy to get at my money, and then you couldn't go through with it? Are you just a cruel, heartless bitch who gets off on ruining people's lives? Are you a con artist? Were you sent from one of my family's enemies to try to bring me down? Why did you pretend to love me?" The last question slips out, and I hate the desperation in my tone.

She bolts up from the chair. "I loved you! I didn't pretend anything. You're the liar!"

I bite back my grin. Finally, she speaks.

# 8

*RAPSODY*

I crumple into the chair, embarrassed by my admission, scared by what I said, how I said it, and the repercussions of my outburst. But when Kol asked why I'd pretended to love him, I couldn't allow him to think that...I just can't explain why.

His face was etched in pain. So much pain after all these years, and I don't understand why. It doesn't make sense for the man I knew him to be, the man he showed me he was with his actions this week, to feel that deeply about what I did after all this time.

"Between the two of us, you're the liar," Kol says with a sneer.

I shake my head, afraid to admit what I found out, why I left, for fear of how he'll react.

"All right then. Tell me. Why am I the liar?" He leans back in his chair and crosses his arms. His shirt sleeves bunch in his biceps. He'll never wrap me in the embrace of his strong arms again, like he once did. "I'm waiting."

I have no choice but to tell him something. "You told me you were a special ops soldier."

His amber eyes narrow. "I was at the time."

"You let me believe that's *all* you were. You didn't tell me you were the son of a billionaire. A billionaire yourself."

A sadistic laugh rings through the room, and I suppress a shiver. "Most women would be happy to marry a billionaire. Especially a dumb one who didn't demand a prenup and was more likely than not to be killed in action."

My stomach twists at the thought of him in danger on some mission. Which is ridiculous since he's holding me captive. "That's not the point. You lied to me. You lied about who you were. How could I ever trust you?"

His head tilts as he studies me. "So you pulled a runaway bride because I have more money than God—that's your excuse?"

I press my lips together and nod.

Kol lays his palms flat on the table, leaning in. "If you're going to tell half-truths, you have to do a helluva better job."

I swallow, unable to tear my eyes away from his gaze. "It's the truth."

"It may be *part* of the truth. So let's start there. How did you find out who I was?"

Panic flares through my veins. I didn't think this far ahead. What if he seeks revenge on not just me? My head shakes back and forth of its own volition. "It doesn't matter."

He assesses me for a moment. "It matters to you, which means the rat is your mother.

Unless you lied to me about how sheltered she kept you."

My eyes widen.

"That's right, sweetheart. You're still a fucking open book to me." He straightens and crosses his arms again, staring at me.

The venomous sound of the word sweetheart from his lips makes my stomach sour. He used to say that word with so much love and reverence.

"What else did your mother tell you?"

I don't know what to do. But if I don't tell him, I'm sure he's going to leave me in this tower for however long until I admit the truth. Maybe the best thing is to tell him and see what happens. Maybe he'll let me go home once he knows why I left that day.

*Or maybe he'll kill you.*

I look into his eyes for any remnants of the man from four years ago and see none.

"What else, Rapsody?"

Tightness wraps around my chest, and I close my eyes and exhale a few deep breaths, calming my anxiety. When I open my eyes, I meet his gaze. "She told me that you killed your father."

Kol blinks and blinks again. Surprise lines his features, but it disappears instantly. "What exactly did she say?"

"First, you have to promise me that you won't hurt her. You have to give me your word." I'm not even sure I can trust his word, but I figure I should ask for it. Maybe it will at least make him think twice before he does anything.

He nods.

That's as good as I'll get, I suppose.

"First she told me who you really were." I've listened to him berate me for causing him pain, but he acts as though what he did to me—his lies—had no effect. Time for him to realize that's not true. "I'd never felt so stupid in my life. Here I'd agreed to marry you after only weeks, so sure of my decision, of us, and then I found out I didn't know who you really are. That you'd lied to me, and I ate your story up, so desperate for a life, for love, that I wasn't even willing to question you."

Kol opens his mouth to say something, but I don't want to hear his stupid excuses anymore, so I raise my hand and continue.

"She said it was proof of what she was always telling me. That the world is filled with lies and deception, evil people who only want to harm others. And you know what? I didn't listen to her. I told her that I did know who you were and that there must be an explanation for what she was saying. That I would talk to you and find out, and that if she just met you, she'd see how wonderful you were." I shake my head at my own naïveté. I was so unwilling to think the worst of Kol that I was willing to start our marriage with a lie.

I can't sit here anymore, so I stand, wrapping my arms around myself, and pace the room under Kol's watchful eye.

"When she couldn't convince me to leave you, she pulled out old news articles about your father's death. They all said that you or one of your brothers was believed to be the one who killed him, but that either authorities couldn't prove it, or they had been bought off. Article after article from reputable news agencies all said the same thing. And when I googled the Voss family and Kol Voss, there was link after link to stories about you or your family that painted a picture of a person so different. I realized then that she was right about all of it. I was just a naïve little girl willing to believe anything from the first man who paid me the smallest amount of attention."

I walk over to the dresser, pick up one of the large elastic bands bought along with my new wardrobe and braid my hair.

"We'd only known each other a couple of weeks, but what I felt for you was real. I thought I'd fallen in love with a man who didn't exist. My entire life, my mother sheltered me and told me how dangerous the world was. How it was full of liars and thieves and people who only want to hurt me and take advantage of me. After everything she told me about you, for the first time in a long time, I felt like she was right." I finish the braid and tie off the bottom.

Kol's footsteps sound behind me, and I turn around. "Why didn't you just ask me about it?"

He doesn't deny the accusation, so I was right to leave him.

"Because she explained to me that a man like you, so used to getting whatever you desire, so dangerous and violent, wouldn't accept being left. My mom thought it was better for us to disappear—change our names and start our lives elsewhere. She knew you'd be angry and come looking for me. Guess she was right about that too."

His mouth forms a thin line, and he steps forward. "I came looking for you because I wanted an explanation."

"And now you have it."

"Jesus." Kol links his hands and rests them on his shaved head, blowing out a long breath. "You should have just spoken to me about it." His voice is pained as if he's upset.

"I couldn't trust you anymore." Tears build in my eyes, but I blink them back. I promised myself a long time ago that I wouldn't cry over him because he wasn't real and what we had wasn't real anyway. "Why didn't you just tell me who you were when we met, if you didn't have anything to hide?"

His hands drop. "My entire life, I've been judged by my last name. But you didn't see any of that when we met. You only saw the man who stood in front of you. And I liked it that way. I didn't want to ruin what we had." I open my mouth to protest, but he scowls. "Don't even try to feed me some bullshit line about how it wouldn't have mattered to you. It did in the end. As soon as you found out who I was in the world, you ran."

He's right. Although it was more than just that. I hesitate for a moment and ask the question that has haunted me since that day. "Are you saying you didn't murder your father?" I hold my breath, waiting for his answer.

His entire face goes blank, void of all emotion. Somehow, that's more unsettling than if he'd exploded in anger. "My father isn't up for discussion."

There's a bottomless well of pain in his eyes. Why? I wonder who his father was to him.

I reach out to touch him. To comfort him maybe.

But he steps back. "Did you actually think I posed a threat to you?"

My heart speeds up. "I don't know. I was so confused. My mom sprang the information on me, and she had proof that you'd lied. Everything she'd told me my entire life rang true, and I felt heartbroken and confused." My face crumples as I bare my truth to him. I'm tired of hiding who I am and what I feel, trying to be someone I'm not anymore. "I have questioned every day for the past four years whether I made the right decision."

I sink to my haunches with my hands over my face. I can't bear to look at him. At the man I once loved but threw away because I let fear and guilt worm their way inside me. Whether that decision was the right one, I'll never find out.

Kol is quiet for a long time, and eventually I stand, not looking at him. I turn and flop down on the bed in the same position I lie in all the time.

"How did your mom find out we were getting married?" He stands across the room, his voice far away.

"I don't know. She ambushed me when I returned home from the grocery store. Usually she went, but she was too frail after returning from the hospital a couple days before, so I went."

Again, I'm met with silence. No doubt Kol is scrutinizing my answers and examining them for any hint of a lie.

I have no idea if he believes me or not, because his footsteps cross the floor, then the door opens and closes, the key turning in the lock.

Why did I expect anything different?

# 9



I'm unsure what awakens me that night, but I get the distinct impression of being watched. I stiffen, listening, but I don't hear anything.

"Kol?"

No answer.

I swallow hard and roll to my other side. A warm glow shines from under the door. My forehead creases, and I sit up in bed to get a better look. Some nights, Kol has left the sconces in the curved stairwell on, and I can see them flickering underneath the door, but this is different. This glow is warmer and brighter.

Rolling back to my other side, I turn on the lamp. It casts most of the room in shadows but lets me see well enough that I can safely walk to the door. I step off the plush rug that surrounds the bed, and my bare feet tread against the cool stone floor.

Pressing my ear against the door, I listen, but there's no sound. I kneel to the floor to peek through the gap, but it's only the same golden light, nothing else. I stand and my hand instinctively goes to the doorknob, knowing it's a useless endeavor. But I freeze when it turns in my palm.

Did Kol forget to lock the door after he dropped off my dinner?

No. I heard him put the key in and lock it. It's a sound I always listen for as if I'm still holding on to hope that I won't die up here.

I turn the knob and heft open the heavy door, peeking down the staircase. The source of the light must be farther down the staircase. Its glow illuminates the stairs in front of me.

After saying a small prayer that the stairwell is empty, I tiptoe down as quietly and quickly as I'm able, still not hearing anything and not coming upon the source of the light. It's almost as though it's moving ahead of me and wants me to follow.

But I don't have time for that. I need to find my way out of this place and away from Kol.

For a moment, I wonder where I'll go, which is something I should worry about once I'm free.

I'll go back to my mom and Alistair, of course. But I realize that I don't want to go back to the same life I had. I want a whole new one. Kol kidnapping me has been a wake-up call.

No matter, the first step is getting away from here. I can figure out the rest later.

When I reach the bottom of the stairway and try to open the door, I almost expect it to be locked, but it opens easily as well. A rush of air leaves my lungs in relief when I step over the threshold. The massive hallway glows to my right. Farther down the hall, a warm ball of light floats in the air, almost like a floating lantern.

What is that thing?

It moves slowly down the hallway. I'm rooted to the spot like an animal trying to prevent detection.

I must be dreaming. There's no earthly explanation for what my eyes are taking in.

The light stops as though it's beckoning me to follow before starting down the hall again. I look at the doorway I just came from, then back at the glowing orb.

Could it be leading me out of here? That thought is fleeting when I'm at the far end of the hallway, and there's no door to the outside. Mustering all my courage, I step in the direction of the light.

I silently follow it down the hall, past the transition into another part of the house through the stained-glass hallway. My gaze snags on the window depicting a lion resembling the one tattooed down Kol's arm. After more twists and turns, leaving me thoroughly turned around, we finally reach a door that leads outside.

The light passes right through the door, and I blink, again trying to wrap my head around what is happening. But I need to move forward. There's plenty of time to puzzle over what this means once I reach safety. I burst through the door, welcoming the crisp night air. Summer isn't fully here yet, but in days or weeks, the blanket of ever-present humidity will cover this place.

The light continues to float over the grass, and since it freed me from the house, I'm trusting that it's leading me to safety.

I trail it for a time unknown. Ten minutes, twenty, a half hour? By the time I come to the huge pond I could barely see from my tower, goose pebbles cover my skin, and my feet are cold from walking over the cool ground. It's too dark to make much out, but a light glimmers on a post on the far side. But on the bank closest to me, a lone figure sits on the grass.

My entire body stiffens. I'd recognize that silhouette anywhere—Kol. Panic fires in my veins, and I turn to find the light, but it has vanished without a trace, as if it never existed.

No matter. I need to go in whatever direction Kol is not, so I backtrack a few tentative steps from the pond. After a few more breaths, I press my lips together, keeping my eyes on Kol. He hasn't noticed me yet, so I still have time to sneak off the property.

But the invisible string that still tethers us together and I can't seem to cut plants my feet in the cool grass.

Why is he out here in the middle of the night? What keeps him up so he can't sleep? When we first met, he told me that he had trouble sleeping. When I asked him why, his only explanation was "the past."

I stand, contemplating my fate.

Is what I'm running toward any better than what I'm running from? Probably in a lot of ways. It's certainly better than being trapped in one room. But I still wasn't free to live my life how I wished, and I was going from living under my mother's rule to being the wife of a man who would run the household and still make all of my decisions.

What would my life look like if I were the one making the decisions? What can I be? Who would I become if I were given the freedom to blossom?

It's those thoughts, along with the memory of the mystery man in that hospital, a man I've seen only a handful of times since he brought me here, that are the reason why I walk across the damp grass, not toward the gates of freedom, but toward Kol.

This could be a mistake, a very big mistake.

I sit beside him. He startles, suggesting he was so deep in thought, I could have escaped without him knowing. Then his eyes widen when he sees it's me. "How the fuck did you get out of that room?"

"The door was unlocked when I woke up." It's a simple enough explanation. There's no way I'm bringing up the light thing when I can't explain it myself.

His face twists, looking just as confused as mine, before his gaze turns accusatory. "Why didn't you hightail it out of here?"

"Had full intentions of doing just that until I saw you."

He doesn't say anything, and we stare into one another's eyes for an uncomfortable length of time. But he's not dragging me back to the tower, so I count it as a win.

Finally, I break the silence. "What are you doing out here?"

He tears his eyes from me and back toward the pond. "Figuring out what to do with you."

"Oh."

We're both quiet again, and for the first time since my arrival, it's not uncomfortable this time. I contemplate what I should say and, in the end, opt for honesty. "I don't want to be locked up anymore, but I don't want to go back to my life either."

I feel a semblance of relief from admitting

that fact out loud, but at the same time, I panic.

"What about your fiancé?" There's a note of anger in his voice, but he manages to keep it in check.

I bring up my knees and wrap my arms around them, pulling my legs into my chest to try to conserve some of my body heat. "I care for Alistair, but I never loved him like one should when they're going to marry. He just represented a little more freedom. But it still wouldn't be enough to really make me happy, and that's not fair to him."

I wait to see how Kol takes my admission, given that he believes I never loved him. Will he think I'm just a conniving man-eater to all men?

But he doesn't get angry or take any shots at me for skipping town when we were supposed to be married. To my shock, he says, "You can stay here if you want." He turns away from the pond and meets my gaze. "Not locked in the tower. You can stay in one of the other rooms in my wing until you figure out what you want to do."

I squash the hope that wants to sprout with the possibility of this being real for fear that he'll tear it all away just to be cruel. "Really?"

He nods. "I shouldn't have done what I did."

My arms drop from around my legs, and my shoulders sag. "I shouldn't have left you without an explanation. I'm sorry."

His eyes flicker with an emotion I can't decipher, then he stands. I wait for him to leave, to give me his back once more, but he holds out his hand. I slide my palm into his big hand and shiver once I'm on my feet.

Kol's eyebrows furrow. "Here."

Before I can decline, he pulls his long-sleeve Henley over his head, revealing his bare chest. My eyes widen. I've never seen a man's naked chest in person, and Kol's is perfection. I want to run my palms over the planes of his hard muscles. Looking at him shirtless with the moon casting down on him makes him look virile and strong and lethal.

His lion tattoo is fully visible. I saw most of it when he wore a T-shirt and pulled it up to show me once, but I've never seen it all. The way the lion's mouth is open in a roar over his shoulder and the body twists around his arm down to his elbow.

I avert my gaze as he holds out his shirt to me. "Put this on."

"You don't have to do that." My limbs shake with a shiver.

"Rapsody." He steps into me, the heat of his body warming me before he pulls the shirt over my head.

The hem falls to my knees, and I feel his body heat as I slide my hands through the arms. His scent, the one I remember so well from our time together, surrounds me. It always reminded me of what I imagined a winter forest might smell like—pine and snow and crisp air.

"Thank you." I look at him, and our gazes lock and hold.

The air between us blends, and the small amount of space crackles with energy, just like the first time we met. His gaze dips to my lips, and he huffs. My tongue slides out, licking my lips. Just when I can't take the tension any longer, and my patience is about to snap, Kol clears his throat and steps back.

"Time for bed," he says.

I follow him to the house, and when I lie down to go back to sleep, for the first time since I arrived, real true hope springs to life inside me.

# IO

*KOL*

I still can't figure out why Rapsody didn't run last night. It doesn't make any sense. She could have left, and I wouldn't have known until morning. She would have gotten so far ahead of me, it might have taken another four years to find her.

But she came to sit by me. Why, after everything I've done to her?

My mind is a jumbled mess, assuming she's got some bigger scheme on the horizon. I don't see how it could be. What would be the point? What would she have to gain?

Which leaves me thinking that maybe she's telling the truth and doesn't want to return home to her mother and the prick.

It's fine. It all plays into my plan anyway. And now it was her idea, so she won't be suspicious of my motives as I get her to fall back in love with me.

She won't just fall in love with me—she'll fall in love with Midnight Manor. I'll steal her innocence, then I'll cut her off at the knees and kick her the fuck out. Then she'll have a semblance of an idea of what she did to me. To know what it feels like for the person you care most about to pull a one-eighty on you.

I rub my palms together. Today is the first day of my plan's execution, and it begins with having her join the family at breakfast. No doubt Anabelle will take Rapsody under her wing and become her new long-lost friend.

Good. It will be one more thing to miss when she's no longer welcome here.

I didn't lock Rapsody's door when I returned her to the spire last night, so I knock on it and wait until she invites me in. I'll have Marcel move her to the guest room directly beside my bedroom today.

The door swings open, and she stands in the frame, looking bright-eyed and fresh-faced. There's little trace of the morose woman who resided in this room yesterday.

"You look like you're in a good mood," I say.

She smiles, and I hate the way my stomach swoops. She always had the best smile. It lights up her entire face with innocence and joy. Two foreign qualities to a man like me, and it makes me covet those pieces of her.

"For the first time in a long time, I feel like I'm free. Like I don't know what the day is going to bring."

"Breakfast first. Go get changed, and we'll head to the dining room."

Her smile grows, which I wouldn't have thought possible. "Not in my room?"

I shake my head. "No."

Her eyes flare with excitement.

"Now go, or we'll be late."

Her head cocks to the side. "Who else will be there?"

"My brothers and perhaps Anabelle, my eldest brother's wife." Her head tilts.

"Anabelle is your sister-in-law?"

I nod.

Rapsody smiles as if she's put the last puzzle piece in place.

She brings her fingers together in front of her and fidgets. "What should I wear? I'm not prepared to meet a bunch of people. I always get so nervous around others. When I first started going to church, I would almost have a panic attack because I didn't know how to be around so many people at once. Sometimes I think I—"

"Rapsody." I grip her shoulders, lowering my chin to look into her eyes. "There's nothing to be nervous about. It doesn't matter what anyone at that table thinks. You're here because I invited you."

While I'm speaking the truth, reassuring her grates on me. Still, it's the role I have to play to accomplish my goal.

Her body relaxes a bit under my hands. "Okay. Come on in. I'll just be a minute."

I follow her into the room and sit on the chair in the sitting area that faces away from the doors to the balcony. Rapsody hurries around the room collecting her clothes and heads into the bathroom to change, but she's in such a rush, she doesn't completely close the bathroom door. Through the crack, I catch a glimpse of bare skin, and my cock twitches.

It's a natural physical reaction, I tell myself. Nothing to do with her specifically.

She walks out wearing a pale purple summer dress with a floral pattern that reaches down to her ankles, paired with gold sandals. Her long blond hair is pulled back into a braid that rests against the column of her spine. Her green eyes sparkle like dew crystals on blades of grass in the morning.

"Is this okay to meet your family?" Rapsody looks at me expectantly, smoothing down the front of her modest dress.

It's amazing how much her demeanor has changed with the opportunity to have a little bit of interaction with others, and it's hard to ignore the swell in my chest at being the one responsible for her happiness. I have to tread carefully. This feeling could become addictive, and I'd be a fool to forget the endgame. Then I'm the one heartbroken, and that will never happen again.

"Let's go." I stand from the chair.

I can't bring myself to tell her what I really think—that she reminds me of the woman I met that first day. So full of sunshine and light that she was blinding.

She follows me down the stairs and walks quietly beside me, but her steps almost skip as we make our way down the cavernous hallway. Her gaze pings along the walls, her eyes widening with each new item. She doesn't even speak until we leave the north wing.

"How old is this place?" Her voice is full of awe as though she's never seen anything as ancient as this manor.

I suppose she likely hasn't, given that she was a prisoner in her own home.

"Old." I pick up my pace, not trusting myself to be alone with her for longer than I have to be.

Jesus, if I can't even handle walking down a hallway with her, how am I going to feign falling in love with her?

"Was it always your family's home?" She seems particularly interested in the art on the walls as we pass through the rooms. If Rapsody had any idea how much it was all worth, she'd probably have another one of her anxiety attacks.

"My ancestors built it many generations ago. The Voss family has resided here ever since."

She must sense from my tone that I don't particularly want to talk about my family's past, and she purses her lips, remaining quiet the rest of the walk to the dining room.

I didn't tell anyone she would be joining us this morning. Wasn't sure if I could go through with my plan. So it's no surprise when we walk in side by side, the conversation comes to an abrupt halt, silverware clanking on plates as four sets of eyes stare at us in shock.

If things go according to my plan, then Rapsody will be intimidated and frightened by the three men sitting at the table and will seek comfort and safety from me, the only person she really knows here. Anabelle might be a challenge for me, with her nurturing side, but I trust that Rapsody will find solace with me.

It's just another puzzle piece sliding into place and sealing her fate for destruction.

# II



*RAPSODY*

I swallow hard as the three men and one woman all stare wide-eyed at us. One of the men actually has a piece of cantaloupe on a fork frozen in front of his mouth. I'd been so excited to have some human interaction and get out of that godforsaken tower that I hadn't thought about who I would be meeting and how I might be received.

"This is Rapsody." Kol thumbs toward me and continues to the right side of the table. He sits while I stand rooted to the spot.

The woman is the first one to break the ensuing silence, pushing back from the table. "Rapsody, it's wonderful to meet you." She walks toward me and envelops me in a hug. "I'm Anabelle, Asher's wife."

Anabelle smells like the wealthy women at church, and when she pulls back to smile at me, I watch as her big brown eyes look me over.

I can't help but return her smile. "Nice to meet you."

She's in a sophisticated dress one might wear to an office and her brown hair hangs wavy to her breasts, but she looks to be about my age. Though I can tell from how she carries herself that her twenty-three is much more worldly than mine.

"Rapsody, we've heard a lot about you," the man seated beside Kol says.

It's nice to hear people call me by my real name rather than Lillian, a name that never felt true to me.

He rises from his seat and makes his way over to me, but instead of hugging me like

Anabelle, he takes my hand and brings it to his lips, pressing a kiss against my knuckles. My face heats when I meet his dark, penetrating gaze. A tattoo of a wolf peeks up over the collar of his dress shirt, and his dark wavy hair has been styled back away from his face.

I can only imagine what Kol must have said about me, so I answer with, "Not good things, I assume."

The entire room breaks out in laughter—everyone except Kol, whose gaze I catch with questions. He seems perturbed by the comment, as if he didn't expect me to speak during breakfast.

Then why did he bring me?

I may not be used to being social, but now that I've been given the chance to interact with other people, you'd better believe I'm going to. Who knows when I'll get the chance again?

"I'm Obsidian, but everyone calls me Sid. Glad you'll be joining us today."

I smile and nod.

"I'm Nero," a man on the opposite side of the table says, raising his hand in greeting. "It's good to meet you."

It's clear to me that he's the youngest of the brothers, and unlike the two brothers I've already met, Nero has blue eyes that contrast with his dark hair.

"Rapsody, I'm Asher," the last man says. "Why don't you have a seat beside Kol?" He gestures across the table as Anabelle returns to the seat on his left.

"Thank you." I nod and follow Sid over to that side of the table, where he slides his breakfast plate to the left.

"You can have my seat, Rapsody." Then Sid gestures to a woman dressed in a housekeeper's uniform in the corner, and she darts away, seeming to read his mind. I hadn't even noticed her.

Sid pulls the chair out for me, and I slide in next to Kol. "Thank you."

Seconds later, the woman returns and sets down a clean plate and cutlery in front of me. I smile and mumble a thank you.

I have a hard time concentrating, my eyes pinging to different locations in the large room. I glance at a crystal chandelier hanging over the long, dark wood table. I've never seen a table with this many chairs before. Despite the chandelier and some flickering sconces on the walls, the room is still dim, and it's hard to tell if the paint on the walls is black or a deep blue. Paintings in ornate gold frames line the walls, and a large mirror hangs over the huge fireplace.

A long buffet table is set against the wall behind the head of the table, and above it is a large painting of a pretty woman with long, flowing dark hair and deep blue eyes. Eyes that hold sadness despite the upward curve of her lips. I admire the way the artist was able to capture such depth of emotion in her eyes, which is no small feat.

"Who is she? She's beautiful," I ask.

Silence greets me, and I still, fearing I've found my way into unwanted territory.

Nero clears his throat. "It's our mother...was our mother."

My chin dips, and I glance at the empty plate. "I'm sorry."

I don't know any details except for what Kol shared with me—his mother was murdered. After I ran off, I did a lot of googling on Kol Voss but never looked up his mother. It just didn't feel right.

"You didn't know," Asher says from across the table. "Now, help yourself to whatever you'd like before these three polish it off." He gestures to the center of the table and the platters of food.

I do as he insists, adding bacon, eggs, fruit, yogurt, and granola to my plate.

"So, will you be staying with us long?" Sid asks from my left.

I glance at Kol, knowing I'm only here because he's allowing it and unsure how long he'll allow me. "I'm not sure."

"You don't have anything important to get back to out west?" he asks.

"Is she on fucking trial?" Kol snipes.

Sid chuckles low in his chest. "Apologies, Rapsody. Sometimes I forget I'm not in a courtroom." He smiles. Though on the surface it appears genuine, there's something predatory underneath.

Anabelle saves me from having to think of a response. "What do you do for a living? Are you still in school?" She radiates warmth, and her smile is welcoming.

Though I appreciate her trying to save me, I'm not sure how to answer. Obviously, Kol hasn't told anyone how I grew up.

"Oh well, actually I... I wasn't working before I came here. I was..." I turn to Kol, but his head is buried in his plate. "I was supposed to be married, and I was going to stay at home and run the house. It's what he wanted."

Shame weighs heavily on my shoulders, and they slump while I push my eggs around my plate with a fork.

"Nothing wrong with that," Anabelle says, clearly sensing my discomfort. "I think running a household is even harder than a nine-to-five job, especially once kids are involved." She kindly doesn't ask anything about my fiancé or the wedding or whether I'm married.

I give her a wan smile.

"Speaking of weddings..." Anabelle leans forward and looks around her husband at Nero. "How are the preparations for your big day going?"

"You're getting married?" I say excitedly, happy to discuss anyone but myself and my sad existence.

Nero grins. "In the fall. We're just putting the final touches on everything now."

"That's wonderful. What's your fiancée's name? How did you meet?" I lean back, knowing I need to tamper down my enthusiasm.

The other three men at the table groan.

"Her name is Maude, and we met when I stopped to help her with a flat tire."

I lean my cheek on my hand. "How chivalrous."

He carries on, telling me about how she's perfect for him and explaining what her vision for the wedding is. It sounds as though it's going to be an enormous affair.

"It all sounds so exciting," I say when he's finished.

"What about you, Rapsody? Would you want the party of the year like Nero's bride, or would you be satisfied with something more subdued?" Sid asks me with a glint in his eye. His gaze flickers past me to Kol but swing back my way as if I wouldn't notice.

"Me?" My eyebrows raise. "Oh no, I'd be happy with a wedding at city hall as long as it meant we were married." The words slip from my mouth before I can stop them.

Kol stills at my side, fork half raised to his mouth.

My breathing becomes loud in my head, and every creak of the wood as people shift in their chairs is magnified.

Heat floods my cheeks. "I'm sorry, I—"

"It's fine." Kol places a hand on my forearm.

Beyond when he was rubbing my back when I had my panic attack, it's the first comforting gesture he's allowed himself to give me. My uneasiness evaporates as I let the heat of his palm sink in.

But his touch is gone too soon. He whips his hand away as if my skin is as hot as boiling oil. I watch his fingers coil into a fist, resting at the side of his plate.

"I'm the same as you, Rapsody. Asher and I had a very small ceremony here on the manor grounds." Once again, Anabelle comes to my rescue.

I take the lifeline she's thrown me and try to hoist myself from the stormy sea. "Oh, whereabouts? I'll bet there are hundreds of beautiful spots to choose from."

"In the center of the hedge maze actually. It's sort of a special spot for Asher and me." She looks adoringly at her husband.

I feel Kol go as still as death next to me, and it feels as though the shadows in the corners of the room creep in closer. When I turn my head in Kol's direction, he pushes back from the table, tossing his napkin beside his half-finished plate.

"You done?" he asks me.

"Uh, sure. Yeah." I push back my chair and stand, looking around the table. "It was nice to meet you all."

"We should have a girls' night sometime soon," Anabelle says with a smile, glancing in Kol's direction.

"That would be great." And I mean it. I've never had a girls' night before.

Kol makes his way toward the exit of the dining room without waiting for me, and I hurry to catch up.

I don't know why what Anabelle said was so upsetting to him, but against my better judgment, I want to be the one to make him feel better. Old habits die hard.

# 12



I follow Kol as he storms through the house, shoulders taut, strides long. I don't dare say a word as we weave through the manor, past the antique furniture and oversized paintings. Each room feels dimmer, shadows lurking in the corners.

Eventually, Kol reaches a set of garden doors and pushes them open with both his hands, bolting outside and sucking in a deep breath as though the air inside the house was suffocating him. He doesn't look to see if I'm still behind him.

I'm not sure if he even wants my company, but he's obviously in pain for some reason, and I can't walk away, leaving him in this state. Regardless of what he did, a huge part of my heart belongs to him, even if he's not the man I thought he was when we first met. I can't... I can't just walk away. Last night proved that when I had the chance to escape but stayed instead.

Closing the doors behind me, I face him and find that we're standing under a portico on a stone patio. Beyond that is a large swimming pool, but there's no sun glistening off the water. The morning is overcast, and a thin layer of mist hangs low to the ground, making the temperature feel cooler than it should this close to summer.

Kol stands with his back to me, hands interlocked on his shaved head.

I'm not sure what to say or whether I should say anything at all. I opt for the most obvious question. "Are you okay?" My voice is soft, tentative.

He blows out a stream of air. "I'm fine."

There's a bite to his tone, but I decide to press on anyway. "What Anabelle said upset you for some reason. I don't under—"

"Just leave it alone, Rapsody."

"If you can't talk to me, you should talk to someone." I want to be the one to bring him comfort, but if it can't be me, all I care about is that he finds someone.

"I said, leave. It. Alone." He whips around to face me and steps forward. His arms land on either side of my head, caging me against the doors.

He stares down at me, those caramel eyes that once looked at me with such softness and love now filled with turmoil. Both our chests heave for breath. A flash of panic ignites in his eyes. The thought that I'm responsible for his rage because I brought up his mother in the painting makes the cords in my throat tighten.

"I'm sorry if I upset you when I asked about the painting."

Pure pain flashes on his face. "You didn't know."

"Still…" I reach toward his face on instinct but drop my hand before I connect with his skin. I don't think he wants me to touch him, even though we're only inches apart. The look on his face reminds me of an animal after he's cornered his prey and is deciding whether to attack or not.

"Do you miss your mother?"

His question catches me off guard, and it takes me a beat to respond. "I…I mean, a bit. I miss the comfort of having her there, knowing she loves and cares for me, but I'd be lying if I said I wasn't enjoying having some space from her."

God, guilt lies heavy on my shoulders, saying that after all she's done for me, but it's true.

"I miss mine every fucking day." His voice is a quiet rasp as though it pains him to speak of her out loud. "I was the one who found her."

My entire body draws tight. I don't know how old he was when his mother died, but I remember he said that he was young. "You must've been just a child."

"Ten." He squeezes his eyes shut for a moment. "I was ten when I found her in the garden with a set of gardening shears plunged into her chest, blood seeping out."

A pained sound leaves my lips, and I bring my hands up to cover my mouth, my eyes stinging with unshed tears. He was so young. So young to have seen such a thing done to his mother. "Who... who did it?"

"A man she was having a long term affair with. He murdered her when she told him she wouldn't leave my father for him. So he stabbed her and left her for dead like she was a piece of roadkill. Like she meant nothing. But she was everything to my brothers and me."

"Kol..." There are no words to say. Sorry is too small a word for the trauma they must have all endured.

"I think about that all the time. What her last moments must have been like. How much pain she must have been in. Was it slow, and she knew she was dying? Or did she die instantly?"

My hands tentatively slide around his taut waist. I step into him, leaving no space between us, and press my cheek to his chest, squeezing him in a hug. "I'm sorry. I'm so sorry."

I'm prepared for him to push me away, but he doesn't. Instead, his arms wrap around me and tuck me into him, his cheek lying on the top of my head. He shudders a breath and tucks his face in my neck, breathing me in.

All traces of the cold, calculating billionaire are erased, and in its place is a vulnerable son, a man who misses what could have been if his mother hadn't been murdered.

"She's at peace now, Kol. I truly believe that." My attendance at church taught me that I do believe that when our souls leave our bodies, we move on to a better place.

He squeezes me harder, and I wish I'd never run off on him. I wish I had stayed and confronted him, and maybe we'd have had more of these moments. Maybe I'd know the real Kol Voss underneath the bridled exterior. If I would have talked to him, maybe we'd be more than whatever we are now—strangers, adversaries, certainly not friends.

But there's no use going down that line of thought. Kol may be letting me stay here until I figure myself out, but his romantic interest vanished the day I decided to run. He'll never give me another chance.

"I hope you're right," he says and pulls away from me, hands clenched at his sides.

He stares at me, gaze coasting over my features. That string pulls taut between us, as if neither of us has the energy or desire to pull apart.

His gaze drops to my lips, and they tingle, my belly fluttering low in my abdomen. Blissful memories of what his lips felt like on mine rise to the surface. The way I'd lose track of anything that wasn't him. The way I'd crave more and more of him. The way I'd think dirty things I'd never thought of before.

My breathing picks up, and I meet his unwavering gaze as he slowly, so carefully brings his head closer to mine. I can almost taste him the closer he gets, and my lips ache in anticipation. His warm breath floats over my face, and my nipples pebble in my bra. Waiting, waiting for him to set his lips on mine.

Our mouths are millimeters apart, and a groan slides up my throat, begging him to put me out of my misery. His amber eyes disappear under his eyelids, and he steps away from me. A cold rush of air whips through me. I'm almost unable to bite back the sound of disappointment that's desperate to be unleashed.

"I'm going to be gone for a week or so. I have some things to take care of for Voss Enterprises." All the lust is stripped from his face. Kol is back to being the man who showed up in Seattle to collect me, as if we didn't just share a moment.

"Oh. Okay." Despair fills my veins that I'll be here on my own without him.

"I don't want you leaving the property while I'm gone."

I wrap my arms around myself. "So I am a prisoner once again?"

"Yes. No." He scrubs his hands down his face. "I know you want to live more during this time away from your mother. But I want to be the one to show you the world. I want you to save those moments for me."

His words remind me so much of when we first met and all the things we talked about doing, the places he wanted to take me.

I nod. "Okay."

"You sure?" he asks as though he thinks I'm going to try to slip off into the night again.

"I'm sure."

"Your stuff is being moved to the room beside mine today. Is there anything I can have brought in for you?"

I ask for the only thing I've been missing from my old life. "Would it be possible to get some paint and canvases?" My breath stays trapped in my chest while I wait for him to answer.

"You still paint?" His head tilts.

"Yeah. Helps pass the time."

Growing up, painting was one of my favorite ways to spend my time when I wasn't doing homeschool classes. While my mom worked from her home office, I must've watched hundreds of videos online before I developed my own style of painting.

Now it's more than just a way to pass the time. It helps center me, helps me make sense of my feelings, and gives me the ability to paint the worlds I create in my mind, since I don't know very much of the one beyond my doorstep.

"I'll make sure you have everything you need."

"Thank you."

There's no hope that the two of us can ever come together again, but the way he looks at me, I curse my wretched heart for wishing we could.

# 13

RAPSODY

Kol has been gone from Midnight Manor for more than a week, and with every day that passes, I become more and more lonely. I keep thinking I should find a phone to reach out to my mother, but I stop myself every time.

I flip in bed, unable to fall asleep.

The darkness filling the bedroom feels heavier, almost oppressive. With a sigh, I reach toward the night table and flick on the lamp. All that does is to further highlight the shadows in every corner the light doesn't penetrate.

I've kept to myself since Kol has been gone. Before he left, he explained that the house manager, Marcel, could take care of any of my needs, so I'd requested that my meals be brought to my bedroom. Eating with the rest of Kol's family when he isn't here doesn't feel right.

Anabelle was nice enough to seek me out one day, and we spent that evening chatting on the seating near the pool. But she's busy with a new husband and her job as his assistant, so I don't fault her for not returning.

The truth is, I just want Kol to come back. He's the most familiar thing in this massive manor, and there's a comfort in knowing he's close, even if he resents me most times.

I huff and yank the blankets off of me, sliding out of bed. Lying here staring into the dark abyss isn't any use. I'm going to go paint for a bit and wait for fatigue to settle in.

I slide my feet into slippers and open the large door to the bedroom. The sconces in the hallway are lit, casting a dim light down the wide hallway. It's hard not to feel as if the darkness is chasing me as I make my way down the hallway.

Very often as I make my way through the manor, that feeling of being watched arises, and tonight is no exception. It's completely silent except for the sound of my slippers shuffling on the floor, but I swear I feel the penetrating gaze of something, or someone, following my movements.

I pick up my pace until I reach the conservatory. It's huge and filled with plants and some flowers, with towering glass walls and a ceiling supported by black iron. Marcel told me that Kol asked him to set up all my painting supplies in here because he thought I would like the abundance of light. He was right.

But tonight, there's not much light since it's the middle of the night.

An idea sparks in my head, something I could never do when I was living with my mother because of the restricted views out our windows. I've always wanted to paint a night scene cast in moonlight. It's not a full moon, but it's close, so I grab a fresh canvas and some paints I'll need. I remember from the night I snuck out that lights surround the manor on the outside, so if I stick close to the building, there should be enough light to see what I'm painting.

Excited for a new challenge, I shake off the creepy feeling I had earlier and gather my supplies. I contemplate going back to my room for a sweater, but I'm wearing a long-sleeve button-up pajama shirt with pajama pants, so I don't think I'll be cold outside. The days continue to get warmer and warmer.

I haven't spent much time outside the manor, so I'm a little unsure which way to go, and I wander for a bit, much of what I pass looking unfamiliar. When I find a door that leads to the outside, I take it. I'm not sure exactly where I am, but I gather that I've come out from one of the other wings since I don't recognize the landscape, even if it is dark.

The moon shines, but I continue walking a little farther to get a better view of the outside. I step through the grass and around some large greenery but stop when I hear murmurs of voices.

I frown, wondering who could be out here in the middle of the night. Maybe it's some of the landscape staff, though I can't imagine why. The sound of tires on gravel intrigues me, and I make my way past another large bush to see what I overheard.

There's a door on the wall of the manor between the two wings, and outside of it are a bunch of parked SUVs. They're all dark with blacked-out windows and remind me of the kind I see celebrities and politicians in on some of the TV shows I've watched.

The door swings open and a few people—two men and a woman—with masks step out. I can't see what's past the door because of the angle I'm at, but as soon as I register the masks on their faces, I innately know that it will not be a good thing if I'm caught here, so I step into the shadow of the large bush and peek out around it.

The three of them get into the back of an SUV, and it drives away, the sound of tires on gravel filling the night. I watch until the taillights disappear around the other side of the manor.

Why were they wearing masks? Why are there so many vehicles here? Is a party or something going on?

Someone else comes out of the door, and I suck in a breath when I recognize the wolf tattoo on his neck. Sid. He wears a gold wolf mask.

What the heck is going on?

A woman in a red dress is at his side and wearing a black mask, with black hair that flows down her back. He escorts her to the back of one of the SUVs, and when they reach it, he grips her chin roughly and says something I can't hear. She grins and runs a fingernail down his chest before he steps back and reaches around her to open the door.

She slides inside, and he closes the door, stepping away right before the vehicle pulls out. Once the vehicle disappears, he slides the mask up so it rests on top of his head and pushes his hands in his pockets, turning to look at the doorway.

I swing my eyes in the same direction and gasp. Kol stands just outside the doorway with a gold mask dangling from his fingers.

He's back.

He's back, and he didn't even bother to tell me.

Sid says something to Kol, and Kol's brows draw down. He says something back to Sid, who lets out a low chuckle. Kol turns in my direction, and I slide completely behind the bush, heart hammering. Did he see me?

I wait one minute. Then two. After I don't hear anything for some time, I risk peeking out from behind the shrubs once more, finding them both gone.

Not wanting to push my luck, I make my way back to the door where I exited, with more questions than ever about the secrets Midnight Manor hides.

# 14



*RAPSODY*

The next morning, I don't wake until mid-morning after being up half the night. I stare at the ceiling, going over the events of last night and trying to make sense of what I saw.

Maybe it was a costume party, but if so, why didn't the guests use the front door?

I'm still pondering while I get out of bed and dress in a pair of leggings and short-sleeved shirt that cuts off just above the waistband. Then my stomach rumbles, so I braid my hair and decide to make my way to the kitchen to see if I can scrounge something to eat.

Marcel will scold me if he finds me there fending for myself rather than just summoning him to take care of it for me, but Mrs. Potter, who is in charge of the kitchen staff, doesn't seem to mind. It still feels weird to pick up the phone in my room and ask someone to do my bidding when I'm perfectly capable. Not only that, I have nothing better to do. Kol may be back, but it's not as though he's bothered to come see me.

I begin the long trek to the kitchen. I'm only a few steps from my room when I hear something that sounds like metal clanking on metal. As I keep walking, I find that one of the doors ahead on my left is open.

The sound gets louder the closer I get, and when I finally reach the door, I peek inside.

I'm surprised to see a gym with mirrors lining the room. In juxtaposition to the age of the manor, the room is filled with state-of-the-art equipment, free weights, and cardio equipment. One side of the room is open with thick matting on the floor.

In the center of the room is shirtless Kol, skin beading with sweat. He holds big dumbbells as he squats. His lion tattoo is on display, along with another one on his pectoral. He looks up, making eye contact with me through the mirror, but he finishes his reps and sets down his weights before facing me.

I step farther into the room. "You're back."

He picks up a white towel from across a bench and wipes his face. "Just got back a couple hours ago. Didn't want to wake you."

*Liar.*

Why is he lying?

"How did everything go on your trip?"

"Fine. Got done what I needed to." He tosses the towel back on to the bench and rests his hands on his hips. "Where are you off to?"

I thumb behind me. "I was just going to grab something to eat."

"Marcel can do that for you."

I nod. "I know. But I'm fine to do it on my own. Not like I have anything else to do." It's a dig, but I'm upset that he's lying. Why is he keeping it a secret that he was home last night? Has he been home even longer than that and just been avoiding me? It wouldn't be hard in a mansion this big.

Kol frowns. "I explained that I would be away."

"You did. But that doesn't explain why you're lying about when you returned home. I know you were here last night, Kol. I saw you."

His entire body freezes. "What do you mean you saw me?"

He arches an eyebrow and closes the distance between us. My breathing becomes labored the closer he gets. He stops close enough for me to touch, and despite my ire, I want so badly to let my finger trail over the ripples in his lower abdomen. I've never touched a man's naked body, and I want to know what Kol would feel like under my fingertips.

"Where and when did you see me, Rapsody?" He leans in, and the male scent of him hits me like a bolt of lightning.

"I saw you by the door outside with Sid, with people wearing masks," I say the words slowly, unsure how they'll be received.

His head tilts. "Are you spying on me?"

I don't tear my eyes from his gaze when I shake my head. "No. I went outside to paint because I couldn't sleep and... and I saw some people leaving the manor. What were they doing here?"

His features go blank, as though someone has pulled the curtain over all his emotions. "It's nothing you have to concern yourself with." Then he walks back over to the weights he set on the floor.

I follow. "Just tell me what it is. Did you have a party or something and didn't want to invite me? Is that why you lied about when you got back? Was I not of high enough social standing to attend?"

Is he embarrassed because I'm naïve and overzealous and would ask people tons of questions? I don't ask though, because that would make me seem vulnerable to him, and I don't want him using it against me.

He whips around to face me, his features a cold mask of fury. "It has nothing to do with you. Drop it."

"Maybe I should just leave and go back to Seattle, or somewhere else and start over. You obviously didn't want me to know you were back." I turn and start toward the door, but Kol grabs my elbow and pulls me around to face him.

"You'll do no such thing."

I'm so sick of everyone telling me what to do. First my mom, then Alistair, now Kol. Everyone thinks I need protecting, but what I want more than anything is to be able to make decisions for myself, to not have people hide things from me because they think the truth might hurt.

"Contrary to what you might think, you don't own me, Kol."

His grip tightens, and the muscles in his jaw flex. "You're right. I won't make the mistake of owning you ever again."

"If you don't want me here, just say it. I'm only here because you said I could stay and sort myself out, figure out what I want to do with my life. But if I'm not welcome, tell me."

"You should go. You should." Our angry eyes test one another. Who will fold first? But the energy shifts, and tensions rise. His touch loosens on my elbow as an ache forms between my thighs. "But that doesn't mean I want you to."

"I—" I want to feel him just once more, damn the consequences.

Our bodies lean in. I try to prepare myself for him to shove me away once more, but he tugs me into his sweaty body, and his lips fall to mine. The familiar taste of him seeps through my body as his tongue roughly pushes into my mouth. Acting on instinct, my arms wrap around his neck, pressing our chests together, separated only by the thin fabric of my shirt and cotton bra.

Kol groans as his hands slip around my waist and move lower to squeeze my ass and pull me into him. His hard length presses into me. I gasp. The space between my legs hums with pleasure.

Everything between us disappears—our past, the promises made and broken, the animosity and hurt. All of it evaporates, and there is only us.

The feel of his tongue against mine. My hard nipples pressed into his heated chest. The stubble under my hand as it crests over the back of his head. Every sensation feels magnified and perfect. I melt into our kiss, wanting more. I don't even know what, just... more. Whatever he'll give me.

But as quickly as the kiss started, it ends.

Kol pushes me away, and I stumble back, eyes wide, the fingers of one hand pressed against my swollen lips.

His eyes are now filled with horror. "Don't ask me about last night again."

Mortified by the switch in his demeanor and how easily I gave into the kiss, I rush from the room.

Why did he even kiss me if he was so disgusted afterward? Was it just a way to shut me up so I wouldn't ask any more questions? God, that man is so cruel.

I suck back my tears and continue toward the kitchen. I don't understand why he got so weird about me asking about last night. I don't understand why he kissed me. I don't understand why he seems to even want me here. I don't understand any of it.

"Are you okay?"

I blink at the sound of a female voice and come out of my daze. I hadn't even realized that I'd stopped in one of the many sitting rooms in the communal part of the manor.

Anabelle walks toward me with a concerned look on her face. "Are you okay?"

"Sorry, yes, yes. I'm fine." I give her as big of a smile as I can muster.

When she reaches me, she rests a hand on my shoulder. "You don't look fine, Rapsody. What happened?"

The genuine concern on her face brings the tears new life, but I somehow push them back. "I just got into an argument with Kol. Sort of. I don't know if you could even call it that."

She frowns. "What about?"

Maybe Anabelle knows something about whatever was going on last night. She probably would, right? I mean, she's married to the eldest Voss brother.

"I asked him what was going on here last night. I saw some people with masks leaving the side of the house."

Her hand drops from my shoulder, and she winces. "Oh."

"Do you know what was going on? Why would Kol be so upset with me for asking?"

Anabelle sighs. "That's something you need to discuss with Kol."

"But I tried, and—"

"I'm sorry, Rapsody, but I can't discuss this with you." It's a small consolation that she appears to actually feel bad.

"Right. Okay, I get it." I walk past her without saying another word.

Message received loud and clear—I'm not one of them. And I'll never be.

The first tear leaks down my cheek.

Will I ever find somewhere I belong?

# 15

*KOL*

The spark on the lighter flares, lighting the joint in my hand. I take a pull and hold the smoke in for a beat before exhaling. I close my eyes against the sunshine that finds its way through a break in the clouds overhead.

"Pass it over," Nero says, sitting on the grass to my left.

I take another pull off the joint and pass it over. God knows he has more to want to forget than even I do today.

We're sitting by the pond, a place I always come when I want to clear my mind. When Nero told me earlier that he'd called off his engagement, I suggested we bring a couple joints and a bottle of whiskey out here and get fucked up together. Forget this day even exists, for more reasons than just his failed relationship.

"You wanna talk about it?" I ask.

He shakes his head. "No."

"Fair enough."

I take the offered joint from him, content to sit in silence and consider all the things we're not saying. Mostly about what went on this day nearly nineteen years ago.

As for the present, I have no idea why Nero would've called off his engagement, but he's clearly pissed and stewing over it. It's for the best, if you ask me. I never liked Maude. She looked good on paper but... something always bothered me about her. Like she was oily under the calm, serene surface.

"What's your plan for Rapsody?"

I blow out the smoke and pass the joint back to him. "No plan."

He scoffs, takes a drag, tosses it ahead of him on the grass, and crushes it with the heel of his boot. "Bullshit, brother. You always have a plan."

"Whatever." I pick up the bottle of expensive whiskey and take a swig.

"I don't know if it's a special forces thing or if it's just you, but you always have a plan. So what is it?"

The truth is, my mind is a mess where Rapsody is concerned. One second I'm trying to draw her in as part of my plan to destroy her, and the next, the rage at what she did to me, what she made me feel surfaces, and I'm lashing out and pushing her away.

She was on my mind the entire time I was gone, and the only reason I didn't tell her I returned Saturday evening was because of what day it was and what I had to do. She surprised me when she confronted me in the gym. Rapsody has a set of claws she's kept hidden, and I found myself just as enamored by that side of her as I am by her innocent one. I might have been impressed if I wasn't so pissed off by her questioning me about shit she has no right to know about.

"I don't know what went down with you and Maude, but if I had to guess, I'd say you might have some idea now how I felt four years ago when Rapsody up and left me."

I look at Nero, and his jaw clenches while he puts his hand out for me to pass him the bottle.

"So you do have a plan." He tips back the bottle.

"Of course I do."

He chuckles and takes another swig.

"I'm going to make her fall for me again. Make her think all is forgiven and that I'm the same man she met back in Atlanta. Show her how wonderful our life together could be. Ruin her, in all the ways that count, and leave her the same way she left me."

I can do it. I have to do it. I'm convinced the only way I'll be able to move on and get Rapsody out of my mind and my life for good is if I claim my revenge.

Nero passes back the bottle, but I set it down in the grass. I feel good now that the weed is hitting me, and I'll just enjoy the high for a while.

"You think you can do that without falling for her?" he asks.

"Of course I can." I glare at him.

Leave it to Nero to voice my own fear.

"She's the only woman I've ever seen you give a shit about. More than that—you were going to marry her, Kol. You've never even bothered to really date anyone other than her. You fuck them for a bit and move on, never even talk about the women with any of us."

"We can't all be Prince Charming, kid." I ruffle his hair, knowing that, coupled with calling him kid, will piss him off.

"Fuck off." He shoves my hand away. "And nice try distracting me, but it's not gonna work."

It was worth a try. "I made the mistake of falling for her once. I won't do it again."

He shakes his head and falls to his back in the grass. "For the record, I think your plan is shit."

"I didn't ask for your fucking opinion."

Nero doesn't know what he's talking about. I can totally do this. I just have to pull Rapsody in rather than push her away when I think of what she did to me and the anger surfaces. It goes against all my protective instincts, but I can make her fall for me again. She kissed me back after all, and she wanted a helluva lot more than a kiss.

*God, that kiss.*

No, fuck. It didn't mean anything. It was just the first step in my plan. And the fact that I enjoyed it—thoroughly—just means that I'll enjoy stealing Rapsody's innocence from her. That's all. It doesn't mean I'll fall in love with her.

I have a feeling she's not going to let go of what she saw on Saturday night. I'll have to think of some story to tell her that will appease her... unless... my thoughts travel.

Yes, maybe that's it. Maybe that's the perfect way to thoroughly destroy her.

The corner of my lips tips into a half smile.

"Do you think we're cursed?" Nero asks, pulling me from my thoughts.

"What do you mean?"

He props himself up on his elbows so he's only half lying down. "This family. This manor. Do you think it's cursed and that's why we've gone through all the shit we have, or do you think it's karma for all the bad shit or something?"

I pull a blade of grass in front of me. "Most people would say we're lucky to have been born into a billionaire's family."

Nero gives me a cutting look. "They obviously didn't know our father."

The mention of our father, especially today, squeezes the air from my lungs. Flashes of images from that day nineteen years ago play like a slideshow in my brain.

"I think some people are just evil, and we happened to be the sons of one of those people. But then we had Mom, and she was… she was everything." I reach for the whiskey and slug back another mouthful. "Maybe karma is just what balances the scales. We had Mom, and we were born into money, so it gave us Dad. I dunno." I pass him the bottle.

He sits up to drink some, then wipes his mouth with the back of his hand. "What happened that day—"

My head whips in his direction, and I narrow my eyes at him. "We agreed we wouldn't talk about it. Ever."

He looks properly chastised, but then a smirk plays on the edges of his mouth when he looks over my shoulder.

"Hey, Rapsody," Nero calls, waving. "Why don't you join us?"

# 16



*RAPSODY*

With a small canvas and some paint in hand, I wander the grounds of Midnight Manor in search of the pond. It would be a pretty place to paint, and more importantly, I need to clear my head after what happened with Kol.

Maybe staying here isn't what's best for me. I feel more confused than ever. Maybe my mom was right all those years she told me I couldn't handle the real world.

I come over the crest of a rolling hill and see the pond down below. But apparently, I'm not the only one who wanted to hang out here today. The sun goes behind a cloud, and I shiver. At least that's the reason I tell myself. It has nothing to do with Kol and Nero sitting near the pond's edge.

Darn it. I definitely don't want to see Kol. I don't think I can take his whiplash moods today, and being around him certainly won't help me sort out my feelings.

I step backward, but before I can get out of sight, Nero spots me. He raises his hand and waves. "Hey, Rapsody. Why don't you join us?"

Kol's body stiffens. He doesn't turn around to look at me.

Not wanting to be rude and turn down Nero's invitation, I slowly walk over. I realize I have a decision to make as I get closer. Will I sit beside Kol or Nero?

I choose Nero since he's the one who invited me, and Kol hasn't acknowledged my presence. When I reach them, I smile and sit, carefully placing the long fabric of my dress over my bare legs.

Nero eyes the paints when I set them down to my left. "You're a painter?"

My cheeks heat. "I don't know if I'd call myself a painter, but I enjoy it. I find it relaxing. Helps to clear my head."

Kol scoffs, and for the first time since I sat down, our eyes connect.

"What?" I snipe, sick of his Jekyll and Hyde act.

"Own it. You're a talented painter."

My forehead creases. "How would you know?"

In the short time we were seeing each other, I hadn't had the opportunity to show him any of my paintings.

"I was in the conservatory this morning and saw your paintings."

I blink several times, not sure what to say. Not sure why he would bother complimenting me.

Nero laughs and shakes his head. "I love being right."

I look at him. "What do you mean?"

"Ignore him. He's drunk. And high," Kol says.

Then I see the bottle of booze on the grass. "Are you guys celebrating something?"

A caustic laugh leaves Nero. "Certainly not. It's a shit day for us Vosses, second only to the day that our mother was murdered. And today..." He leans in and looks me straight in the eye. There's a glassy glint to his stare. "Today is especially shitty for me."

"What happened?"

"Called off my wedding." He rests a hand on my knee.

"I'm sorry." I place my hand over his and squeeze. No wonder he's getting drunk.

"You could help me feel better, Rapsody. I can think of some ways you could help me forget all the—"

"Cut it out, kid." Kol's voice is as frosty as the tips of the Rocky Mountains in winter.

Nero laughs and removes his hand from under mine. Then he reaches into his pocket and pulls out a joint. "Want some?"

I shake my head. "No thanks."

"Suit yourself." He holds his hand out to Kol, who places a lighter in his palm, then Nero lights the end of his joint.

The musty scent of a skunk wafts past me.

Nero inhales, then exhales and offers it to Kol, who waves him off.

"You two are no fun. I'm gonna go see if I can find some trouble. Get my mind off things." Nero gets up off the grass and wobbles a bit before finding his equilibrium. "See you two lov... see you two later."

I watch him stumble his way up the hill. "Is he okay to be alone?"

"He'll be fine. Probably go pass out some-where and sleep it off."

I think back to what a mess I was the day I left Atlanta. "He must be upset about ending his engagement, even if he's the one who called it off."

"You'd know better than me what that feels like." Kol meets my gaze. Rather than the hatred I'm used to seeing, this time there's only hurt.

I sigh, shoulders sagging. "I'm tired of looking back, Kol. I can't change the past any more than you can. Maybe if you'd told me the truth from the beginning, we'd be happily married right now. Maybe if I'd come to ask you about what my mom told me, I wouldn't have run away. I don't know. Neither of us does. I'm sorry I hurt you, but I hurt myself in the process too. You seem to forget that part."

Kol rips grass blades up from beside him and tosses them forward. "You're right. We both could have done things differently, I guess."

"I just know that I need to look forward. You've given me the chance to figure out what I want for my life, and to do that, I can't keep looking toward the past. I need to look ahead, figure out what I want. I understand if you can't do that, but if that's the case, then I should probably leave."

His penetrating gaze meets mine. "Where would you go? Back to Alistair?" Kol says his name as if it's a curse.

I shake my head. "No. That's one good thing to come from you kidnapping me, I think. I shouldn't have ever said yes to marrying him. I didn't feel about him the way..." *The way I felt about you.* "I was marrying him for the wrong reasons, and that's not fair to him. Though I should probably call him at some point to resolve things."

Kol's eyebrows draw together at that suggestion, so I drop the topic for the time being. "You can stay here as long as you want, Rapsody. I'll stop bringing up the past. Let's start fresh."

Hope springs buoyant in my chest, like a life raft floating on the water. "Really? You think you can do that?" I hold my breath, waiting for the answer, realizing that's what I want more than anything.

The corners of his lips press in, but he nods. "Yeah, I think I finally can."

Without thinking, I draw him into a hug. "Thank you, Kol."

His body is rigid at first, but he wraps his arms around me slowly and returns the hug. The sun peeks from behind a cloud and warms the top of my head and my shoulders. We draw back, and the light makes the amber flecks in his eyes sparkle.

Tension draws taut between us, and I clear my throat and reposition myself with my legs crossed in front of me, leaning back on my hands.

"So, what do you plan to do to figure out what you want next?" he asks.

I raise my face to the sun, closing my eyes. "I'm not sure exactly. Try things I've never done before, I guess. Experience life. That sounds stupid probably, but I've never had any of the experiences that most people have at my age. I've only ever seen them in TV shows or movies." I lower my chin when the sun goes behind a cloud, and my attention snags on the bottle of whiskey. "Take that for instance. I've never even had a drink before."

Kol's eyes widen in disbelief. "You've never had a drop of alcohol in your life?"

I shake my head. "My mom didn't keep any in the house. If she did, I probably would have snuck some just to see what it feels like to be drunk." I chuckle.

Kol picks up the bottle by the neck and holds it out to me. "Probably not the best experience, drinking it straight from the bottle rather than in a mixed drink, but here."

Excitement bubbles in my chest. "I shouldn't..."

"But you want to?" He arches an eyebrow. "Nothing is stopping you from doing what you want anymore. You said so yourself, you wanted to know what it's like." There's a gleam in his eye as if he's daring me.

But he's right. I don't have to be the cowering little girl anymore. I'm sticking around here so I can make decisions for myself, good and bad, so be it. One drink isn't the end of the world, right?

I take the bottle from him, hesitantly bringing it up to my lips. I swallow a mouthful and cough immediately, my eyes watering. Kol laughs and swipes the bottle from me, taking a swig of his own.

"That's awful!" I bring my hand to my throat, willing the burning sensation to go away.

He shrugs and hands the bottle back to me. "Like I said, probably not the best introduction to alcohol, but you made the decision for yourself."

A grin spreads across my face because he's right. No one told me what to do, no one insisted I do one thing or another. I got to make the call. The grin remains on my face as I tilt the bottle to my lips again, taking a smaller sip this time.

What's the worst that could happen?

# 17



Sometime later, I'm not even sure how long, I can't stop laughing. For no real reason, laughter is billowing out of me like a cloud of smoke.

"Well, I think you can check getting drunk off your list." Kol holds out his hand. "Here, why don't you give me the bottle now?"

I raise the bottle over my head, grinning. "No way! This is fun."

He shakes his head. "Maybe so, but you'll

regret it if you drink any more than you already have, trust me."

I guffaw. "I think you just don't know how to have fun."

Kol gives me a "really" look. "I'm twelve years older than you, spent over a decade in the military, and was raised by a billionaire, and you think I don't know how to have fun?" He arches a dark eyebrow.

I burst into a fit of giggles. "I guess when you put it that way."

He shakes his head and props up on his knees to pull the bottle away from me, but I don't let go. Instead of him plucking it away from my hands, I go with the bottle, losing my balance and falling forward. Kol falls back onto the grass with a grunt, me on top of him, the whiskey bottle rolling out of my hand onto the grass.

He looks up at me, his gaze intense, and I feel every bit of his muscular body underneath me. Both our breathing is shallow as our eyes scour the other's. Kol's gaze dips to my mouth, and I can't help but slide my tongue over my lip, wishing it was Kol's tongue.

A low groan rumbles in his chest beneath me, and I suck in a breath. I want so badly to lower myself so that our mouths collide. He clears his throat and takes my hips in his hands, maneuvering me off of him.

I frown and straighten myself until I'm sitting on the grass again, avoiding his gaze.

"What's wrong, Rapsody?"

Do I dare confess to him my feelings? Tell him that I think about him all the time, think about the things I imagine us doing together with our bodies?

Oh, the hell with it.

"I thought of something else I want to explore moving forward." I keep staring at the dark water of the pond, afraid I'll chicken out if I look directly at him.

"What's that?"

"My sexuality. I want to know what it means to be desired, to give my body to someone else."

Kol doesn't say anything for a beat, and the urge to turn my head and see what he's thinking is so strong, but I resist, afraid I'll see either disgust or judgment.

"Um…" He clears his throat. "Does that mean you're still a virgin? You and Alistair…"

I blink a few times, realizing he probably assumed if I was marrying Alistair, we would have. "No, we never… we just kissed. He wanted to wait until marriage."

"Isn't that what you wanted, too?"

I meet his gaze, and the air rushes from my lungs like a burst balloon when I see the look of possession on his face. "Not anymore. I want to live. And I think I'll come to find that's a big part of feeling alive."

Kol's Adam's apple bobs as he swallows, pupils growing larger by the second. "And where do you plan on finding someone to explore all of this with?" He drags his fingertip from my shoulder down to my wrist, leaving goose bumps in its wake.

"I don't know." My voice is breathy, barely there. "I suppose I'll have to go looking for someone who's willing and able. Maybe Nero—"

Kol's hand whips around to clutch the back of my head, weaving into my French braid. "Finish that sentence, Rapsody, and you'll regret it."

My nipples pucker in my bra. "Does that mean *you* want to help me?"

Kol growls. "You know the damn answer to that. I'll kill anyone if they get in my way."

He leans toward me, and his lips crash into mine, firm and insistent. I open for him, sighing in relief when his tongue crests over mine. It's only now that I realize how desperate I've been to feel him like this again.

His hand tightens its grip on the back of my head, and he uses the leverage to move me where he wants. My body heats, and a moan escapes me. What I want, I don't know, but I know I need more of whatever he'll offer.

Kol pulls away, and I whimper. He rests his forehead against mine, breathing heavily. He doesn't say anything for a beat, and if he pulls away again, I may just find someone else.

Seconds tick by, his eyes searching mine.

"Fuck it," he says. "Let's explore."

His hands slip down to my waist, and he lifts me as if I weigh nothing at all. He hauls me over his lap, spreading his legs and setting me between them. I'm facing away from him so that my back is pressed against his firm chest.

"What... what are you doing?" My breathing is shallow.

"What you asked for. Helping you explore." He tugs my braid to one side so it rests between my breasts and drags his tongue from the base of my neck up to my earlobe. "Let's find out what you look like when a man makes you come, shall we?"

Anticipation twists in my abdomen, and I nod eagerly. Kol chuckles as his hands coast over the fabric of my dress, over my breasts. I can't help but arch into his touch, wanting more. But he continues his descent until he reaches my upper thighs. He pulls the fabric of my dress up until it lays at my waist, exposing my white cotton thong.

Kol brings a hand to the waistband, trailing his fingers back and forth under the elastic. My body feels alive in anticipation, but he goes no further.

"Kol, please."

He pushes his nose into my hair with a dark chuckle. "All good things to those who wait, sweetheart."

"I've waited a lifetime."

He tilts his hips, and the hard length of his arousal presses into me from behind. My eyes drift closed, and my head falls back onto his shoulder, offering myself for him to do what he wants.

He breathes me in as he finally pushes his hand under my panties, his fingertips trailing down to my mound. He cups it in his large hand.

"Fuck, Rapsody." He groans. "Do you know how long I've waited to touch this pussy? Make it mine?"

His vulgar words do the opposite of what I would have thought they'd do—they ratchet up my arousal to a level I've never experienced before. My hips gyrate of their own accord.

"Ah, you like that, do you? Like me talking about your cunt and how much I crave it?"

A moan escapes my lips.

"Answer me, Rapsody."

"Yes."

He dips his fingers between my folds to find me wet and wanting, and he slides his finger over my clit. I buck up off his lap, my legs drawing together on instinct. Kol wraps an arm around my middle to keep me in place.

"You're not going anywhere, sweetheart. Now bring your legs over my thighs."

I do as he says, spreading myself wide. I'm rewarded when he spreads my arousal up over my clit and moves his fingers.

"That's my good girl."

"Oh, god." I arch my back again, but his arm around my middle keeps me in place.

"Me. I'm your god, Rapsody." Kol increases the pressure, moving his fingers in a steady rhythm, and I move one rung further up the ladder. He tucks his face into my neck and inhales deeply. "You always smell so fucking good. Drives me crazy."

The pressure throughout my body mounts, and all my muscles feel as if they might snap.

Kol opens his mouth on my throat as though he might bite me, but instead holds himself there like a predator asserting his dominance over his prey. And god, does it do something to me, that feeling of being at his mercy, under his control. Every part of my body warms, and my limbs and lips tingle.

He increases the tempo and pressure again. I won't last much longer, and I can't really tell if I want to or not. This feels so, so amazing, but I can only imagine what my climax might feel like when it comes.

The sound of Kol's slick fingers working me and the feel of the sun coming out from behind a cloud will stay with me for eternity. My brain tries to commit every single sensation to memory.

My hips move, desperate for more friction. I suck in a breath and hold it as I reach the crest of the mountain Kol led me to, and I cry out.

"That's it, sweetheart. Come all over my hand. Give it to me. Only me."

Air leaves my lungs in a whoosh as stars settle over my vision, and I feel as if I'm the shooting star. I have no idea if I say anything, what I'm doing with my body, nothing. All of it is secondary to the feeling of bliss when my body comes apart and slowly, slowly starts piecing itself back together.

I've never experienced anything like that sensation in my life. Of course, I've masturbated before, but I've only ever had the use of my own hand, and even when I finished, the results were... tepid at best.

But with Kol... I'm not sure I even have words to describe what I just felt. I didn't know anything could ever feel that way.

He says nothing as I lean back against him, catching my breath. My inexperience puts me at a disadvantage. I don't know what to say or do. What do people do after they fool around? Do they talk about it? Pretend it never happened? Am I supposed to reciprocate now?

Feeling a bit like a fool because I can't answer any of those questions, I pull my dress down so I'm covered, then crawl out of Kol's lap. When I dare to look back at him, he's leaning back on his hands, chin up, eyes shut, and his nostrils flared. He almost looks as if he's in pain.

"I—"

"Just give me a minute," he rushes to say.

"Are you okay?" Did I hurt him when I came? I sort of blacked out, so I'm not really sure what I did. Maybe my head jerked back and hit his chin, or maybe I accidentally hit him in the—oh.

Oh wow.

Kol's erection is pushing against his shorts,

looking as though it might tear the fabric, and the outline... is... huge.

Not like I have anything to compare it to, but I thought the average guy was supposed to be six inches or something? I mean, I can't see the whole thing, but there is definitely more than six inches pushing against those cargo shorts.

"Fine. I just need to get this hard-on under control." He sounds pissed off. Maybe I am supposed to return the favor.

"Do you want me to..." I gesture toward his lap.

His eyes whip open, glaring at me. "Talking shit like that isn't gonna help, Rapsody."

I press my lips together. "I'm sorry, I just don't know what I'm supposed to do now." My hands fidget in front of me.

"Talk about something. Anything that'll get my mind off how badly I want to rut inside you right now."

My cheeks heat at what I'm choosing to think of as a compliment, and I search my addled brain for anything. The first thing that comes to mind is something Nero mentioned earlier. "Nero said that today was a bad day for the Vosses. What did he mean?"

Kol sighs. "Yep, that'll do it."

He looks down at his lap. I can't help but look, too, and I realize the bulge isn't as pronounced as it was.

"If you don't want to talk about it, that's fine." Though I really want him to trust me and open up.

He sits up straight and reaches for the whiskey bottle that's lying on its side and somehow still has some liquid in it. He brings it to his lips and takes a generous swig before passing the bottle to me. "Today is the day my father died."

My stomach takes a freefall off a high rise. "I'm so sorry." I lift the bottle to my lips, cringing as the alcohol slides down my throat.

"Don't be. He was the worst sort of human being. I was happy when he died."

What kind of man must his father have been for him to feel that way?

I'm not sure what to say, but the raw pain in Kol's eyes has me reaching out to take his hand. He lets me, linking our fingers together.

"It's not that today is hard because I'm mourning my father. It just brings up all the shit from my childhood that I'd rather forget."

I don't know how, but some instinct tells me not to ask what he's referring to. At least, not today. So instead, I try a different tactic.

"Well then, I guess I understand why you and your brother were on a mission to get drunk, so let's do it," I say with false cheer.

It seems to work though, the corner of his lips creeping up ever so slightly. "Let's then."

I take another swig from the bottle and pass it back to him.

An hour later, I realize why Kol tried to warn me as he holds my hair back while I throw up into the grass.

# 18



A couple days later, my hangover still lingers behind my eyes. I don't know why people subject themselves to that. It was fun, but heaving my guts up and waking the next morning feeling like a mining crew was digging in my brain wasn't worth it.

Still, I'm thankful I can check off getting drunk. Now I know for myself why I won't be doing it again.

I didn't leave my bedroom the entire day, but Kol came to check on me once, bringing me ibuprofen to help put me out of my misery. Today, I only saw him in the dining room at breakfast.

Everyone was quiet, seeming content to sit in silence and eat. I couldn't help but wonder if it was because of Nero calling off his wedding or because the anniversary of their father's death was still hanging over the brothers.

Usually, Anabelle would try to make conversation with me, but even she was quiet. I wonder if that's because of how I acted when I asked her about the people in the masks. I'll have to apologize to her. It's not like I can expect her to forego her loyalty to her husband to fill me in on something that is obviously supposed to be a secret.

Basically, breakfast was uncomfortable, and I couldn't wait to get out of there. I ate as quickly as I could and excused myself from the table.

I'm not sure if Kol's avoiding me after what happened at the pond. I hope not, because ever since my headache subsided enough for me to think clearly, I'd been reliving our time together in my mind. And I want to do it again. That and more. But I'll have to follow his lead for fear that if I push him too far too fast, he'll strip me away entirely.

I spent the day outside because I overheard Marcel talking to Mrs. Potter about how a storm is due to sweep in tonight.

My paintbrush flicks over a canvas in an arch as I hear the first raindrops hit the glass roof of the conservatory. What starts as a light sprinkling quickly turns to the pounding of big raindrops on the glass, the wind picking up. Lightning streaks across the sky, lighting up the room for moments and casting shadows where there weren't any before. Rolling thunder follows, shaking the glass in its iron casings.

My work area is bathed in light courtesy of the ring light Kol provided, but it's hard not to feel as though something is lurking in the surrounding darkness, watching, waiting. A shiver runs down my spine as I look away from my lit-up canvas at the room beyond. I shrug off my unease and start to paint again, but the feeling of being watched causes the hairs on my neck to rise.

"Hello?" I call, but there's no answer.

I stay still for a moment, keeping my breathing shallow and listening, but only the sound of the pelting rain on glass rings out.

"Don't be such a scaredy cat," I mumble to myself and bring the paintbrush to the canvas again.

A loud crack of thunder echoes through the room, and I yelp, dropping my paintbrush. My hand flies to my chest as my heartbeat races in the rapid-fire staccato of a machine gun, my breath strangled.

"Darn it."

I bend to retrieve the brush when another crack lets loose from the sky, so loud that it sounds as if God is playing the cymbals right above the glass roof. When I startle, I jerk up and hit the edge of the easel.

"Ouch." I bring my hand to the edge of my hairline and grimace.

A flash of lightning bathes the room in its ethereal glow before the room plunges into darkness. I still, waiting, waiting, waiting for the lights to come back on, remaining in darkness.

"Shoot." Reaching out blindly, I find the small table with the rest of my brushes and paints on it and set down the brush.

How am I going to find my way back to my room in the dark? This manor is creepy enough in the middle of the day, but at night with zero light and being as big as it is, navigating it feels like an impossible task. I decide to sit tight for a few minutes and see if the lights come back on. If they don't...

Lightning strikes again, and this time, I'm looking outside when it does. Everything out there feels threatening in the middle of the storm. The trunks of the trees look like soldiers at attention. The natural rise and fall of the lawn make me think of the undead pushing up from their graves, and a big, black creature streaks across the lawn.

There's no way I'm spending the night here. I'll have to somehow find my way back to my room, even if it means I have to wait for every lightning strike to see where I'm going and make only a little bit of progress at a time.

On the next lightning strike, I turn toward the door and mentally map out the way to get there. Then I walk slowly in the dark with my hands out in front of me. I miss the mark a few times and stumble into something, but when the lightning flashes again, I'm closer to the door.

As I walk, I think I must be close now, though there's no real way to tell. Lightning flashes again, and I am indeed only mere feet from the door. A massive silhouette enters the doorway, and I scream, stumbling back.

A light shines in my eyes, blinding me, and a hand grips my arm. I scream louder, trying to free myself, until the sound of his voice cuts through my panic.

"It's me."

I still, panting hard. "Kol?"

"What the hell happened to you?" His voice booms through the dark room like a bass drum.

"The lights all went out, and I couldn't see... I... I didn't know it was you."

He lets go of my arm, and with his other hand, he shifts the light on what I now realize is his phone and brings it to my face again. I squint.

"You're bleeding."

"What?" I touch my head where I hit the corner of the easel, and it comes away wet. When I bring my hand down in front of me, Kol points the flashlight at my fingertips, where red liquid paints my pale skin. The ground feels as though it swells up underneath me, and I sway, feeling woozy.

"Shit," Kol says as I fall into his arms.

Kol wraps me in his arms while he stomps through the house. Of course, he knows his way even in the dark. He's lived here his entire life.

"I'm going to get you all bloody." I'm still lightheaded, so I don't lift my head, even though I want to so I don't get his shirt bloody.

"That's the least of your concerns." Kol sounds pissed, so I decide to shut up until we get wherever he's taking me.

He's quiet as he walks through the manor. I've never seen it this dark before, even at night. It does nothing to quell the unease I had in the conservatory.

Eventually, another bolt of lightning reveals the stained-glass lion as we walk into the north wing. I can't help but think of the tattooed lion on the arm that's holding me right now.

Kol bypasses my room in favor of his own, and I secretly thrill at getting to glimpse his room for the first time, even if it's pitch black. I can't make much out as he weaves through the room toward the bath, and once we're inside, he gently sets me on the counter.

"Stay put," he snaps and pulls his phone from the pocket of his pants, pressing on the flashlight.

As he riffles through the vanity drawers, the flashlight is directed down at the drawers and casts a shadow on his face, highlighting and deepening the angle of his jaw, the strong line of his nose. He appears even more intimidating than normal.

When he finally finds what he's looking for, he slaps it on the counter beside my hip. "Let me get a better look at this. Close your eyes."

Light shines brightly behind my eyelids. Then there's a whooshing sound, and it gets even brighter.

"The lights are back on, but maybe you shouldn't open your eyes, so you don't pass out." Once again, he sounds annoyed by my reaction to the sight of my own blood.

"I think I'm okay now that I know what to expect," I say in a small voice.

"You sure?"

I nod and slowly open my eyes. They meet Kol's amber hues immediately. He stands in front of me with his arms open, hands inches from each of my arms in case I sway to the side again. I glance down and find that blood has dripped onto my shirt. I swallow hard, pushing back the nauseated feeling crawling up my throat.

"You good?"

I nod slowly. "Yeah, I think so."

He nods and unpacks the first aid supplies. "Head wounds bleed a lot. It probably looks worse than it is. I won't know until I clean you up and take a look."

"Okay."

Once he arranges everything like a skilled surgeon, he walks over to the linen closet and pulls out a clean washcloth, then he wets it under the faucet.

"I'll be gentle, but this might hurt." He brings the washcloth to my face and wipes away blood.

I close my eyes to make it easier for him and wince when he gets closer to the cut at my hairline.

"I take it the sight of blood isn't your thing?"

I thank him for making conversation in an effort to distract me even though his question comes out sounding forced. "I guess not, though I didn't really know that until now."

When I open my eyes, he gives me a questioning look.

"I didn't have the usual childhood experiences of playing outside and skinning my knees and stuff." I shrug, feeling inadequate somehow after admitting it. "It's not like I've never scratched myself or anything, but I've never seen that much blood before."

He nods and tosses the washcloth in the sink, then rips open a small package. "I need to disinfect the wound to make sure it doesn't get infected. This will sting." He holds the wipe up near my head and the strong scent of alcohol wafts up my nose. "Ready?"

He meets my gaze, and I nod. Gently, he brings the wipe to the cut on my head. I wince when it touches my open wound, and the stinging sensation feels like fire on my skin.

"Just another second. There, done." He turns and tosses the wipe in the garbage. "Some ointment and a Band-Aid, and you should be good in a few days."

"I don't need stitches?"

He shakes his head. "No, it's a small cut. It's already clotting." Kol applies the antiseptic cream, then puts a small Band-Aid on my forehead and steps back. "Done."

"Thank you for fixing me up."

Our gazes lock and hold, and he swallows hard, stepping closer. "You need to be more careful."

I watch his lips move, and all I can think about is how I want them on me. "As long as the lights stay on, I should be good."

I inch forward on the counter, close enough that our breaths mingle, imploring him with my eyes to kiss me. His breathing picks up, and his gaze diverts to my lips, and my belly tugs.

Disappointment rolls over me like a wave when Kol steps back and clears his throat. Here we go again.

"You probably want to get back to your room and change." He motions to my shirt and the blood there.

"Right." I hop down off the counter, putting on my best smile. "Thanks for coming to my aid and fixing me up."

He nods and rubs the palm of his hand over his cropped hair.

The shower turns on before I've even left the room, and my disappointment doubles that he didn't ask me to join him.

# 19



*KOL*

I squeeze my eyes shut and pinch the bridge of my nose, willing the image of Rapsody covered in blood to leave my brain. It's been on repeat for days now, ever since I found her in the conservatory, blood dripping down her face onto her shirt.

I've seen a lot of shit. Enough shit that a small cut on a head shouldn't have been so alarming, but the image is haunting me. Which is why I've been avoiding her. Which is fucking stupid since I'm trying to woo her into loving me again. Kind of impossible to do when I'm keeping my distance.

If I'm really honest with myself, it's also because of what happened at the pond and how much it affected me. Watching Rapsody fall apart courtesy of my fingers, knowing I was the one responsible and that no one else had ever come before me—fuck, that was enough to almost have me busting a nut in my shorts.

Sweet, innocent Rapsody has a naughty side, and now that I've discovered it, it's impossible to ignore. Every time she's looked at me since our encounter, it's there on her face— she's craving more. She's hungry for me to show her all the ways I can bring her pleasure—which should be fine, it's part of the plan.

What is not part of the plan is me relishing the opportunity. Me being thirsty as well.

I blow out a breath and shut the laptop on my desk, slumping back in my chair with a sigh. I need to decide what I'm doing, and whether this plan is feasible anymore.

Can I make Rapsody love me without falling for her myself? Do I even want to still?

I think back to where this all started... me waiting on the steps of city hall, taking in every pedestrian on the street, sure that she was around the corner, and it would be like the parting of the sea for Moses. The woman I knew could save me from myself would be there to commit her life to me and mine to her, and it didn't matter what had happened in the past, what I had done. If someone like Rapsody could love me, then I must be worth loving.

But the minutes ticked by, first one, then five, then fifteen. By the time an hour had passed, my stomach was on the concrete, and my heart had gone eight rounds against the heavyweight champion in the ring. It was a beat-up, pulpy mess. Devastation is too weak a word to describe how I felt when I knew that Rapsody didn't want to marry me anymore.

I shouldn't have been surprised, I guess. Everyone who has supposedly loved me has left, one way or another.

Anger rises to the forefront as it always does when I think about all the people who have let me down over my lifetime.

Yes, I can do this. I can show Rapsody what it feels like when someone plays with your emotions without thinking of the consequences.

With that thought in mind, I push back from my desk and leave my bedroom. When I knock on Rapsody's door, there's no answer. Frowning, I continue down the hallway until I reach the communal part of the manor.

I quickly check the conservatory, but I don't find her there. I take a moment to admire the painting she's working on of a night sky, moonlight bathing the world below.

Continuing on my quest, I decide to check the kitchen. It's always alive with activity. Surely someone there might know where I can find her.

Halfway to my destination, I come across Marcel speaking with his partner, Finn, in the hallway. When they notice my footsteps, they take a step back from each other. They must think they're being stealthy and none of us know they're a couple.

"Where's Rapsody?" I don't bother with pleasantries.

Marcel turns to face me, chin up. "I saw her leave the manor a few minutes ago."

"Where was she heading?"

"I'm not sure, sir, but she went out the door closest to the maze." He motions in the general direction.

The maze. Just fucking great.

I don't say anything as I move past them, hurrying to catch up to her. I have no idea if she's planning on going into the maze, but if I don't beat her there before she goes in, my plan for the day will be a bust. Having to spend time there during Asher and Anabelle's wedding ceremony was bad enough. If I ever have to go in there again, it will be too soon.

A couple of minutes later, I step outside and find her standing at the entrance to the maze.

"Rapsody," I call, jogging over to her.

She looks at me over her shoulder and smiles.

God, that fucking smile could light up the sky if the sun weren't already out.

"What are you doing?" I ask when I reach her.

She motions to the maze. "I was thinking of going in to check it out, but when I got here, I was worried I might not be able to find my way out."

I swallow.

"Do you want to go in with me? You must know your way around. You were probably in here a million times when you were a kid."

The blood drains from my face as a cold sweat breaks out on my forehead.

Rapsody steps toward me. "Are you okay?"

"Yeah, yeah... I..." My gaze goes over her shoulder to the maze and the twelve-foot hedges that feel as though they're towering over us.

All of those memories from my childhood assault me at once, like bullets ripping through my calm demeanor. When Rapsody takes my hand, the frenzy of thoughts calm so they're not so overwhelming.

"Do you want to go somewhere else?" She squeezes my hand.

"Yeah. I came to find you to see if you want to go to the pond with me."

She looks over her shoulder at the maze then back at me. "Let's go."

We walk in silence for a while, which is good. It gives me time to put myself back together. I avoid that fucking maze whenever possible because it's a damn trigger. Asher offered to cut it down for me at least a decade ago, but my mom's prized rose bush is in the middle, so I didn't have it in me to say yes. It would have felt like severing a tie to her.

Rapsody seems to be in tune with the fact that I need to get my shit together and doesn't speak until the pond comes into view.

"How come you wanted to come here?" she asks as we walk down the slope toward the water.

She's in front of me, and I pull her to a stop by taking her hand. "I thought of another experience you could have. Something I doubt you've ever done before."

A spark lights in her emerald eyes, as sure as if I'd struck a match. "What is it?"

"Skinny dipping."

She blinks a few times then laughs. "Are you serious?"

"Totally." I walk past her, stripping off my shirt and letting it fall to the grass. Then I toe off my shoes.

"What if someone else comes?"

I turn to face her and find her looking back the way we came. "No one is going to bother us."

She turns back around and looks at me as I'm sliding off my shorts, revealing my black boxer briefs. "But Nero was here just last week."

I shrug then turn around. "He was here with me. This is my spot, not his." Then I push down my boxer briefs while I walk, stepping out of them when they fall to my ankles.

Since I'm not facing her, I can't be sure, but I'd bet money on the fact that she's checking out my ass right now. The water is a little chilly when I step into it, but nothing terrible.

Once I'm in it to my waist, I turn and face her. "Come on. It's refreshing."

She chews on her bottom lip, looking unsure. "My hair will be a rat's nest if I go in there."

I tilt my head and give her an incredulous look since her hair is pulled back in its usual thick braid.

"It's true! You have no idea what kind of maintenance is involved with hair this long."

I don't doubt it for a second. "Come on! You wanted new experiences. If you want, I'll turn around while you get in."

She looks over her shoulder one last time

then back at me. "All right, fine. Turn around."

Thank god my dick is underwater so she can't see how fast it salutes her decision.

# 20

*RAPSODY*

Once Kol has turned his back toward me, I pull my T-shirt up over my head. I can't believe I'm doing this, but at the same time, a rush of excitement flows through me. Partly for the new experience, but partly because I'm going to be naked—with Kol.

Next to go are my shoes and socks, then my leggings. When I unclasp my bra, I take a deep breath before I let it fall to the grass. I've never been naked with a man before. Never has a man seen my bare breasts. Finally, I push my panties down my legs and step out of them.

The sun warms my body as I take tentative steps toward the edge of the water.

Kol's back muscles tighten when he hears me step into the water. "Let me know when it's safe to turn around."

Once I'm waist deep, I crouch down so that my chest is covered. "You can turn around."

When he does, he meets my gaze. "Another thing you can check off your list."

"I guess so."

"Want to go deeper?" He arches an eyebrow.

This is it. This is my moment to be brave. Without saying a word, I push up to my full height. Water sluices over my breasts, and I stand there for a moment while Kol takes me in. His eyes grow wider with a predatory gleam as he stalks toward me.

I force myself not to look away from him, but it's easier than expected. The way his gaze devours me makes me feel wanted and beautiful.

"Fuck, Rapsody." His voice is rough like sandpaper.

"Do you still want to go deeper?" I ask.

He shakes his head, meeting my gaze. "No, now I want to suck on your glorious tits." I press my thighs together underwater, but Kol smirks as if he can read my mind. "You gonna let me worship these tits, sweetheart?"

My nipples pucker even tighter than they already were, and a low chuckle leaves Kol. He's finally in front of me, only inches away, and I watch as he lowers his mouth to my right breast. He does it so slowly that I'm practically panting by the time he flicks his tongue against my turgid peak.

My head tips back, releasing a breathy exhalation, when he closes his mouth around the bud, pulling my lower half into him. His hard length presses against me, and an involuntary shudder works its way through my body. Kol's tongue flicks and swirls around my nipple, and he sucks hard before softly biting the tip. A mewl crawls up my throat, and my hips move of their own accord, rubbing his erection against my tummy.

Kol releases my breast and backs up a few inches. "Want to check another thing off your list?"

I *do* want. I want to know what his length feels like in my hand, if he feels as hard and smooth as I imagined. Tentatively, I reach under the water and grip him. He shuts his eyes with a curse. When I move my hand up and down his shaft, he groans. Heat floods my body, even in the lukewarm water.

Kol brings his head down to my other breast, and his tongue slides over my nipple, causing the peak to glisten. He brings his hand up to my other breast, massaging and tweaking the nipple with his finger and thumb.

I grip him tighter, and his hips slowly move back and forth. The vision of him doing that while entering my body comes to mind, and my free hand runs down the back of his head. The friction of his stubble against my palm only adds to the chorus of sensations racing through my body.

Kol bites my nipple, harder this time, and tugs. I cry out. Not because it's painful, though it is in the most delicious way, but because it feels like electricity racing straight from my breast down between my legs. My clit is swollen and desperate for attention, and I'd bet anything Kol knows that.

"Kol, I..." I don't know how to finish my thought.

"Don't worry, sweetheart, I know what you need."

Without warning, his hands grip the backs of my thighs. He tugs me up out of the water and wraps my legs around his waist. My yelp turns into a moan when his length centers between my legs. Oh god, if it feels this good just to have him *near* my entrance, what would it feel like to have him inside me?

Kol's lips meet mine, and he doesn't stop kissing me the entire walk out of the pond. It's all I can do to stop myself from grinding against him. My clit pulses. Once we're a few paces from the water, Kol gently lays me on the grass, then straightens back up to stand over me. I get my first good look at his naked body.

It's glorious. There's a brutal sort of beauty about him from the muscles apparent under his olive skin and the tattoos on his body. The way he holds himself, hands clenched, chest heaving—all of it comes together to make the perfect package. Even the scars I assume he must have gotten while he was in the military only add to his coarse beauty.

His eyes soak me in, and he lazily strokes his cock while his gaze roams my body. When his gaze reaches the apex between my thighs, his hand stills. "Fuck, sweetheart, did you shave that pussy bare for me?"

"Yes." I think back to my decision a couple of days ago to do so and know I made the right one when the need to conquer me shines in his eyes.

"Jesus." He squeezes the end of his cock as if the sight of my body is too much. "I'm gonna make you come with my tongue. That alright with you?"

My hips shift just thinking about having Kol's head between my legs. I nod. What will it feel like to have his tongue on me when his fingers undid me with such ease?

Kol falls to his knees and slides his hands up my thighs, spreading me open for him. "Are you on birth control?"

My eyes widen. I thought he said mouth? Are we doing this now?

He chuckles, clearly reading my thoughts. "Not today, but birth control takes a while to kick in. When I take this pussy, I have to go in bare."

I squeeze my legs together to stem the insistent thrumming between them, but Kol holds my thighs wide open with his hands.

"I'm on the Depo-Provera shot. I started it before my wedding, so I have another... five or six weeks left before I have to get another one."

Kol's jaw tightens for a moment at the reminder of why I went on birth control in the first place, but he seems to set those feelings aside and his jaw relaxes. "Good."

He lies down between my legs and his whiskey-colored eyes stare up at me. I'm going to paint this image one day. Not for anyone else to see, but to cement it in my mind.

Kol uses his thumbs to spread me wide, then his tongue takes a thorough swipe from top to bottom. I almost internally combust. The sensation is too much, yet I yearn for more.

A moan rips from my throat as he leans in and gets to work. It feels as if he's French kissing my clit. The sounds slipping out of him awaken my arousal for him even more.

It's not going to take me long to finish at this rate.

Kol sucks on my clit, and I feel as if I'm levitating, but he holds me to the ground with the firm push of his hand on my hips. I moan, not caring if anyone nearby overhears me. The sun bathes us in heat while my hands find my breasts, squeezing them both. Kol watches me from between my legs, and it's so erotic. His heated gaze takes me up another level, and I tug on my nipples. An electric current rushes from my nipples to where his tongue is centered on me.

I pant, arching my back, pressing my head into the grass. Kol flicks my clit with his tongue while his fingers explore my entrance. He doesn't push them inside, and I turn more desperate, gyrating my hips, longing to feel any part of him inside me.

I'm so close. I feel like a bomb about to detonate—full of so much pent-up energy that I'm liable to take out the entire manor.

He sucks hard on my clit, and I come on a cry, grinding my hips into his face while he devours me whole.

When I come down from my orgasm, I lie limp in the grass, staring at the sky and the white clouds passing overhead.

"Do you have any idea how good you taste coming on my tongue?"

I look away from the sky and heave myself up on my elbows. Kol is still between my legs, but he's on his knees, fisting his cock.

"You gonna let me come all over this virgin pussy, sweetheart?"

My insides clench with his words. "Yes, yes."

His arm with the lion tattoo jerks roughly on his rigid cock. I watch, studying his movements so that the next time we're together, I can replicate his actions and take him where he's taking himself.

"Play with my balls."

I move so that I'm half sitting up, leaning back against one hand and reaching out with the other. The heavy weight of his balls rests in my palms, and he tilts his head back with a groan, continuing to jerk himself.

Feeling a little braver now that I've seen his reaction, I fondle his balls, moving them in my hand and squeezing lightly.

"Fuck! I'll bet you can't wait for me to come inside you, painting your insides."

"Kol..." I squeeze harder on his balls.

The cords in his neck tighten, and he roars as his cum spurts onto my lower abdomen and the top of my mound. Watching this man come apart so thoroughly because of me—a sense of power I've never felt before washes over me.

Now that I know what it feels like, I want more.

Kol drains himself onto my skin, making sure every last bit is out before he collapses on his back beside me. With one arm above his head and the other over his abdomen, he stares at the sky while he catches his breath. Eventually, he picks up his shirt and wipes my stomach clean before tossing it aside and lying back down next to me.

Kol doesn't seem like a cuddler, but I take a chance and roll onto my side, bringing my leg up over his legs and resting my cheek on his chest. He stills at first but relaxes. He doesn't put his arm around me, but it's progress, I guess.

"Can we do that again?" I ask.

His deep rumble of a laugh echoes through his chest to meet my ear. "I've created a monster."

I trail my fingertips over his chest, enjoying this feeling of intimacy with him almost as much as what we just did. "Maybe I'm a nympho and didn't know it until now."

He chuckles again. "You're still a virgin."

"True. But we could fix that right now if we wanted to."

He's silent. Probably contemplating, because Kol doesn't make rash decisions. "I think we've done enough for one day."

His words sting, but he does bring the hand on his abdomen over and covers mine. We lie in silence for a minute or two, and my mind wanders while listening to the birds chirping in the nearby trees—to what we just did, what I hope we'll do next, to when Kol found me in front of the maze.

I don't want to ruin this rare moment between us, but the panic and pain in his eyes when I asked if he wanted to go in the maze with me is now at the forefront of my mind.

"Kol, can I ask you something?"

"You want to know when I'm going to fuck you?" I can hear the amusement in his voice, and for a moment, I think maybe I shouldn't ask him.

But I want to know. I want to bring him comfort if he needs it. I don't know for sure, but I don't get the feeling that he opens up to many people. "Why did it upset you so much when I asked you to go in the maze with me?"

He moves his hand off mine.

"You don't have to talk about it if you don't want to. I just... want to help if I can. Even if it's only by listening."

He's silent for so long that I fear he's going to push me away and storm into the manor.

"It's because of my father, and what he did."

I ease up onto my elbow and look down at him. His eyes are clouded with pain and grief.

"What did he do?" I whisper.

Kol brings his arm down from over his head and gently forces me back into the position I was in, so my cheek is pressed against his chest, and I can't see his face. Only then does he continue.

"My father was a bastard. And that's putting it mildly. His way of resolving conflict was with his fists—even when it came to his wife and his children."

I don't dare move a muscle for fear that he'll stop talking.

"It didn't even have to be something big. Accidentally spilling your drink at the dinner table could be enough to set him off sometimes. I don't have a clear memory of when it started, how old I was. It seems like it was always like that. Growing up with him as a father was like walking a tightrope and never knowing when you might make a misstep, but knowing if you did, it might be your funeral next."

He exhales audibly and scrubs his face with his palm.

"The maze thing..." I hear him swallow hard with my ear pressed against his chest. "When I really pissed him off, he'd drag me into the middle of the maze in the darkness of night. There's a small courtyard in the middle. He'd leave me there all alone. The first time he did it, I was so scared I pissed my pajamas."

I squeeze him with the arm I have wrapped around him. "How old were you?"

"The first time I must've been around five, maybe six."

I work to keep the tears in my eyes from falling. And to think that I once judged Kol for having something to do with his father's death. Maybe he did. Maybe he didn't. I don't care at this point, knowing what a monster his father was. I'm glad he's dead. Otherwise, I might have killed him myself.

"He always thought I had too much pride, and it pissed him off when that pride showed. Maybe he was right. I'm sure pride is partly why I flew across the country to kidnap you." He laughs, but there's no humor in it. "Funny, my pride is one of the things my mom always said she loved most about me, and it was the thing he hated the most. Guess that's a good indicator of why they had such a shit marriage."

"Kol—"

"Anyway, that's why every year when this anniversary rolls around, all four of us are in shit moods. We're all glad he's dead, but it churns up a lot of stuff from our pasts. Asher and Anabelle got married in the maze a few months ago, and I told them I could handle it. That I could spend an hour in there if I had to. But when the day rolled around, I got high as fucking kite just to get out of my head enough to step inside."

I lift up onto my elbow again and take him in.

"Don't you dare look at me like that." He narrows his eyes.

"Like what?"

"Don't pity me." He pushes off the ground and steps over to his clothes that lay discarded in the grass.

With a sigh, I get up too. "I don't pity you, Kol. I can feel badly for what you went through without pitying you." I slide on my panties then reach down to grab my bra. "No child should ever have to go through what you did."

"Maybe I deserved it." He pulls his shorts up to his waist, then sets his hands on his hips and stares at the ground.

I clasp my bra and walk over to him, then clasp his face in my hands. "No one deserves that, do you hear me? No one."

He meets my gaze. Though the pain is still there, something like understanding lurks under the surface. "I guess neither of us got what we deserved growing up."

His comment strikes true, like an arrow nailing me in the center of my heart.

# 21



Kol directs us on the path that will lead down to the stables. The day is overcast, and dark gray clouds roll by. Though it's still pretty hot, it feels more like a late fall day on the West Coast than a summer day in the south.

"I'm surprised you haven't ventured down to the stables already," Kol says.

"I didn't want to come on my own. I've never been around an animal as big as a horse before."

Kol looks at me with a frown. "Sometimes I forget just how sheltered you were before I stole you away." He takes my hand.

My heart flutters like hummingbird wings. Since our day by the pond when Kol told me about what his father did to him, I feel as though we've turned a corner. I hope I'm right.

"Didn't you and Alistair ever go on dates?"

I'm surprised he's asking, though his voice is strained. Kol gets upset any time anything to do with my ex-fiancé comes up.

Which reminds me, I really need to call Alistair and apologize.

"Not really. At first, we'd just chat before and after church service. Then I started attending more group meetings throughout the week to get out of the apartment, and he started showing up to them."

"Your mom didn't attend church with you?"

The stables come into view in the distance, looking more like the exterior of an expensive home than somewhere horses sleep and eat.

"No, she never did. I invited her to be polite and offered for her to come with me when I first started asking to go, but she never would. I don't know why." I glance at Kol, who has a contemplative look on his face.

"So what did you and Alistair do then?"

"A lot of our time was spent at church. It took months for me to convince my mom to let me go out to eat with him after church. No one was more surprised than me when she finally agreed. I kept pushing, so I think she could tell that I wasn't letting it drop."

Once the words are out of my mouth, it dawns on me that I could have done the same when she confronted me about Kol. I could have begged and pleaded for her to let me see him again to see if he had an explanation for everything she'd told me. I know why I didn't... maybe it's time he understands too.

"Kol, there's something you should know."

He pulls us to a stop with our joined hands. His forehead is wrinkled, and I can tell he has no idea what I'm about to say. "What?"

"The reason why what my mom told me affected me so much…" I nibble on my bottom lip.

He squeezes my hand. "Just tell me."

"I was conceived the night my mother was raped by a man she was out on a date with."

White-hot anger burns in his eyes. "How did you find out?"

I sigh. I hate talking about this on a good day, but at a time when I'm hiding out from my mother, it's a reminder of how much she loves me, how much emotional turmoil she went through to have me…

"I got nosy once when I was younger and went through all the photo albums. I realized there weren't any pictures of my mom when she was pregnant and none of me when I was an infant. When I asked my mother, she got upset and told me never to ask again. But me being me, I wouldn't let it drop, and she eventually admitted the truth. She found it so hard to come to terms with the reality of my conception that she couldn't bear to take any pictures until I was a little older."

Kol drops my hand and steps forward, tucking some of the hair that has escaped my braid in the warm breeze behind my ear. "I'm sorry, sweetheart. That must be a hard thing to deal with."

I nod, tears building in my eyes. "My whole life, I grew up knowing and hearing about how violent and selfish and what liars men are. I was a by-product of that fact." I look down between our bodies. "When my mom showed me all those articles about you and explained who you really were... I don't know. It just felt like she was right. She was right, and I was the naïve, sheltered little girl she'd been right about all along. I didn't trust my own judgment."

Kol tips my chin up with his finger. "I should have told you from the beginning who I was to the world. I'm the one who proved her right by lying."

"I should have spoken to you before I ran away scared. I'm sorry I hurt you."

Something flashes in his eyes, too quick for me to make sense of, and he places a slow kiss on my lips before he pulls away. "I'm sorry too."

Having that off my chest feels so good. I feel better now that he knows, and I know, with his own background, he's not likely to judge me for it.

"Ready to go get your first look at a real live horse?" he asks.

I appreciate his attempt at lightening the mood. "Giddy up!"

He chuckles and links our hands again before we continue down the path.

When we reach the stables and go inside, there are a couple of people working inside, but they quickly find something else to do outside. The building is far more expansive than I imagined. It's a giant A-frame building built mostly of wood, and running down the point of the A are skylights that allow the sun in, if there were much to be had today. It's much cleaner than I would have expected, and several horses pop their heads out from their stalls. One of them grabs all my attention.

"Oh wow. Who is this?" I can't help but be drawn to the black horse with a coat that almost sparkles.

Kol steps up behind me. "That's Asher's horse, Poe."

The horse is huge, way bigger than I expected, and when he brings his head up and down, I step back into Kol's chest.

"He's a little shit. Got loose the night of the storm. Took Jack and some of the other stable hands two days to get him back."

I chuckle and look at the black beauty. I swear his eyes glimmer with amusement. "Can I... touch him? I mean, is that okay?"

"Sure."

"Where should I touch him?" He seems like a nice horse, but he's so big that it's intimidating.

Kol walks closer to the stall. "Come here." When I do, he positions me in front of him, and he strokes Poe's neck. "Just do that. Only go with the direction of his hair. Ready?"

I nod, reaching up to the giant's neck.

"Don't be scared. He can read your energy," Kol says.

I take a deep breath and pet him. To my surprise, Poe seems like he relaxes at my touch. I turn my head and smile at Kol. "I think he likes it."

"What male wouldn't like you running your hands over his body?" He squeezes my ass, and I yelp, causing Poe to nicker.

After Poe, Kol takes me around the rest of the stables to introduce me to the rest of the horses. All of them are beautiful in their own way.

"You want to take one for a ride?" he asks a while later.

My eyes widen. "Maybe another day. I think just saying hello is all I have in me today."

The idea of being seated on the back of one of them terrifies me, but I want to. One day. I want to see if I love it or hate it. Whether I'll be scared the whole time or able to get my nerves under control.

"That's enough firsts for today?" He arches an eyebrow.

"You're all about showing me my firsts, aren't you?" I smile.

"I thought you knew that by now, Rapsody. I want all your firsts."

I hold his gaze, and my heart swells with emotion. Lately, being with Kol has felt so much like when we were falling for each other before, but somehow even deeper. But I'm glad he said he wants all my firsts because it will make it easier to talk to him about what I want today.

"What's going through that head of yours?" He taps my temple just below where my now-healed cut is.

I step into him and wrap my arms around his neck. "That's exactly what I want. You to have my firsts. In fact... I want you to take me to bed. I want it to be you, Kol."

I've never meant anything more in my life. I have no idea if this tryst with Kol is headed anywhere. I'm too afraid to ask. But I do know that I'll regret it if anyone but him takes my virginity. That truth is embedded in my soul.

He tugs playfully on the thick braid that hangs down my back. "We're getting there."

"I'm serious, Kol. I don't want to wait anymore."

His smile fades. "If that's really the case, there's something you should know." From the tone of his voice, it's serious.

"Okaaaay, should I be scared?"

Instead of answering me, he unwinds my arms from around his neck and tugs me out of the stables. We walk in silence for a few minutes until we come to a large tree that appears as if it's been on the property for centuries, it's so big. Kol sits down under it as though to escape the sun even though the landscape is bathed in shadows from the thick clouds.

"You're scaring me," I admit once he's seated across from me.

"I needed to make sure no one overhears what I'm about to tell you."

"Still scared." I chew on my bottom lip while I wait for him to fill me in.

"It's about what you saw that Saturday night when I wouldn't tell you what was going on."

I exhale a sigh of relief though I really don't know if I should. But just knowing the topic of our conversation alleviates some of my worries. "Alright."

"I'm going to be blunt about it. I don't know any other way to be, but what I tell you, you can't share with anyone else. Ever. Understand?"

He's serious. I don't need to ask what the consequences will be if I do. It's clear to me that they'll be dire.

I nod. "I won't say anything."

He scrubs a hand over his face. "My brothers and I run a sex club out of the basement of the manor called the Ritual Room. It's pretty much a meeting of the one-percenters of the world, and it runs one Saturday a month. That's who you saw in the masks—some of our... guests. The club started by my father, and after he died, we carried it on because it gives us leverage and information on other wealthy families, which is never a bad thing if we need to use it."

And here I thought it was a costume party he was embarrassed to bring me to. This is a whole other level. I sit stunned, trying to make sense of what he just said. He watches me silently while I sort through information and figure out what to say.

I probably shouldn't be surprised that my mind snags on the fact that Kol is a member of a sex club. Kol has sex with other women in that club, right? The night I saw him...

"Do you... do you have sex at the club?"

He meets my eyes and doesn't look away. "Yes."

"Right, of course you do. I mean, look at you." I motion to him while my stomach turns over on itself. "So the night I saw you, you..."

Jealousy rages like a beast in my chest, clawing to get out. I want to lash out and smack him, push him down onto the ground and pound away on his chest, but I have no right to.

He reaches for my hand, but I tug it away. Kol meets my gaze again with a frown. "I didn't do anything that night. I tried. I wanted to, if just to prove to myself that you didn't still have a hold on me, but I couldn't do it. There's a ceremony that happens every year, and I'm usually the one leading it, but this year..." He shakes his head almost as though he's disappointed with himself. "I just couldn't. Sid took over for me."

My stomach settles with that knowledge, and I can think a little more clearly. "Everyone had masks on. Why?"

"Each color mask denotes something different. White is a watcher, red is a waiter, and black is a doer."

"But the mask in your hand and Sid's mask were gold."

A small smile tilts up the corners of his lips. "We're special. We're the founders."

I nod, putting all the information together. "I

get the watcher thing, but what do the waiter and doer mean?"

"People in the red masks haven't decided what they're up for that night. It'll depend on what opportunities present themselves. Anyone can suggest something to someone in a red mask, and they might decide to join in, maybe not. The people in black masks are down for anything. You don't have to get their consent for each thing. They want people to do whatever they want to them. It's part of what gets them off."

"So which are you?" I hold my breath, waiting for him to answer. I haven't even had sex. I don't know what I would classify myself as. I'm so out of my league right now.

He tilts his head. "What do you mean?"

"You have a gold mask. Are you usually in a white, red, or black mood?"

"If you're asking what I like to do when I'm down in the club, it's simple. I like to fuck in front of everyone else. I want to be the one to put on a show. I'm an exhibitionist."

It's not what I expected him to say. Knowing Kol, I wouldn't have thought he'd want to be the center of attention, but maybe that's the only place he feels comfortable exploring that side of himself.

I try to push away the images of Kol having sex with other women while people watch. It's nearly impossible. How will I ever think of anything else now?

"Why are you telling me all this? I'm glad you did, but I guess I don't understand what it has to do with me asking you to take my virginity."

"You should know the man you're asking, that's why."

In some weird, messed up way, I find it kind of sweet. Jeez, what is happening to me that I even think that?

My head drops, and I push my fingers into my hair, before pulling them out and probably making a mess of my braid. "So you're telling me because you want me to know that even after you take my virginity, you're going to sleep with other women once a month in the club, is that it?" My stomach sours.

He scowls. "No, I'm telling you because I want you to join me in the club."

Oh hell. I want the experiences, and I want to live, but does he even understand what he's asking of me?

# 22



Rapsody's eyes widen, the green of them matching the grass underneath us. This is the most shocked she's looked during this whole conversation.

I didn't know today was going to be the day I told her about the club, even if it was part of my plan all along to get her down there. Nothing screams debauched and ruined like sex in a club.

But when she pressed the issue of her virginity, something I've been holding off on god knows why... that's a lie. I know exactly why.

Because the idea of taking her virginity as part of some revenge plot makes me feel like the worst kind of person. Which is saying a lot after all I've done.

But I knew I couldn't do it without her knowing about the club and knowing that some fucked-up part of me wants her down there with me. If I can't be honest with her about my intentions, the least I can do is be honest with her about that.

Hell, I can't even be honest with myself about my intentions these days. I don't even know where my head is at.

"You want me to go with you?" Rapsody's soft voice draws me from my thoughts.

"I do. It's clear to me that I'm not going to be able to fuck anyone else, so I want you there with me. I want to show you yet another first."

She puts up her hand. "To be clear, you want me to lose my virginity to you in front of a bunch of strangers."

Shit. I should've explained this better. My thoughts are a riot in my head.

Am I fucking nervous? Jesus. I've been on missions with a high probability that I would not return, and I never felt this anxious.

"No, that's not what I'm asking. There's an initiation into the club that anyone who wants to be there has to go through. There's no getting out of it, and it's for everyone's protection."

"What's the initiation?"

"You'd have to do whatever I wanted in front of everyone. No mask. It's videotaped, and the tape becomes the property of my brothers and me. It's kept as leverage in the event that someone wants to get chatty about what goes on in the Ritual Room."

"So you *do* want me to lose my virginity in front of everyone, just without a mask." Rapsody doesn't even appear scandalized. Why doesn't she look scandalized?

I rub my hand over my shaved head. "No, I'd think of something else. I like being in front of others, but I wouldn't want them seeing that."

It bothers me that I even care. Who the fuck am I? A month ago, I would've fucked her innocence out of her in front of everyone and not cared one bit that she might come to regret losing her virginity with an audience.

"Oh, I see." Is that disappointment in her voice?

"You don't have to give me an answer right now, but you won't have much time to decide. The next gathering is this weekend."

She leans closer to me, and her pear-and-vanilla scent wraps around me. "I don't need time to think about it."

"Rapsody…"

She comes even closer, setting her hands on my shoulders and pushing so I'm forced to lie back. Then she moves over me so that she straddles my lap. My dick twitches at the feel of the heat between her legs.

"I already know my answer. Yes." She presses her lips to mine, but when she tries to deepen the kiss, I force her back by the shoulders.

"Are you sure? You don't have to do this."

She nods, biting her lip. "I'm sure. I want adventure. This sounds like the biggest adventure I may ever have."

I hold her emerald gaze, searching for any sign of reluctance and finding none. "All right then. It's a date."

Wasting no time, I slip my hand behind her head and drag her down to my lips.

The next morning after breakfast, I meet my brothers and Anabelle in Asher's home office. Everyone's eyes are glued to me by the mammoth fireplace, hands on my hips, looking at where they all sit on the couch and chairs.

"I've got an overseas call in twenty minutes," Asher says, glancing at his Patek Phillippe watch. "Can we get on with this?"

Anabelle, the only one who can ever settle the asshole, moves her hand to his knee as if telling him to cool it. He takes her hand and lifts it to his lips, kissing her knuckles.

Why the hell does that feeling hit my chest

when I see it? It feels something like longing, which is fucking ridiculous.

"Yeah, brother. What's up? Rapsody finally send you over the edge? You need help burying the body?" Sid says with a sly grin.

I narrow my eyes.

Nero doesn't say anything. He's unkempt and has bags under his eyes.

I nod in Nero's direction. "What's up with you? You just get in?"

"Don't worry about me. Just get on with it already."

Asher and Anabelle share a concerned glance.

There's nothing to worry about though. I went on benders and fuck-fests after Rapsody left me, determined to prove to myself that I didn't care. Nero's probably just doing the same.

"Fine. I'll be initiating Rapsody into the Ritual Room on Saturday."

Anabelle gasps.

Asher glares.

Sid chuckles.

And Nero gets up with a, "Fine. Whatever," and leaves the room.

"You can't initiate her," Asher says.

I thought this might be an argument I'd have to have with him, so I'm not surprised. "Did it sound like I was asking for permission?"

"I don't care if you were or not. We don't initiate just anyone, you know that. Flights of fancy aren't indulged when it comes to our membership."

I scoff and motion toward Anabelle. "What the fuck was Anabelle if not a flight of fancy?"

The hand with the bear tattoo fists on Asher's thigh. "She is more than that, and you know it."

"But you didn't know that at the time."

Asher's head tilts. "Last I heard, your plan was to seduce and ruin Rapsody, then send her packing."

I glare at the door Nero just left through, knowing he opened his big fucking mouth.

Anabelle's mouth drops open, and she looks between Asher and me. Obviously, this is the first she's heard about it.

"Things have changed," I say.

Have they? I don't even really know myself. All I know is that lately, revenge hasn't been at the forefront of my mind and hasn't felt as important.

"Do tell," Sid says with a shit-eating grin. A grin I'd like to wipe away with my fist.

"All you need to know is that I've prepped her on everything, and she'll be there. End of story."

Asher stands from the couch, stepping over to me. "If she breathes a word of this to anyone..."

He doesn't have to finish that sentence. I know what it means. Just as I know I'd probably be the one he asked to do it.

I nod. "It's not going to be a problem."

He looks as though he's not too sure, but he says, "Fine. She can join as long as she knows the consequences if she steps out of line."

My gut twists, because I'm fairly sure the consequences will be more dire for me than her.

# 23



*RAPSODY*

It's the night of the initiation into the sex club, and what was excitement in my belly when I said yes has turned to nerves and nausea.

I don't regret my decision. I just wonder what Kol is going to do in front of everyone, and if I'll react properly or if I'll mess up and embarrass him.

I'm wearing the outfit he left for me—a pale purple lingerie set that consists of a lace bra and panties, along with a thin elastic belt that sits at my waist and attaches to garters that rest mid-thigh. Along the top of the bra and the belt are small flowers that match the color of the lace.

When he said he was going to buy me my outfit, I envisioned leather with grommets or bright red lace, but this is pretty, sweet, innocent. Which is likely why he chose it.

I smooth my hair back into a high ponytail and braid it as Kol requested. It's heavy on my head as it always is, and I stretch my neck side to side to alleviate the discomfort. Lately I've thought about cutting my hair. I've always worn it to my waist because it's what my mother likes best, but it requires so much maintenance. I just think that maybe I'd like to try something different.

The thought of my mom threatens to drag my mood down with guilt, since I haven't reached out to her yet, but I push it aside. I'm not going to think about her tonight.

I'm walking out of the bathroom when a knock lands on my bedroom door. A moment later, Kol strides through. My arms stretch to cover myself, but the look in Kol's eyes stops me. There's a hunger alive in them. Hunger for me. So I force myself to not hide from him.

He strides toward me. "You look... phenomenal." His gaze rakes over my body like a caress.

"Thank you. You look..." I eye his bare chest and white linen pants. "Different."

He laughs, and I admire the crinkle at the sides of his eyes and the way it changes the angle of his jaw. It's not something I've seen often enough.

Kol looks down at himself. "The theme tonight is summer solstice. This is what I came up with." He shrugs.

"There's a theme?"

"There's always a theme." He rolls his eyes as though maybe he and his brothers have had fights about having themes, and he lost the argument. "This is for you."

He hands me a white robe lying over his arm. I slip it on, noticing that his mask was hidden under the robe, hanging from the crook of his arm. My chest tightens when I think about how I'm the only one who will be without a mask tonight.

"May I?" I gesture to his mask.

He slides it off his arm, handing it to me. It's heavier than I assumed and resembles the lion tattooed on his arm. It must come down over his nose because it even has the top two canine teeth.

I recall the mask Sid wore, a wolf's mask like his wolf tattoo on his neck. I wonder if Asher's is a bear like the bear tattoo I've spotted on his hand. Which makes me curious about Nero.

My chest squeezes tighter when I realize something I hadn't before. "Your brothers are going to be there. Anabelle?"

He nods. "Yes."

Blood drains from my face, and my windpipe squeezes. I struggle to get air as my heart pounds. The first signs that I'm panicking and going to have a panic attack.

Kol pulls me into his chest and rubs my back. "I know it might seem weird to you, but it's not, I swear. Asher and Anabelle just end up going into their private room now. If I do my job right, you won't be thinking about anyone but me and the pleasure I'm giving you."

I nod into his chest, but I'm not sure I can make it not weird.

"You can back out. It's not something you have to do," Kol says softly.

My throat opens a bit with my next breath and a little more with my next until eventually I can breathe normally again. I pull away and meet his gaze. "I'm okay. I want to do this. I just hadn't thought about them being there, that's all."

He smiles with that proud look I love to witness and takes my hand. "Let's go then."

The sun has long since set as we make our way through the dim manor, sconces flickering against the walls.

Kol leads us to a large wooden door and slips a skeleton key from the pocket of his pants, opening the door. In front of me is a long stairwell that's dark at the bottom. A few lanterns dot the wall beside the stone stairs, but not enough to see below.

He directs me down the stairs. When we reach the bottom, he hangs my robe on a hook there. Music is playing at the end of a long hallway with an abundance of doors. I guess I'll find out where they lead.

Before we move again, Kol slides on his mask and faces me. The result is arresting. He's still Kol, but somehow not. In fact, he reminds me a lot of the man who showed up at the church to steal me away from my wedding. His appearance is different, the way he holds himself. More severe. More serious than he's been with me the past couple of weeks.

We walk down the hallway and step through an archway into a cavernous room that's carved from stone. Music pumps throughout the room, and the bass vibrates in my chest.

Everyone in the room turns to face us, as if they somehow knew we were coming. I guess we are the main act tonight. It's impossible to read their expressions to know what they're thinking, which brings back my nerves.

Kol gives my hand a reassuring squeeze and leads me to the other side of the room. The crowd parts as though Kol is the king of the jungle, leaving a path straight to a dais. I avert my gaze on the way, not wanting to see the eyes that will be watching us. It's easier said than done though when I feel all their eyes on me, assessing.

Are there women in the group who have slept with Kol? Who are silently nitpicking me for not being good enough for him? Wondering why I'm so special? I push away all the doubts because he asked me, and that's why I'm here.

Kol helps me up onto the dais and pulls me into his chest, leaning down and whispering in my ear, "Still time to change your mind."

When he pulls back, I meet his gaze through his mask. Steeling myself, I nod.

Yes, I'm afraid, but maybe that's exactly the emotion I should be feeling. And isn't that what I've been yearning for? To feel the array of emotions from living life? Not only the boredom of being stuck in an apartment? Besides, I want to do this with Kol. No one else, just Kol.

He nods, and his jaw sets hard. His eyes go blank, and he says loudly enough to be heard over the music, "Get on your knees."

I suck in a breath and fall to my knees, staring at him.

We haven't done this before. Correction—I haven't. I've never given oral sex to someone, and I worry that I'm going to mess something up, accidentally bite him or something. But I look in his eyes, and my worry dissipates. Kol knows that I have no experience with this, and I trust him to guide me through whatever he has planned.

He runs his palm down my face, tilting my head farther back. "Take out my cock, sweetheart."

My gaze flicks to his waist where the hard length of him presses against the linen pants. Swallowing hard, I undo the button on his pants. My fingers tremble on the zipper, but I slide it down. Sliding my hands around the sides of his hips, I tug the pants down and they crumple to his ankles. I've seen Kol's member before, but the size and width still take me back.

"Let's give everyone a good show, shall we?" He smirks.

The kind, reassuring man from upstairs is replaced by his usual cocky, stoic demeanor. The man standing in front of me, cock splayed for any to see, is a different man entirely.

"Run your tongue from my base all the way up to the tip, then suck the head into your mouth."

I'm still nervous, but just listening to his instructions makes me wet between the thighs. I push everyone else out of my mind, let the thrum of the music fill my body, and bring my tongue to the base of his thick cock, running it up his hard, smooth length until I reach the top. I wrap my lips around his tip and suck the head as he instructed.

"Fist the base and jerk me off while you suck on the head."

I do exactly what he requests, the way I saw him do it before, and his chin tips up toward the ceiling on an exhale. Not sure what to do with my free hand, I splay it on his upper thigh, feeling the hard muscle beneath his heated skin twitch.

I grip him a little harder, testing it out, and he groans, looking at me with wide pupils and amber eyes full of lust. That powerful feeling at being the one to make him make those sounds arises inside me.

Determined to please him, I open my mouth wider and bring him farther down my throat, until he hits the back. I gag and think maybe that's a bad thing until a pleased look pierces Kol's face, as though he's proud of me.

For the next several minutes, I use Kol's reactions as my guide. When he flexes his hips into my mouth, I almost smile around his cock. He wraps my braid around his hand several times, using it as leverage to keep me from moving, keeping me in place while he pumps his hips. My eyes water, and I gag on the length of him, drool running out of my mouth, but more noises and curses fall from Kol's lips.

"Men are jerking off to you right now, sweetheart. How does it make you feel to know that you're turning them on so much they can't help but fist their cocks?"

My insides flutter at his words, and my nipples draw tight. I'm desperate for some friction on my clit, but rather than use my hand to satisfy myself, I bring my hand to his balls and take the heavy weight of them in my palm. Kol grows harder in my mouth, and he unwinds his hand from my braid in favor of placing his hands on either side of my head.

"Relax your throat for me."

I force myself to do as he says though it takes me a few tries to be successful. Then he pistons into my mouth, using me for his pleasure. I meet his feral gaze, shocked at how much it turns me on.

"I'm going to paint you with my cum, you want that?" he growls.

I give the smallest nod, and the feline smirk that tilts his lips, along with the satisfied gleam in his eyes, is a vision I commit to memory, it's so damn hot.

Kol bucks into my mouth a few more times, then he drops his hands from my head, dragging his cock all the way out and leaving a stream of saliva between my lips and the tip. Jerking himself a few times, he cries out as his seed pours onto my collarbone and chest. Then he brings the tip to my lips, and I seal my mouth around it, swirling my tongue and lapping up what's left while he watches with a satisfied grin.

He holds my gaze for a few beats before he bends at the waist and tugs up his pants, then fastens them. "I think you deserve to be rewarded."

He holds out a hand to me. I take it, getting up off my knees and standing before him. He whips me around so that I'm facing the audience, his one arm over my collarbone and the other around my waist. My back is pressed to his front, and my chest heaves from my heavy breathing—partly from surprise and partly because I'm so horny over what I just did that I'm desperate for him to make me come. I don't care if it's in front of all these people.

Not wasting any time, he brings the hand on my waist down into my panties, finding my swollen clit and spreading my arousal over it with his fingers. I sigh and lean back into him, arching my hips, wanting more. More of whatever he's willing to give me.

Seeing the audience from this angle gives me a whole new insight. Some of the men are indeed jerking off, watching the show Kol and I are putting on. Some of the women have their hands between their legs too. A surge of shame flares for being turned on, but I push it aside. I can examine my feelings later. Right now, I just want to enjoy this moment.

Kol brings his mouth to my ear and nips at my earlobe while his fingers circle my clit. A moan escapes me, and he must like what he hears because he brings his mouth to the space where my neck meets my shoulder, opens his mouth, and bites down. I cry out as the pleasure below my waist mixes with the pain above it.

I'm so close to coming that my hips move of their own accord.

"All these people are about to watch you fall apart. Watch you come on my fingers. Do you think they'll be remembering it days from now when they're at home, rubbing one out?" He doesn't wait for me to answer, which is fine. My mind is so overloaded with sensations right now, I'm not sure I could form a sentence. "I know they will, because I know what you look like when you come, Rapsody, and it is fucking glorious."

He doubles down his efforts. Every muscle in my body draws taut right before a swell of sensation fills my veins and shatters my thoughts. I come apart like shattered glass ricocheting through the cavernous room. My body vibrates with bliss, and the air in my lungs seizes until I start slowly knitting myself back together.

I sag against Kol's chest, unable to stay standing on my own.

He tucks his face into my neck and inhales me. "See? Glorious."

My eyes close. I don't have the strength to open them, even when I feel him pick me up and step down off the dais. I don't know where he's taking me, but I wrap my arms around his neck and tuck my face into his bare chest.

He smells like he always does—crisp air and pine, a scent that is intrinsically Kol, and it comforts me in ways I've never felt before.

I didn't expect what we did to be so intense and overwhelming. I don't know if it's because of the audience and setting, the fact that I gave someone head for the first time, or because what we just did felt more weighted with emotion than just the physical aspect.

Kol places me on a mattress, and I open my eyes to see where we are. We're in his room, and just the bedside lamp is on, leaving the vast space beyond the bed in shadows. Kol stands over me, looking down with a mixture of ownership and awe. The look makes my chest ache because I realize that's what I've wanted from him all along.

I may have begun staying here because I wanted some breathing room from my mother and my old life, but the truth has always been that I really want him. I want the Kol I had back in Atlanta. But I found something even better because this Kol, the one he's shown me, is the real Kol. All of him. The broken and shattered pieces, the jagged edges, all of it. It's all a part of what makes him who he is, and he is so beautiful when he lets me see him.

I'm tired of waiting.

It's time I take what I want.

# 24

*RAPSODY*

"Come here." My voice is soft, and I reach for him.

He takes my hand, and I pull him down, wordlessly asking him to cover me. He does, and the weight of his delicious body pressing against mine feels perfect. This is how it was always meant to be. We just got lost for a little bit.

He brings his mouth to mine with a slow, sensual sweep of his tongue, and I sink into the kiss. There's so much emotion in this kiss. So much we're not saying with words, but I *feel*.

I pull away and frame his face in my hands. "I want you to make love to me, Kol. I want to know what it feels like to have you inside me, to be joined with you."

His eyes flash with some emotion I can't quite place, almost like a mixture of fear and acceptance. But it's gone in an instant, then he's trailing his nose down my body, slowly undressing me and kissing each new piece of skin he bares.

My hand goes to the back of his head when he closes his mouth around my nipple, tugging gently with his teeth. Each pull from his lips tugs on my core.

"Please don't make me wait any longer," I whisper.

He raises his head, looking at me with a warmth in his eyes I haven't seen in four years. He dips his head and brings his lips to mine. Kol kisses me as though I'm the air he breathes and uses his knees to spread my legs wider, settling between them.

I feel how hard he is and nearly cry out when he pushes up off of me, the muscles in his chest and arms flexing, and sits back on his haunches. But I relax when his hands move to the waistband of his pants, and he unfastens them, straightening to get them to his knees, then hovers over me again, using his feet to pull the pants all the way off.

"You're sure?" he asks before settling between my legs again with the firm press of his rigid length.

I brush my hand over some of the bristle he's grown over the last couple of days on his face. "You know I am. Please, Kol."

A soft smile transforms the severe lines of his face. "How could I ever say no when you beg?"

Bracing himself on one arm, he slides his fingers between my folds, finding me wet and ready. When he grabs the base of his erection to line it up with my opening, I get a little nervous for the first time since we arrived in his room.

I'm really going to do this. *We're* going to do this.

I look down the line of my body and watch as he pushes into me, notching the head into my entrance. He's so large that he's stretching me even though he's barely inside. He must know because he leans down and kisses me until I forget the discomfort.

"You ready for more?" he asks.

I nod. He flexes his hips again, pushing inside me another inch and halting so that I get used to him. And so it goes for several minutes until we both feel him reach the barrier.

"This will hurt." Kol's voice sounds as if it's going to hurt him more than me. "Ready?"

I suck in a deep breath and nod, trying to brace myself.

"Just try to stay relaxed." He kisses my forehead at the same time as he pushes inside me, and I gasp at the burning pain, tears welling. "You're okay, you're okay."

He kisses me again. It takes a minute for the

pain to lessen, and I let myself relax and enjoy the kiss.

"You okay?" he asks when he pulls away.

"I think so."

He pushes a little farther, waits for me to get used to his size, and repeats the process until he's fully seated inside me. It's a foreign sensation, the way he's filling and stretching me. At first, it's uncomfortable, but as my body grows used to him, I settle into the feeling.

Kol pulls back slowly before pushing in the same way. He does this a few times, and each time it feels better and better until I grip his shoulders and pull him down to kiss me.

"More," I murmur against his lips.

He increases his pace as I moan into his mouth. He pulls away from our kiss and buries his face in my neck. "Holy fuck, sweetheart. You're like a fucking vise."

That makes me smile. I want him to move even more. I *need* him to. When I wiggle my hips, he gets the message and slides out of me, then pushes back in with some force this time.

Oh. My. God.

There's a bit of discomfort, but every single one of my nerve endings is singing hallelujah. After a few more thrusts, the discomfort disappears all together and absolute euphoria passes through me.

One look at Kol's rigid jaw above me, and I can tell he's still holding back, and I don't want him to. I may be a virgin, but I'm not a porcelain doll.

"More, Kol."

He increases his tempo and holds himself inside me for a beat before he drags himself back out. I grow slicker around him. The sound it makes where our bodies join is vulgar and erotic, ratcheting my desire higher.

He stares into my eyes the entire time. I couldn't look away even if I wanted to. It's as if a tether is connecting his gaze to mine, and it rocks me because I see a depth of feeling in his eyes I wasn't sure he could ever feel for me again.

Within minutes, he's no longer holding back. The first flutters of my climax deepen in my womb, and Kol's must be close too because he brings his one hand between us and strokes my clit. My back arches, and my breathing picks up while Kol watches me, almost studying my reaction. The sensation rises, rises, and rises until there's no way for me to hold off.

My orgasm hits me like a rolling tide, and I scream out, fingertips pushing into Kol's skin.

"Oh fuck, I can feel you coming. I'm gonna…" His voice is rough and shakes as he spills inside me.

He holds himself there, tucking his face into my neck again and breathing me in. He twitches inside me with the last traces of his orgasm. Then he pulls out of me, rolling off to my side.

I immediately miss the feeling of him between my legs. He pulls me into his chest and wraps his arms around me, saying nothing. Though I want this moment to last forever, it's not long until the steady tempo of his heart lulls me to sleep.

I don't know how long I drift off for, but I wake up wrapped in Kol's arms.

His hand lazily coasts down my arm. "How are you feeling?"

I tilt my head up to look at him. "A little tender, but okay." I position myself on my elbow so I'm looking down at him, tracing a fingertip down his chest. "I liked it. The parts that didn't hurt anyway. I'm guessing it gets better from here."

Amusement flicks in his eyes. "It does. But plenty of time for that. You need to heal, so it'll be at least a few days before I'm bending you over and taking you from behind."

Kol's words make my insides clench.

His face grows serious. "How do you feel about what we did downstairs?"

"I want to do that again too."

A small smile lifts his lips. "You do?"

I nod. "I wasn't sure whether I would like it or not, but it turned me on to have all those people watching. To know that they were turned on because of me... us." My cheeks heat at the word us, though I don't know why after everything we've just done.

"Guess I'll have to think of something for us to do next month then." He groans and rubs the top of his head with his palm, looking at the ceiling. "Fuck."

I frown. "What's wrong?"

"I'm going to be preoccupied with this for the next month, picturing all the things I could do to you."

My anxiety eases. "Just know that I'm a willing participant."

Without warning, he rolls us so he's over me again, and I yelp. "Good... we're going to have a lot of fun checking things off the list."

I stare into his eyes, smiling, but at the same time, I'm wondering if that's all this is for him...fun. Because I know it's not for me, even if it might have started that way. The way I've been feeling for him lately... no. I force myself to stop those thoughts right where they are. I'm not going to ruin this moment.

"Can't wait." I run my hand up his arm with the lion tattoo, for the first time studying it up close. "Why did you decide to get a lion tattoo?"

My question is innocent enough, but when pain flashes on his face, and he rolls off of me to lie at my side, I know I've stepped into unwelcome territory. Sometimes talking to him feels like walking through a minefield, but damn do I want to diffuse each one.

At first, I don't think he's going to answer me. But then he sighs and speaks. "My mom used to call me her little lion." He gives me a sad smile.

"How come?" Maybe I shouldn't pry further.

"She always said I had too much pride, but that I had a lot of courage and wanted to protect the people I cared about. That I always wanted to be the dominant one of my brothers when we were all together, even if I wasn't the oldest. Growing up, I kept my hair long and she always used to say it re-minded her of a lion's mane because of how thick it was." A bemused little laugh leaves his lips.

"Look at you now." I run my hand over his shaved head.

He takes my hand and kisses my palm. "That's why I joined the military—because of everything she said, I figured I would be suited to that kind of life and because I thought it would make her proud. Well, that and to get away from Midnight Manor and all the memories here."

My chest squeezes at the reminder of every-thing he went through as a child.

"But now you're back," I say softly.

He nods. "Now I'm back." Kol appears deep in his thoughts for several moments before he speaks again, almost as though he's trying to decide whether he wants to tell me. "It was time to stop running. To come home and take my role at Voss Enterprises. Asher had been asking me to for years, and by the time I met you, I finally felt ready."

"Well, I'm glad you did." If he hadn't, we might not have met, and I wouldn't be here with this amazing, if complicated, man.

Kol places a chaste kiss on my forehead. "Why don't we go take a bath? It might help with the discomfort."

"Ohh, that sounds nice."

Ten minutes later, Kol stands beside the large soaker tub, holding my hand and helping me step into the warm water. I sigh as I sink down into it, and the water cocoons my body like a warm blanket. Kol slides in behind me and immediately reaches for my long braid, removing the elastic from the bottom to unravel my braid.

I don't mind—in fact, this ponytail is so heavy on top of my head that taking it out will be a blessing—but having my hair in the water means I'm going to have to wash it and then painstakingly brush it so that it doesn't become a nest birds can live in.

"How would you feel if I cut my hair?"

Kol stills in his unraveling of my braid. "It's your hair to do what you want with."

"Sure but... would you still..." I don't know how to voice my insecurities without feeling like an idiot.

Kol drops my braid and wraps his arms around me, squeezing me tightly and bringing his mouth to my ear. "Would I still think you're as beautiful and sexy as I do now? Damn straight. No haircut is going to change that, sweetheart."

The tension in my body eases, and I relax back into him. "I think I might then. Maybe Anabelle knows someone who can do it."

"Let me guess, your mother didn't want you to cut it."

I shrug, for some reason feeling a little defensive of my mother even though he's right. "I guess. She didn't want me to cut it, but I grew to like it the longer it got, and I didn't really fight back when I'd suggest cutting it, and she'd complain."

We're quiet for a few minutes, in our own thoughts and content to enjoy the warmth from the bath seeping into our bones.

"I was wondering something," Kol says, breaking the silence. "Why did your mom start letting you go to church? When we met, it was pretty clear she didn't let you leave the house except to see a doctor or dentist, things like that, so what changed?"

Out of all the questions, I didn't think this would be one. We briefly talked about it before.

"After I got my first taste of freedom when she was in the hospital, it was hard to go back to the way it was before. I tried to fall in line, but I'd already seen more of the world in the month she was in the hospital than I had my whole life, and I couldn't stop thinking about it. I begged and begged for her blessing to let me leave the house and do some things, but she wouldn't budge. Said it was too dangerous, and my relationship with you was proof that I wasn't a good judge of character."

Kol runs his hand up and down my arm from my shoulder to my elbow as though he can tell how uncomfortable I am reliving this.

"One day I saw a commercial on TV for one of those at-home DNA tests, and I asked her if she'd consider letting me get one. I thought maybe I could find some third cousin or something and try to connect with them, but she refused. We got in a huge fight—probably the biggest one we'd ever had, and I threatened to leave. Shortly after, she agreed that I could go to church. Up until then, I didn't know anything about religion, but it didn't matter. She could have offered to let me go wash dishes in a restaurant, and I would have said yes."

Kol chuckles behind me then grows quiet. "Do you miss him?"

I know who he's asking about. I turn in his arms and look at him over my shoulder, holding his gaze. "No."

He nods, and I think he believes me.

"Though I probably should reach out to him. I owe him an explanation." When he opens his mouth to say something, I add, "Not the real one, but just to let him know that I never should have said yes in the first place."

His jaw flexes, as does his hand on my arm. He clearly wants to tell me no, there's no reason for me to speak to Alistair, but he seems to get that impulse under control and nods.

I turn back around and wiggle a bit so I can lean into him. "You asked me if I enjoyed everything we did tonight, but did you?"

"That's not even a question, Rapsody."

I roll my eyes. "Obviously, I know you enjoyed it to a certain extent, but was it everything you wanted it to be?"

He chuckles, squeezing me in his arms and pulling my ass back into his lap. "I think you can feel how much I enjoyed it. Just you bringing it up has me rock hard again."

I wiggle against his erection, smiling at the mild buzzing sensation that starts between my legs. "Maybe we can—"

"Nope." He eases me forward and stands in the tub before stepping out. "You need a break. I'm going to take a cold shower."

I laugh and watch the muscles in his perfect ass flex as he walks over to the shower. I lean back and close my eyes, anxious for the days to pass so we can do it again.

Maybe I am a nympho.

# 25

*KOL*

Every instinct in me roars not to let her do this as I set the burner phone in her hand, but yet I still let go. I may not understand why she needs to call her ex-fiancé and explain, but clearly Rapsody thinks she does. After the way her mom raised her, I don't want to force her to do or not do anything, unless it's down in the Ritual Room. She'd just end up resenting me the same way she clearly resents her mom.

So even though it's killing me, and the green-eyed monster claws come out, I walk over to the other side of my bedroom and stare out the window with my arms crossed as she dials the number. That doesn't mean I won't be listening to every single word that comes out of her mouth.

"Hello, Alistair? It's Lillian."

My jaw flexes at the mention of her fake name.

"I'm fine, I'm fine. I'm sorry it's taken this long to call you... I know, I'm sorry."

She's quiet for a long time. I swear to Christ, if I get the impression that he's giving her a hard time, I'm going to reach through that phone and rip out his vocal cords.

"I'm glad my mom called you like I asked her to. I just wanted to call to apologize. I never should have said yes to your proposal... I know you did, but you deserve someone who loves you with her whole heart and that wasn't me."

I swear I feel her eyes on my back after she says that.

"You're right I shouldn't have run away like that, but I was scared."

I spin around to walk over and rip the phone out of her hand, knowing he's saying something unkind to her, but Rapsody raises her hand, so I stay in place. He says something else that has her shoulders sagging—whether in relief or guilt, I can't be sure, but this fucker better hope it's relief.

"I wish I had done things differently. I hope you'll forgive me."

My hands clench at my sides.

"Thank you. I'm sorry if I hurt you... I agree it's better this way. I know you'll find someone who will make you happy... Okay, you too." She pulls the phone from her ear and ends the call.

The need to pin her on the bed and fuck her raw burrows inside me, but it's only been one day since I took her virginity. She's not ready yet. Especially for the way I want to dominate and own her body right now just to prove that she's mine.

And she is. Mine.

The moment I pushed inside her, I knew there was no going back. That my feeble attempts at keeping my feelings at bay were all for nothing because this woman fucking owns me. Always has, and always will.

So I force myself to set aside the fact that she was talking to another man, a man she was all set to marry if I hadn't shown up. "Feel better now?"

She nods and stands from the edge of the bed. "Yes, thank you." She walks over and hands me the phone.

I slip it in my back pocket. "What did he say?"

She arches an eyebrow, something I don't think I've seen her do. "I think you have a good idea of what was said." She smirks, knowing I was listening to everything.

"Fair enough. You ready to go eat dinner now?"

"Yeah, sure." She places a kiss on my lips.

It starts out innocent enough but quickly progresses into making out. When I can see the direction we're headed, I step out of her arms.

"I think we should cut it off there, otherwise we're not going to make it to dinner."

Rapsody sticks out her bottom lip in a pout, and it makes me want to nibble on it. She's made it perfectly fucking clear that she wants me to fuck her again, and I will. Believe me, I'm counting down the damn days until I can be inside her again.

"Fine. Let's go."

I take her hand and lead her out of my bedroom. We make our way through the manor, past the centuries-old furniture and the paintings of ancestors I never knew. I'm used to the gloom and oppressive feeling inside the manor, but I wonder what she thinks of it. I'm afraid to ask.

When we reach the communal part of the property and are headed down the hall that leads to the dining room, Anabelle calls out from behind us.

"Where's Asher?" I ask when I see she's

alone. Those two are attached at the hip these days.

"He's finishing up a call. I was starving, so I told him I'd meet him there."

I smirk. "Bet he liked that."

Anabelle rolls her eyes, but she knows I'm right.

"I'm glad you caught us," Rapsody says. "I had a couple of things I wanted to talk to you about."

My sister-in-law's head tilts. "Everything okay?"

Rapsody drops my hand and plays with her fingers in front of her as though she's nervous, but I have no idea why. "I wanted to apologize for how I spoke to you the night I asked you what goes on in the basement."

Anabelle's look of concern softens to understanding. "Don't worry about it. I know exactly how you felt. There was a time I was questioning Asher about it, and he wouldn't tell me. I get how frustrating it can feel to know you're the only one without the information."

Rapsody smiles, seeming relieved. "Still. I shouldn't have given you attitude."

Anabelle squeezes Rapsody's hand, and this weird feeling, warmth or something, fills my chest at seeing my brother's wife be so kind to my... my what? She's not my fiancée anymore, but we're certainly not *friends*.

Rapsody's voice pulls me from my thoughts. "There's one other thing I wanted to ask."

Anabelle smiles. "Of course."

"I want to get my hair cut shorter, and I thought that maybe you would know someone who can do it."

Anabelle grins, appearing excited. "Yes! I can get you an appointment with my girl in town. Magnolia Bend only has one place, but I swear she does a great job."

Now Rapsody knows the name of the town we're in. She hasn't asked up to this point, and I haven't offered.

"Really?"

"We'll make a whole girls' day of it. We can get our hair done and go to dinner, maybe have a drink. It'll be so fun."

I frown, wanting to shut down the idea of a whole girls' day, but when I see Rapsody's happiness, I can't do it. This is probably the first female friendship she's tried to cultivate in her life.

"Oh my god, I can't wait!" Rapsody looks over at me.

I force myself to smile at her no matter how much I don't like the idea of her being out of my sight. It's hard not to worry that she's going to disappear again after what happened last time. But as much as my instincts push me to shut down this shit, I can't keep her chained to me. I can't be the same person as her mother, and I suspect I know why.

Because despite my best efforts, it's over. I've fallen back in love with her.

# 26

It's not until the following week that Anabelle can get me an appointment with her hairdresser. I've been counting down the days even though I'm nervous about what I'll look like without my long hair. But this change feels necessary, like the next step in my journey to discover who I really am.

Kol has filled my days, though—first by taking me to the horse races and Go-Cart riding, which was a bit of a disaster since I've never driven anything in my life. I saw Kol hand the guy money for the dented barriers I couldn't stop running into.

The best part of my nights and days is him having sex with me. Lots and lots of sex.

Since the initial few days passed, he has been insatiable. Well, I can tell he's still holding back. As much as I insist I'm not made of glass, he won't listen. I figure it will take him time to come around.

Anabelle parks her expensive car on the side of the road outside an older building with a sign over it that says Scuttlebutt Salon.

"I take it that a lot of gossiping goes on here?"

She laughs. "Yes, but don't worry, no one here is dumb enough to ask about anything that happens up at Midnight Manor. No one talks about the Voss brothers."

I frown. "Are they scared of them?"

"You could say that." She climbs out of the car, so I follow suit.

The bell above the door dings when we enter, and everyone turns to face us. Anabelle doesn't appear fazed, strolling up to her hairdresser. I hope to have confidence like her around people one day.

"Dorothy, this is my friend, Rapsody, that I told you about." Anabelle motions to me at her side.

A plump woman in her late fifties smiles at me. "Well, look at you." She laughs and touches my forearm. "You need a trim."

My cheeks heat. "More than a trim really."

"Don't you worry, I'm gonna fix you right up. Now come on over, and have a seat, tell me what you're thinking." She walks over to a worn blue leather hairdresser's chair and pats the back.

I walk over and sit, looking at Anabelle over my shoulder in the mirror. She's giving me an encouraging smile.

"I want a change. A drastic one. I want you to cut it to my shoulders."

"Now we're talking!" Dorothy says. "All these other women are worrying about a half inch here, a half inch there. You just made my day." She inspects my hair and meets my gaze in the mirror. "Do you want to donate what we cut off?"

"Donate it?" I look at her, confused.

"Yeah. I'll put it in a ponytail and cut right above where the hair is secure. They use it to make wigs for cancer patients who have lost their hair."

Oh, that makes me happy. "Definitely then."

Dorothy sets about collecting what she needs, and Anabelle sits in the empty chair to my left.

"Are you nervous?" Anabelle asks me.

I nod. "Yes, but more excited than nervous. It's time for a change."

"Okay, let me just get this in a ponytail." Dorothy gathers my hair in a loose ponytail down my back and picks up her scissors, placing the open blades around my hair. "Ready?"

I suck in a cleansing breath and nod. "Ready."

She presses on the shears, and I feel her cutting through the pile of strands until a giant weight lifts off my head—literally.

Dorothy holds up the long ponytail to my side. "The hardest part is done, sweetie. You still good?"

My eyes glisten as I admire the long, cumbersome locks in her hands. Not because I'm sad I cut it off, but because it's a physical representation of the transformation I've been going through since arriving at Midnight Manor, and it feels right. "I'm good. I'm happy."

Dorothy gives me a knowing smile. "All right, we're cooking with gas now. Let's finish the job."

An hour later, I leave the salon feeling like a new woman. Not only did I get my hair cut, but a woman who is a makeup artist declared today a makeover day for me and squeezed me in. She didn't go crazy with the makeup, but it's enough to make a difference. Everyone was so nice.

I've never worn makeup before. I used to beg my mom when I was a teen, asking if I could buy some to play around with, and she always said no. Told me it sexualizes a woman, and there was no need for it.

"I can't tell you how much I love it," Anabelle says for probably the fifth time.

"Me too. I didn't think I'd like it this much. I mean, I knew I needed a change, but I didn't know I'd love it this much." I giggle like a schoolgirl. "And my head feels so light."

I still can't stop swishing my head side to side, amazed by how light my hair is.

"Kol is going to lose it when he sees you, trust me."

I stop midstep. "You think he's going to be mad?"

Anabelle throws her head back and laughs. "No, he's going to be turned on."

"Oh." My cheeks heat, but I hope that she's right, and this is what makes him give up on treating me like a valuable piece of porcelain when we sleep together.

"What do you want to do now? Are you hungry? Do you want to grab a drink?" she asks.

"That Black Magic place looks interesting."

She raises her eyebrows. "Black Magic Bar? Sure, let's go there. We can get some drinks, and they have food too."

I smile at her. "Lead the way."

We walk the short distance down the street, and Anabelle opens the door to let me walk in first. I've never been in a bar, so I don't know what to expect. But what I see is what I think most people would term a dive bar, if it had creepy vibes. Lined up on shelves against an exposed brick wall are bottles of liquor, voodoo dolls, portraits of tarot cards, half-burned candles of different colors, crystals, and skulls. There's more of them throughout the bar too. Stools are lined up along the bar, and there are worn wood tables littered throughout the space.

Anabelle comes in behind me and waves to the woman working behind the bar, so I follow Anabelle over there.

"Hey, stranger. It's been a while. How's married life?" she asks Anabelle.

"It's perfect. Which is why I haven't been here much."

The woman laughs. "I bet."

Anabelle turns to me. "Cinder, this is Rapsody. Rapsody, Cinder."

"Nice to meet you." Cinder gives me a warm smile and extends her hand over the bar.

She's really beautiful, and if I wasn't feeling so good about myself right now, I might feel self-conscious in her presence. Her long blond hair hangs in waves to her large breasts, and she's wearing a tight white tank top and short denim shorts that showcase all her curves.

I take her hand. "Good to meet you."

"What can I get you ladies?" Cinder asks.

Anabelle looks at me. I don't plan on drinking after my last experience.

"I'll just have a sweet tea please," I say.

Cinder nods and looks at Anabelle.

"Wine spritzer for me since it's not even dinner time yet."

Cinder laughs and nods down toward the end of the bar at a couple of men who look to be in their early forties who have obviously been partaking for a while. "Not everyone waits until dinner."

We laugh while Cinder works on our drinks.

Anabelle turns to me. "Want to sit at the bar or go get a table?"

I glance down at the dress I'm wearing. It reaches my knees, so I should be fine to sit on a bar stool. "Let's sit at the bar. I've never sat at one before."

Anabelle gives me a quizzical look and slides onto a stool, motioning for me to take the one next to her. She doesn't say anything for a second, and I'm sure she's wondering what planet I just descended from.

"You mentioned in the salon that you've never worn makeup and then you just said that you've never sat at a bar... I was just wondering—and I hope it's not rude of me to ask, I just want to get to know you better—

did you grow up in a really religious home or something?"

I don't blame her for asking. I'd be curious, too, if I were her and met a twenty-three-year-old who was such a novice at so many things. So I explain to her the way my mom raised me, though I don't mention the why of it. I may have shared with Kol that my mother was assaulted, but it's not something I feel right about telling everyone.

"That must have been really difficult," she says.

"It was honestly fine until I reached my teens. I guess I didn't know any better, but then when I started watching certain TV shows and surfing the internet, I realized there was this whole world out there I was missing out on. But at the same time, I was afraid of the idea of experiencing it."

Cinder slides our drinks in front of us.

"Thanks," I say before taking a sip of mine.

Before she can answer, one of the guys at the end of the bar calls, "Hey, sweet tits, get yer ass down here and fill me up." He raises his beer mug.

My eyes widen.

"You should kick them out," Anabelle says in a low voice.

"Their bark is bigger than their bite, believe me. And they tip well." She winks before heading to the end of the bar.

"Are all guys like that?" I ask Anabelle. Maybe my mom was right about most men. Perhaps Kol and his brothers are the exception and not the rule.

Anabelle shakes her head. "Not at all. But alcohol doesn't usually bring out the best in people."

I nod, leaning in to take another sip of my drink. "So what is this place? It's kind of..."

"Weird?" Anabelle laughs. "Yeah, it's not your typical dive bar, that's for sure. Local urban legend is that the woman who owns it is a witch."

I blink rapidly. "Really?"

She nods. "Yeah. She's not really here any-more because she's older. Mostly has other people do the day-to-day for her now."

"Do you think she's a witch?"

Anabelle considers it while she sips on her spritzer. "Not sure. It's possible, I guess. Wouldn't be the weirdest thing that has hap-pened around here."

I want to ask what she means, but I get the sense she'll probably blow me off if I do. Maybe if we become closer, in time I'll be comfortable digging a little more.

We chat for a while, Anabelle telling me about her life, where she went to college and how she came to be in Asher Voss's orbit. Eventually I need to pee.

I slip off the stool. "I have to go to the re-stroom. I'll be right back."

"Okay." Anabelle pulls her phone from her purse as I set off toward the hallway that has the restroom sign above it.

I use the facilities, and as I wash my hands, someone says my name. I look into the mirror to see who would know me here. My stomach drops.

Because it's my mother.

"Mom!" I wheel around and face her, pulling her into a hug. "What are you doing here?"

When I draw back, she's looking somewhat frantic. "We have to go. Now." She grips my arm, but I yank it free.

"Go? Go where?"

"Away from him. Now let's go." She heads toward the door.

"I'm not going anywhere, Mom. I don't want to."

She whips around to face me, hurt and anger glowing. "I knew he'd sink his claws into you. He's brainwashed you."

"He has not."

"You think you can handle someone like him? He's evil. Look at all the people he's killed—in the military, his own father, probably his mother, and who knows who else."

"He has not!" I stomp my foot like a toddler.

"Look at you." My mom waves her hand up and down my body. "Short skirt, your hair is all gone, and you look like a trollop with that makeup. Is this all in an effort to keep him interested? Mark my words, Rapsody, one day he'll tire of you and set you aside as if you meant nothing. And you'll be heartbroken and all alone. A man like Kol Voss, a man who can have anything and anyone he wants, isn't going to stay satisfied with the likes of you."

Her words cut deep.

"He will not." I wish I sounded more confident, but despite myself, her words are penetrating the cracks in my self-esteem formed by being raised in a locked apartment.

A caustic laugh erupts out of her, and she shakes her head. "You'll see. And I'll be ready and waiting when you do."

She slips out the bathroom door, and I'm taken aback that she just gave up. A big part of me wants to follow her. I miss my mother. But I can't live under her reign any longer. And the things she said... I know she's only trying to help me, prevent me from being hurt, but no. I'll show her. When Kol and I are still going strong in a few months, I'll reach out to her, change her mind about him. Maybe the three of us can get together, and she'll see that he's not who she thinks he is.

I gather myself before leaving the bathroom. When I glance around the bar after entering the main room, there's no sign of my mother. How did she even know where to find me?

Sliding into my seat beside Anabelle, I give her my best version of a natural smile. I'm still shaken by my encounter with my mom.

"I was about to send in the search party," she says, bringing her wine glass to her lips.

"Sorry, I was just making sure my makeup still looked okay." It's a lame excuse, but it's all I can come up with.

"No worries. Now tell me about how you and Kol first met. I've never heard the story."

Yes, that's exactly what I need. A reminder of the Kol I first met and the man who emerges a little more every day.

# 27


*KOL*

Where the hell is she?

She's been gone for hours. How long can it possibly take to get your hair cut?

I've been trying to keep myself busy with work shit that needs to get done, but that's been ineffective. I can't concentrate for more than a few minutes, so I shut my laptop with a sigh and stand from my desk.

Asher.

Asher will know what's going on.

He's as protective as, if not worse than, me and surely he tracks Anabelle.

I make my way through the manor from my wing over to his, the west wing.

It took every ounce of my willpower to let Rapsody walk out of here after lunch. The fear that she may disappear and not come back like she did once before is a living, breathing nightmare. I made sure to have Anabelle promise not to let Rapsody out of her sight, but it still isn't enough to satisfy me.

I'm possessive where Rapsody is concerned. More than I should be. More than is healthy, I'm sure.

I walk into Asher's office without knocking.

He looks up from behind his desk, sees me, and leans back in his chair. "To what do I owe the pleasure of your company, brother?" A sly grin creases his lips because he fucking knows why I'm here.

Asshole.

"Have you talked to Anabelle?" I shove my hands in my jeans to calm them.

Asher may wear designer suits to work from home, but the fuck if I will.

"I talk to her all the time. In the morning, during the day." He points toward her desk on the other side of the room. "Nighttime. Well, I don't talk to her a lot at night, but there is talking." He waggles his eyebrows.

"Cut the shit, Ash. Have you talked to her since she left?"

He steeples his fingers, enjoying this. "I haven't. I'm trying to be less... domineering about checking up on her per her request."

I knew I wasn't alone. "They've been gone for a while."

He nods.

"Well, can you tell me where they are?"

He purses his lips. "I just told you I haven't spoken to her."

I tilt my head. "You expect me to believe you don't track your wife?"

Asher rolls his eyes and pulls his phone out of his suit pants pocket. I knew it. It's the same thing I'd do with Rapsody if she had a phone.

After a minute, he looks at me. "Do not tell my wife I have a tracker on her phone."

I roll my eyes.

"They're at Black Magic Bar," he says.

I scowl. "What the hell are they doing there?"

"My assumption would be that they're having a drink."

"I don't like it." I set my hands on my hips.

Asher chuckles.

"What?"

"I didn't realize how far you've fallen for her. Didn't think it was possible, if I'm honest." He holds my gaze for a beat, and we're both thinking about our shared past and all we endured. "I'm glad to see it though."

I scowl. "Fuck off." Then I stalk to the door.

"Remember you didn't find out from me!" he calls after me because we both know where I'm headed.

I park in the lot beside the bar and step out of my car. When I round the building, I do a double take at a familiar car parked well down the street.

What the hell is Nero doing in town? As a rule, the four of us Voss brothers keep to ourselves in Midnight Manor. We're not out shooting shit with the townies. I tuck the fact that Nero's here in the back of my head to deal with later and enter the bar.

My eyes scan the bar, but Rapsody isn't here. Then I hear her laugh and follow the sound to a woman standing by the end of the bar. That is *not* the woman who left the manor this morning. Her hair rests on her shoulders. And it makes her look sophisticated and closer to her age. It's not only her hair; she's wearing makeup. I've never seen Rapsody wear makeup, and I couldn't care less whether she chooses to wear it or not, but it's sexy as fuck on her. Gives her a sultry, wanton look that my dick takes notice of.

My attention snags on the drunk douchebag chatting her up. And from the looks of it, even though she and Anabelle appear to be making it clear they're not interested, this fucker isn't getting the message. I'm more than happy to help.

Fists clenched at my sides, I approach the bar. Anabelle spots me first, her eyes widening in alarm.

"Rapsody," she says to get her attention.

But as Rapsody turns toward Anabelle, the man on her left grabs Rapsody's arm to force her to face him again. Unlike when I was in combat and had control over myself, rage boils inside me, turning me into a pressure cooker about to explode.

"Get your fucking hands off her," I say right before I remove his grip from Rapsody's arm and toss him to the side.

Her eyes widen, full of worry.

"Are you okay?" I ask.

She nods and lets out a ragged breath.

"What the fuck, man! I was just talking to her!" His words are slightly slurred, but I don't give a shit if he's drunk.

No one touches what's mine.

No one.

"Get out of my sight before I use your face as target practice for my fist." I attempt to rein in my fury, but it's proving more difficult with every word out of this guy's mouth.

"Why don't you mind your own business, asshole?" he says and steps toward me, puffing out his chest.

This fucker just doesn't know when to quit. The lion is banging on the cage doors.

"Back off, douchebag. Now apologize to the lady." I motion to where Rapsody is behind me.

He laughs. "As if. I almost had her talked into coming home with me, didn't I, sweetheart? She was drooling for this dick." He punctuates his words by grabbing the limp dick in his jeans.

His words crack the cage doors, and the lion crashes through. I don't think, I just react. My fist hits him in the face with enough force to knock him to the floor. I straddle his body, falling on top of him and punching him again.

I hold my fist over his bloody face, threatening to continue. "Now tell the lady you're sorry."

He turns his head and spits a gob of blood onto the floor. "I'm sorry, okay? I'm sorry."

"Now get the fuck out of here." I stand, turning to find Rapsody and Anabelle standing behind me with shocked expressions.

My adrenaline is sky high now, and my thoughts are moving a mile a minute, but even in my state, I detect Rapsody's horror at what just happened. What I just did.

I flick my gaze to Anabelle. "Go home, Anabelle. I've got Rapsody."

She double-checks by looking at Rapsody quickly. Normally, I'd be mad, but she's Asher's wife, and I like the way she's looking out for Rapsody. Anabelle nods, gathering her purse before heading to the door. Rapsody watches her leave, and for a second, I fear she's so disgusted by what I did that she'll ask Anabelle to take her because she's afraid to be with me, but she doesn't.

People scatter to their seats in the bar as the idiot drags himself off the floor and makes his way to the exit.

"Go back to whatever you were doing!" I shout.

Everyone diverts their eyes, and murmurs fill the room again.

"Come with me." I take Rapsody's wrist and drag her behind me to the washrooms, going into the women's and locking the door behind us. I'm too amped to wait until we get back to the manor to have this conversation.

I position Rapsody against the wall, staring up at me with her big green eyes that have the power to undo me. The need to show my ownership over her, to prove that she's mine is scratching to come out.

My hand flies up and grips her chin. She flinches from the blood coating my fingers, but I don't care. I have to make her see.

"You're mine," I growl.

She looks at me for a beat and blinks.

"Say it." I squeeze her chin a little harder.

"I'm yours."

"Then why are you looking at me like you're afraid of me? I would never hurt you, Rapsody. Never. I'd hurt myself before I let anything happen to you."

She cradles my face with her hand. "I've never had anyone stand up for me. If it were my mom, she would have blamed me and said it was my fault. So, thank you."

I smash my lips to hers. There's nothing loving or thoughtful about our kiss. It's frantic and animalistic and demanding.

Rapsody's hands clutch my shoulders and a moan erupts deep in her throat. My hand trails down her body and under her dress to find her wet and wanting. I bite her bottom lip harder than intended, and the coppery taste of her blood fills my mouth. I start to pull away, but she grabs my shirt, pulling me back to her. I tease her clit with my fingers, and she becomes liquid heat in my arms.

"I need to take you rough, sweetheart. I need to show you that you're mine."

"Please, Kol…"

I take my hand out from under her dress and whip her around to face the wall. She splays her hands beside her head, her cheek pressed against the cool tile wall.

"You're so ready. Your cunt is practically begging for me."

"Yes," she groans, offering her ass to me.

I undo my belt with one hand and push down my jeans far enough for my cock to spring free. I flip up her skirt and rip off her panties, discarding them on the floor. I slide my cock through her folds a few times before lining up with her entrance and savagely thrusting inside her.

She cries out, eyes closed as I take her rough, like an animal that's been caged for too long.

I watch my glistening cock slide in and out of her, covered in her arousal. Then I press my chest to her back so she's trapped against the wall.

"Who." I thrust into her. "Owns." I thrust again. "This." I thrust another time. "Cunt?" Again, I thrust, but this time, I hold myself inside her until she answers me.

"You."

"Damn right me." I plow into her again, changing my angle.

"Oh god," she groans.

My face falls to her neck. "I'm your god, remember, sweetheart."

I pull my length from her and step back.

"No!" she cries out.

Hands around her waist, I lead her over in front of the mirror. "Hold on to either side of the sink. I want to see your face when you come."

She does as I say, always so good at following my instructions. As soon as she's bent over with her hands on either side of the small sink, I flip her dress back up, exposing her ass, and sink inside her.

Rapsody's eyes flutter closed as I drag myself in and out of her. My speed increases until the only sound filling the bathroom is our skin slapping together. She's fucking drenched for me, so much so I'm surprised she's not dripping onto the floor.

Someone knocks on the door.

"Fuck off!" I shout.

I bend over her and bring my fingers to her swollen clit, and her hips buck. Rapsody whimpers and sinks farther down toward the sink.

"Head up. I want you to watch us."

Her head bolts up, so much easier now with her short hair, and meets my gaze in the dirty mirror.

I play her clit as though it's my own personal instrument I've been playing for years, knowing just what to do to get her off. In less than a minute, her entire body goes still before her head drops, and she cries out, climaxing.

Her pussy milks my cock, and with one final thrust, I hold myself in her, spilling inside.

We stand joined, gathering our breath, gathering our wits.

Finally, she raises her head to meet my gaze in the mirror. "Wow. You didn't hold back."

I grin at her. "And you took it like a fucking queen."

I've been holding back with her, even on the night I took her virginity, not wanting to push her too far, too fast, for fear that she'd retreat from me. She's experienced some of what I want to do to her, but we haven't even scratched the surface yet.

Now, she has a better idea.

I withdraw from her and our mixed arousal drips down her thighs. Rather than getting her some toilet paper like a gentleman would, I rub it into her skin between her legs.

"I'll lick it off when I get home."

Intrigue boils in her eyes as she straightens up. She turns and wraps her arms around my neck, kissing me.

I am so fucked. If this woman ever decides to leave me again, I'll be destroyed.

I want to believe she won't, but everyone who has ever loved me leaves me.

I really fucking hope she's the first one who won't.

# 28



Sometime in the middle of the night, I awaken to find myself alone in bed. I roll over and my hand runs over cold sheets. I sit up and look around the room, noticing the glow under the door to the hallway.

All the little hairs on my body stand on end. I turn my head in the other direction and see the curtains are open. Only darkness fills the outside. It's even darker than it should be, as if there's no light left in the world. I can't make out anything beyond the glass.

When I glance back, the warm glow still rests outside the door. I debate what to do and decide that once before the light led me to Kol, the night that things began to change for us, so I trust it will lead me to him again.

I slide out of bed naked and reach for Kol's discarded shirt on the floor. Slipping it on, I walk over to the door, holding my breath and trusting my gut, and open it.

Once again, the light moves down the hallway.

I hurry to catch up, moving through the shadows that feel as if they're chasing me. I leave the north wing, pass the stained-glass lion, and follow the light to one of the doors that leads outside.

My footsteps halt as it moves through the door. I nibble on my bottom lip, unsure what to do. It was different, going outside in the middle of the night, when I was trying to escape. But this time, I have an ominous feeling about leaving the manor.

The light stills, waiting patiently for me to

decide. With a deep breath, I step forward and turn the handle on the door.

"I better not regret this," I mumble to the light, but when I look up, it has vanished.

It takes me a minute to figure out why the light led me here. The thick fog sits heavy near the ground, but I spot Kol sitting on one of the chairs on the patio. He's slouched back, holding a bottle of booze.

I approach quietly, taking him in. When I draw closer, he's clearly deep in thought about something, but I have no idea what. It's obvious from the way he grips the neck of the bottle and from the look of agitation on his face as he stares into the darkness.

It's been a few days since Kol found me at Black Magic Bar, and he's been attentive and is no longer holding back in bed, something I'm grateful for. His mood has been good, stable. But something must be bothering him for him to leave our bed in the middle of the night and come out here.

"Hey."

His head whips to me. "You look like a ghost."

"Is that good or bad?" I ask, closing the remaining distance between us.

He doesn't answer.

"What are you doing out here?" I glance down at his bottle of booze. If the scent coming off him is any indication, I'd guess that he's been out here longer than I knew.

"Needed to shave my head. I usually do it out here because it doesn't make as big of a mess."

My head tilts. "You decided you needed to shave your head in the middle of the night. And what, you just happened to find a bottle out here?"

He gives me a lopsided grin. "Actually, I decided on the alcohol first, then I decided on the haircut."

I frown. "What's wrong?"

He inhales a deep breath and sighs. "Nothing for you to worry about."

"Kol..." I slide onto his lap sideways and wrap my arms around his neck. "You can tell me."

He brings his face to my neck and inhales deeply. "Just got some news. Not sure what to do about it, that's all."

"Concerning work?"

He nods against my neck.

"There's no clear-cut answer?"

He shakes his head.

I frown again. It's clear that whatever this decision he has to make at work is weighing on him. I rub his chest. "I'm sure you'll figure it out."

"Yeah." I hear the clank of the bottle meeting the patio as he sets it down, then he brings his hand to my hip. "Do you want to shave my head for me?"

For some reason, his request makes my belly flutter.

I pull back to see if he's serious. "You want me to do it?"

Kol shrugs. "You can't be the only one looking good." He runs his fingers along the end of my hair.

"Okay." I hop off his lap. "Should we go inside so I can see what I'm doing?"

There's a light on at the side of the house, but with the fog, it looks more like a lighthouse on some distant shore.

"Here's fine. There's not much to it." He reaches for the electric razor on the table to his left, stretching out, and his T-shirt rising gives me a glimpse of the hair that disappears under the waistband of his pants. A faint buzzing sound fills the night. "Just run it bottom to top, front to back." He demonstrates the direction to go.

"Okay." I take the shaver from him and start at the side of his head.

After a few swipes, I get more comfortable and get the hang of the technique. In no time, I've made it around to the other side. When I step in front of him, his hands slide up my bare legs and under his large T-shirt to rest at my hips.

"I like seeing you in my shirt."

The hunger in his voice tells me that if I looked down right now, I'd probably see an erection tenting his lounge pants.

"I like being in it." The moment feels intimate now that I'm in front of him.

I run the razor from the front of his head to the back, leaning in when I get close to his crown. My breasts brush against his face, and Kol nuzzles them and sighs.

His hands squeeze my hips. "Don't leave me." His voice is as rough and worn as the floor at Black Magic Bar.

"I'm not going anywhere." My voice is soft and reassuring, and I hope he hears the truth in my words.

My run-in with my mother has been on my mind, but I have no urge to run back to her, though I do know eventually I'm going to have to call her and try to find some common ground. But I keep pushing it off. I love this little bubble Kol and I have created for ourselves, even if I know it won't last forever.

Kol's hands slide around to my ass, and he squeezes.

I stifle a moan. "I'm going to mess this up if you don't hold still."

Kol leans forward and bites my nipple through the T-shirt, and I yelp. He laughs before sucking the fabric into his mouth along with my pebbled nipple, and my legs go weak. His hands delve between my legs from behind, and he groans around my breast, finding me wet. My head lolls back, eyes closed.

"I'm all done," I say through a haze of lust so thick it battles the heaviness of the fog around us.

His hands drop, and he leans back in the chair, sliding down his lounge pants. I lick my lips at the sight of him and move to go down on my knees, but his hands grab my elbows.

"I want your cunt."

I bite my lip and straddle him. He pulls me down and pushes into me. We both release a satisfied sigh, the feel of him always so perfect. Everything with him is always so perfect.

He's worried I'll leave him, and I'm worried I might not be enough one day, but moments like this makes me believe we're destined for one another.

# 29



A few nights later, I walk out of the bathroom after my shower, and Kol isn't in the bed, but a gorgeous pale purple dress is strewn across the bed in his place.

I love that everything he buys me is purple.

I get a closer look and gasp. The sheer fabric overlaying the dress has a bunch of small flowers sewn to the skirt, up the bodice, and over the two straps. It's gorgeous, and it had to have cost him a small fortune.

On the floor beside the bed is a pair of silver heels. They have a crystal snake that wraps around the heel and comes up to wrap around my ankle and lower leg.

I whip my head right and left, checking for Kol, but I'm met with the usual shadows that darken the room. It's then I notice the note on the night table, folded in half with my name scribbled on the outside.

With a smile, I walk over and read the note.

*Meet me in the conservatory.*

*K*

I grin at the paper. I'm not sure what this is about, but I don't care. I rush to grab some underwear, then think better of it, deciding to go without.

Anabelle gifted me hair and makeup products a couple of days ago, so I head into the bathroom to get ready. I'm no expert, but I do an okay job, probably because makeup just feels like paint for your face.

Once that's done, I slide into the dress and put on the heels. I walk over to the full-length mirror like a baby calf since I don't have any experience with heels, and when I see myself, tears well in my eyes.

I've never felt this beautiful. Not even when I put on my wedding dress for my wedding to Alistair. I look so...alive. How far I've come in such little time. I feel like a flower opening for the sun. The more Kol loves me and allows me to find myself, the more I blossom.

With one last look at myself, I leave the room and head into the dark hallway. Nothing, not even the oppressive darkness of the shadows that linger between the flickering sconces, can bring me down. I feel like when winter turns to spring, and all of nature's beauty shines in vibrant colors.

By the time I reach the conservatory, I've somewhat figured out how to walk in heels. Which is a good thing, because as I enter through the doorway, I almost stumble at what I see.

The room is lit up with candles casting a yellow glow that's reflected on the glass. In the center of the room, to the side of the easel and the piece I've been working on, is a small table for two. Music plays from a speaker, loud enough to be heard, but soft enough not to take over.

The sound of shoes clicking on the floor draws my eye past the table as Kol makes his way over to me. He has a glass of wine in hand, and he's wearing a dark gray suit with a black shirt underneath, sans tie. It fits him perfectly, and there is no doubt in my mind it's a custom piece.

His eyes soak me in, and I preen under his attention, knowing he likes what he sees. He sets the glass of wine on the table as he passes and continues toward me.

"Christ, you look so beautiful." He looks at me in wonder, as if he almost can't believe that I'm here with him.

"You look so handsome." I too feel lucky to be here, especially after I messed it all up four years ago.

With the way he's looking at me, I assume he's going to kiss me, maybe ravage me before we eat, but he does no such thing. Instead, he leans in and kisses my temple, his hand falling to the small of my back.

"What's all this?" I ask in a soft voice.

"I thought you might enjoy dressing up and having a fancy dinner. Kind of like if we'd met under normal circumstances, and I was dating you."

I smile up at him. "Thank you, I love it." *I love you,* I want to say, but I'm too afraid to scare him off—or worse, that he won't believe me.

"Come." He links his fingers with mine and leads me to the table where there are two plates with silver domes over top. "I hope you're hungry. I had the kitchen prepare your favorite."

My forehead wrinkles. I don't remember ever telling Kol what my favorite food is. He goes to one chair and pulls it out for me, waiting until I sit to push it back in. Then he lifts the lid, uncovering a burger and fries.

I laugh and look up at him. "All this"—I motion around us—"and we're having a burger and fries?"

He sits across from me and removes the silver dome from over his plate. "You ordered it when I took you to the horse races and go-karting and inhaled it both times."

My eyes widen, and my mouth drops open. "I did not!"

He chuckles. "You did. And it was cute as fuck, so don't stress about it."

I smile, looking at the meal and back at him. "I can't believe you noticed that."

He doesn't blink as he says, "I remember everything when it comes to you."

I look away from the intensity of his eyes. "Thank you, this is wonderful."

"Bon appétit." He sets his napkin over his lap and picks up his burger, taking a bite.

I do the same with my napkin. I feel a little silly as I bring the burger to my lips, this dressed up and eating something so unso-phisticated, but the moment I bite into it, I stop worrying. This is better than the two I shared with him previously.

"Mmm, that's so good."

"I'll tell the chef you said so. Do you want some wine?"

"With my burger?" I laugh. "No, thank you. I'm still reliving the memories of the last time I drank."

He looks at me with amusement. "Fair enough." We quietly enjoy our meal before Kol speaks again. "What do you think you'd want to do if you could do anything?"

I finish chewing my fry. "Work-wise?"

He shrugs. "Sure. How would you spend your time?"

I ponder his question for a minute. "I'm not sure. I've never had the option to think about it before, but I suppose it's something I need to consider."

My stomach clenches. So many possibilities. What if I choose wrong?

Oh god, I've been so presumptuous, haven't I? Assuming I was free to stay here for as long as I wanted without contributing anything.

"If you're asking because I've overstayed my—"

"Stop." Kol frowns. "That's not why I'm asking. I'm asking because I want you to be happy here."

The tension in my shoulders lessens. "I am happy here."

"For now. But eventually your excitement about this newfound freedom of yours will wear off. I don't want you to want to leave in search of something new and exciting. I'd rather you found that here."

Where is this coming from? He said something similar about me leaving at Black Magic Bar, but why?

"Kol"—I reach across the table for his hand—"I'm not going anywhere. And if anything changes with how I feel, I'll talk to you about it."

He studies me for a long while. I don't flinch, don't even blink until he gives me a small nod.

"The question stands. What would you want to do?"

I put another fry in my mouth since that's all that's left on my plate. Kol was correct, I do inhale burgers. "The only thing I really love to do that I know about is painting. I guess I could try other things. I'd have to. I'm not talented enough to be a professional painter."

"That's bullshit. I've seen your paintings. Especially that new one you're working on. It's a masterpiece."

My head tilts. "You think so?"

"I know so."

I've been dabbling in something other than landscapes lately—erotic art. I enjoy painting the body and mimicking the way it moves, the stretch of the muscles, and since Kol always has me hot and bothered, the erotic nature of the paintings just kind of came out.

Kol sets his napkin on the table and stands, walking over to the easel. "This is really good. And it's fucking hot."

I push back, leaving my own napkin on the table, and join him. "I don't know..."

"Well, I do." He stands behind me and wraps me in his arms.

"Would you ever pose for me?" I voice the question I've been wondering about lately—as soon as I began fiddling with the change in direction of my paintings.

"I'd be honored."

That makes my chest warm, and I get an idea, but I'm not sure if Kol will be up for it. Rather than worrying too much about it, I decide to trust my instincts and step out of Kol's hold, turning to face him.

I find the zipper on my dress, and his eyes follow my fingers as I slide it down tooth by tooth until it stops. Sliding the straps down one arm then the other, I let the dress fall to my ankles, leaving me in only my heels.

He focuses on my bare breasts, adjusting himself in his suit pants. "What are you doing? We haven't even had dessert yet."

"I was thinking... I'd love for you to be my subject, but maybe tonight you could be my canvas." I break the distance, and my pebbled nipples brush against the expensive fabric of his suit. "Why don't you get undressed?"

Kol makes record time of taking off his clothes while I prepare what I'll need. Once we're both naked and standing in front of each other, I pick up the palette with all the paint and turn to face him. The candlelight highlights every dip and crest of the muscles in his strong body. If I paint him one day, I want it to be in this lighting.

He watches intently as I dip a finger in the paint, choosing a pale blue, and step forward, trailing my finger over his round shoulder. Next, I choose a green and wipe it across his lower abs. His breath fans over my face while I continue to work until he's covered with all the colors of the rainbow, resembling a kaleidoscope.

"My turn." His voice sounds pained, but in the best way.

I pass him the palette, and of course he chooses purple first, swirling a circle over my left nipple. The stimulation causes a buzzing between my thighs. Kol chooses yellow next, running it from my ear to the base of my throat.

God, is this how he felt while I was doing it to him? I'm so on edge. I want him to just toss the palette aside and devour me. But I'm enjoying the intimacy that's growing between us.

Once my legs and arms and torso are covered in paint, Kol steps back to admire his work. "You're a treasure."

My cheeks heat at his praise.

The song playing through the speaker finishes and a new one starts.

Kol walks past me and sets the palette on the small table, then reaches for me. "Dance with me."

My stomach flutters with nerves, and my cheeks heat. "I've never danced before. I don't know how."

He offers me a soft smile, one I've never seen on him before. "Another first then."

I take his hand and step into him. "I'll probably be terrible."

His fingers brush my cheek, and the gooey feeling of paint presses into my skin. "I don't care. This is another first of yours that I want. I'm greedy for them all. I'm always so greedy when it comes to you."

I relax into his hold, my nipples brushing his chest.

"Stand on my feet, and I'll lead you around."

I rear back and look at him. "I can't do that."

He rolls his eyes. "You probably weigh a hundred pounds less than me. Yes, you can."

I do as he says, and he wraps his arms around me, resting them on my lower back. I wind mine around his neck, pressing my cheek to his chest, and more paint smears on my face. But I don't care because I feel so safe and loved.

He moves us, and he's right, I likely could have handled this, but I like how close our bodies are. The man sings about being undeserving and not understanding why the woman he's with loves him just the way he is. We dance around the room, and I hope the song is a coincidence, and Kol didn't pick it on purpose. He's so wonderful, and I want him to see himself the way I do.

We rotate in the candlelight, and the emotion in my chest builds and builds until I can't contain it any longer. I look at him and pull him down for a kiss. It's slow and languid, unrushed as if we have all the time in the world.

Kol's hands slide down to my ass, and his erection grows harder between us. Soon his hands are around my waist, and he's pushing me away from him. "We haven't even had dessert."

I hum. "This is even better than whatever's on that table under the silver lid."

His face grows serious. "I'm trying to show you that I don't just want you for your body, but you're making it very hard."

I bring my hand to his cheek. "I don't think that, Kol. But right now, I feel so close to you that I want to make love to you."

My words snap his tether, and he pulls me back into him. The paint on our bodies is turning into a brown mess, but he's the most beautiful thing I've ever painted. He kisses me with more gusto, and I rub my bare breasts against his chest, desperate for friction.

Eventually, I pull away from the kiss. "Lie down on the floor."

He does as I say, for once seeming to be fine with not being the one calling the shots. I lower myself, straddling his waist. I don't waste any time gripping his length, sinking down until he's fully seated inside me.

I slow the rotation of my hips as he watches me with lust-addled eyes. His hands cup my breasts, and he gently uses his thumbs to brush my paint-covered nipples. I rest my hands on his chest, and his eyes devour me. Eventually one hand moves from my breast and up behind my neck, pulling me down to him.

I throw all the emotions swirling in my chest into that kiss, willing him to understand how I feel about him and to understand that I'm never going to leave him. He groans into my mouth, hands laced through the hair at the back of my head.

When we end the kiss, I sit back up and rest my hands on his thighs, arching my back and giving Kol a good view of his cock sliding into me.

"Fuck, sweetheart. You look so good taking me in like that." His voice is hoarse. "Touch yourself."

His words are missing their usual authoritarian tone, but I follow his orders. I bring my fingers to my mound and gently massage my clit.

"That's it. Apply a little more pressure now," Kol coaxes.

I do as he says, moaning at the first ripple of my orgasm deep in my womb.

"Keep at it. Pretend it's my fingers. Can you feel how good it is?" he says.

I continue to ride him, faster as the intensity of my orgasm builds until it's as unstoppable as a landslide.

"Fuck yeah," he says when I grind down on him. "Now finish yourself off. I want you milking me."

His words combined with my fingers send me over the edge. My body jerks a few times on top of him, incoherent words leaving my lips, as my climax drowns me.

Kol sits up and drags me back down with him, so our chests are pressed together. His hips rise and fall, fucking me with hard, powerful strokes. All I can do is grip him and enjoy the ride of ownership he takes my body on.

He stills, holding himself inside me. "That's it. Oh fuck, sweetheart."

His cock jerks, and he spills inside me, leaving me filled with a sense of satisfaction.

He kisses me so long he grows soft inside me. I gaze into his amber eyes, believing this must be what real love feels like. I can't imagine anything greater than what I feel for this man.

Kol tucks a piece of my sweaty hair behind my ear. "I think I might take up painting too."

I laugh and bury my head in his chest. "It's not usually this exciting, I assure you."

He grins. "Do you want to go have that dessert?"

I nod. And I do, but first there's something he needs to know. "Thank you, Kol. No one has ever made me feel this special before."

Something flicks across his gaze that I can't decipher. "You deserve it. I'm always going to do what makes you the happiest. I need you to always know that."

It feels as though there's some underlying meaning to his words that I'm not picking up on, but as I think over everything he's put together tonight, I must be wrong and reading too much into his words.

"Of course I believe you."

He sighs, the tension in his body relaxing under mine as he pulls me in for another kiss.

# 30



When the next Saturday for the Ritual Room rolls around, I'm not nervous at all. In fact, I'm looking forward to it.

Kol explained to me that the theme for tonight night is vampires and vixens, so he's going dressed as Dracula, and I'm going as Medusa.

My costume has green fabric that drapes straight down my chest, leaving a wide gap to my belly button where a gold belt holds the dress in place. Around my neck is a thin snake choker that wraps around several times and matches the gold heels wrapping around my calves. The head piece I'm wearing might be my favorite part, though, with all the snakes coming off it.

A knock lands on the bathroom door. "I'm getting impatient, Rapsody. I want to see."

I told him I wanted to get ready without him seeing me so the finished product could be a surprise. He wasn't happy about it, but he indulged me nonetheless.

"Coming." With a final check in the mirror, I walk over and open the door.

Kol's gaze moves along my body from top to bottom in a slow perusal. "You'll definitely turn some cocks as hard as stone tonight, Medusa." Kol adjusts himself in his pants. "You look fucking hot."

I take in what he's wearing. It's reminiscent of the *Dracula* movie—a dark gray suit from yesteryear. The jacket has tails, and the suit pants are pinstripe. The vest over the shirt matches the rest of the suit, and rather than a tie, he wears a cravat. Does this man look sexy in everything? Now a huge part of me doesn't want to wait until we reach the basement to undress him.

"You look really good." I lick my lips.

"Tongue back in your mouth, or we'll never make it there." He takes my hand and drags me out of the bathroom. "Let's go."

Seems he's as anxious as I am to get this started.

We walk through the dim house, not speaking, and even though I don't feel nervous, my heart rate picks up speed with every step closer to our destination. When we reach the door to the basement, he pulls out his skeleton key and unlocks it, motioning for me to go first.

"Do all your brothers use this door?" I ask as I make my way down the stairs.

"This is our private entrance. Everyone else uses the side entrance you saw before."

When we reach the bottom, Kol puts on his lion mask while I slide on a gold mask he gave me earlier. He told me I didn't have to wear a white, red, or black mask because the only person I'll be doing anything with is him. I didn't complain. I like when he shows the ownership he feels over me.

Once it's situated, Kol takes my hand and leads me down the long hallway. We enter the main room and find it full of people in masks. I feel a jolt of nerves when they all shift their attention to our arrival.

I lean into Kol. "What should I do during this part?"

He explained to me earlier that the evening starts with everyone mingling before the fun gets started. "Stick with me. You'll be fine."

And I am, because as it turns out, Kol doesn't like to associate with many people. It's clear he hasn't nurtured friendships with any of these people, so for a good part of the evening, it's just the two of us. All his brothers come by at one point or another, and I chat with Anabelle for a bit.

Kol is seated on one of the lounge chairs with me on his lap, his hand on my thigh. His thumb keeps drifting back and forth, and that one little movement is driving me crazy. Crazy horny. It doesn't help that he's been hard under my ass for the past hour.

I lean in to speak directly in his ear so he can hear me over the music but no one else can. "When can we... you know?"

When I pull back, he grins at me, then he slides my black thong to the side and runs his hand between my legs. "Seems like you're primed and ready, aren't you?"

He drags his fingers through my wetness and brings them to my mouth. I open and suck on his fingers, twirling my tongue around them.

"C'mon." He takes my hips in his hands and helps me off his lap, standing behind me. Then he takes my hand and leads me toward the hallway.

A few of the people standing around take notice of us. When we reach one of the doors closest to the stairs, Kol uses his skeleton key to unlock it. After he pulls me inside, he doesn't close the door.

The room is dim, and the music from the main room is being pumped in here. It takes me a moment to orient myself because the entire room is encased in mirrored glass. All the walls and the ceiling.

A bed sits at the far end of the room against the wall. In one corner is a large wooden X that looks as though it has restraints on each end, then there's a black dresser in the opposite corner.

In the center of the room hangs what I think is a sex swing. I don't really know anything about them, just what I've seen in pornography online before I came here.

Kol steps over to the swing and pulls on the harnesses to test the strength. He looks at me with a wicked grin. "I had this installed just for you."

A full body shiver works its way down my spine as he steps over to me. When he reaches me, he grips me by the nape and roughly draws me in for a kiss. His other hand slips under one of the slits on my dress and pushes past my thong, delving into my folds. His fingers coast over my clit, and a needy noise slips into his mouth that causes him to hum.

When he pulls away from the kiss, he strips off my panties, takes my hand, and walks me over to the swing. Kol turns me so my back is facing the swing, and with two large hands around my waist, he lifts me and gently sets me so one strap rests across my upper back and the other rests in the middle of my ass.

It takes me a moment to get used to the sensation. But all thoughts of that go out the window when I notice a few people have trickled into the room. My insides clench at the knowledge of our observers.

Kol pays them no attention. He adjusts a couple of straps so that I'm in more of a seated position, and my legs naturally fall open.

"Hold on up here." He guides my hands above me and wraps my fingers around the handles, adjusting the length of the straps so that my elbows are slightly bent. His concerned gaze meets mine. "You good?"

I smile and nod, appreciating him checking in with me.

As soon as I've nodded, his demeanor changes, like flipping a switch. He's more rigid, his pupils bleeding lust out of his irises. Kol yanks both pieces of fabric currently hanging down between my legs up and to the side so that I'm totally exposed. The green fabric drapes on either side of my hips.

Kol licks his lips before meeting my eyes again. He leans in so that only I can hear him over the music. "I'll be right back. Let them enjoy gazing at this little bit of perfection, knowing they will never have it."

He slides the fabric over my breasts to the side and steps away from me. I look in the mirror to my left and see that he went to the black dresser. He opens one of the drawers, and I look away, back at our observers. More people have joined, maybe six or seven, an even mix of men and women.

Kol pulls something from the drawer, but I can't see what it is until he steps back in front of me. The dim lights flicker along the sharp edge of the knife in his hand.

My eyes widen and panic causes my heart to beat even harder.

"Trust me?"

I swallow and stare at the sharp tip of the knife for a beat, then I nod. I do trust him. I trust that whatever that knife is for, it's all in the name of pleasure. No part of me believes that Kol would cause me pain just for the hell of it.

My nod satisfies him. He brings the knife to his mouth and clutches the dull side between his teeth while he strips off his overcoat, vest, and shirt, leaving him in just his pants where his large bulge presses against the fabric.

He steps forward and slowly drags the knife down my body, using the dull side, starting at my collarbone. When he reaches my chest, the cold metal kisses my nipple. I suck in a breath, watching while it travels along the curve of my breast down to my belly button. My breathing is shallow, and anticipation thrums through my veins. He drags it farther down, over my mound, until he reaches my inner thigh. So quickly it takes me a minute to even figure out what happened, he nicks my inner thigh with the knife.

Blood pools there, leaving the spot burning. Not a lot, but enough so I'm aware of it.

Kol lifts his lion's mask to rest on top of his head, leaning in, and closes his mouth over the wound, sucking the blood. It's like a direct pull on my clit.

I moan, arching my back and causing the swing to move. He grips the straps and tugs me forward, swirling his tongue, tasting my life's essence. His eyes meet mine as if he's checking in on me, and I smile at him in pleasure. With every flick of his tongue, the pressure builds.

My moan echoes through the room above the steady beat of the music.

Movement behind Kol gains my attention, and I look over to see some of the men have their dicks out, stroking them. My insides clench.

Kol repeats the gash on my other inner thigh, sucking again. When he finally lowers himself to his knees between my thighs, there's still blood on his tongue. He uses the swing to pull me closer and lap on my pussy.

The moment his tongue skims my entrance, I buck, savoring the feeling but wanting, *needing* more. He makes quick work of bringing me to the edge, then he pulls back and looks at me, stark need in his amber eyes.

"Do you get off on all these men and women watching, wanting what's mine, knowing they'll never get a taste?"

The possession in his words speaks to some dark part of my soul. "Yes."

"How many times should I make you come while they watch?" He latches onto my clit with his mouth.

I open my mouth, but no words come out. All I can do is moan and writhe, a needy piece of flesh with no thoughts.

I watch in the mirror to the side of us and groan at the image of him kneeling before me, ravenously delivering me pleasure with his mouth. When I look up at the reflection of us below, my hands grip the handles even tighter. It's so erotic to bear witness to this in the same way that everyone else in the room is.

Kol pulls his mouth from me and watches me as he pushes two fingers inside. "Who owns this pussy, Rapsody?" I cry out when he curves his fingers and presses on my G-spot. "Who owns it, sweetheart?"

I still can't find the words to respond, and he withdraws his fingers from me and pulls the mask back down over his face.

"You own it!"

With a smirk, he pushes his fingers back in. "Do you think everyone knows that? Or do you think some of them are still wondering if they can join us? Whether they'll get to feast on this delicious pussy and know what it feels like when your cunt milks my cock?"

I glance over his head at everyone surrounding us. There are more people. Some of the men even have women between their legs, sucking them off while their attention is riveted on us. I make eye contact with one man in a black mask, and he bucks harder into the woman's mouth.

Kol works his fingers in and out of me, and my climax draws closer and closer. "Do you know how badly some of them want to push me out of the way so they can fuck you and try to make you theirs? But they'll never get the chance because you have always been and will forever be *mine*."

He growls the word mine from behind his lion's mask, a true predator who will rip out the throat of anyone who treads on his territory.

Kol stands from his knees and curves his fingers again, then uses his thumb to circle my clit. His other hand holds onto the strap to keep the swing in place while he works me. Every muscle in my body tightens more and more, until I can't hold back, and my orgasm explodes from within, shattering me into a million pieces.

I'm not aware of anything else but the sensation inside my body until it begins to ebb. Then I look at Kol.

He's fully undressed, stroking his cock, staring at me with so much hunger it should probably scare me. "Time to really show everyone here that you're mine."

As if I didn't just orgasm, I clench in anticipation.

# 31

*KOL*

I've never felt this possessive in all of my life.

Yes, I've fucked other partners in front of everyone before, and I get a certain kind of high from knowing they all want what I have. But those partners are free to do what they want with whoever once I'm done with them.

The same doesn't go for Rapsody.

I will *never* share her. Anyone who tries to take her from me will end up six feet under.

It's almost comical to think that at one point, all I wanted to do was push Rapsody away and make her feel as much pain as I did. Oh, how the mighty have fallen.

Standing here with all these spectators at my back, all I want is to prove to everyone that she belongs to me. Mark her, possess her, and dominate her.

I loosen the straps across her upper back so that she's lying parallel with the floor and let my greedy gaze take in her perfect body.

*Mine* is the only word that comes to mind as I slowly feed my cock into her needy pussy. She whimpers as though she can't handle how good it feels. I hold her waist to keep her in place as I pull out slowly, then slam inside her. Her tits jiggle with every thrust of my hips, and I lick my lips, wishing I could wrap my lips around her pert nipples.

Rapsody's tight pussy clenches around me when I switch up my angle. I gaze down at the two small cuts on her inner thighs, and my balls tighten.

I still can't believe how much she trusted me. I thought for sure when she saw the knife she'd refuse, but of course she didn't. Because she's just so damn perfect for me.

All these people at my back, watching us, wishing they were me can go fuck themselves because there will never be another man between this woman's thighs. At the idea of how jealous all those motherfuckers are, pride swells in my chest, and my thrusts grow sharper and more staccato.

"You." *Thrust.* "Are." *Thrust.* "Mine." *Thrust.*

"Yes, yes, yes." Rapsody flicks her head back and forth, as if she doesn't know what to do with the pleasure coursing through her body.

I feel like a predator gazing down at her. The need to own her is a primal part of me that can't be denied. I spear into her like an animal, and she accepts me, wanting everything I'm giving her.

Tingling starts at the base of my spine, starting a debate inside me as to whether I want to spill my seed inside her or all over the outside of her pussy like a branding.

I bring my thumb to her swollen clit, and she goes off, her pussy clenching around my steel length. The choice is made—I'm going to paint her insides.

With a roar, I come, holding myself inside her until she's milked every drop of me, and I have nothing more to give.

I hold her hips, both of us heaving for breath.

I help Rapsody up out of the swing and don't let go of her waist until she's solid on her feet, then I slip the fabric of her dress back over her tits before I put my own pants back on.

Taking her hand, I turn to make our way to the door. Everyone has left because they all know the deal—they don't get to mess around in my private room unless they're invited.

I lead Rapsody through the door, then I let go of her hand so I can lock it before slipping the key back in my pocket. When I turn to take her hand again, I spot one of the guys who was in the room approaching.

"Fuck off." I grab Rapsody's hand and tug her toward the private staircase back into the manor.

I did that guy a favor not letting him speak whatever words he intended. I'm pretty sure they were going to be something along the lines of "can I have a turn with Rapsody?" and if he'd said them aloud, I might have killed him.

When we make it back to my bedroom suite, I head into the en suite and turn on the shower. Rapsody didn't say a word on the walk through the manor, and it dawns on me that maybe she regrets what we did—the bloodplay, fucking in front of others, all of it perhaps.

"Undress and get in the shower. When you're done, I'll put some antiseptic ointment on your cuts and bandage them. I'll be right back."

I step out of the bathroom so I can gather myself.

I wouldn't blame her if she regrets it. Maybe I've done her a disservice by introducing someone as pure and so full of light to the depravity that courses through my veins.

I'm not a good man. The things I've done— some in the name of my country and some in the name of family... could she love me again if she knew what I'm capable of? If she knew what I've been keeping from her for my own selfish reasons?

I run my palm over my shaved head and blow out a long, steady stream of air. There's only one way to know for sure.

RIGHT AFTER THE SHOWER, Rapsody fell into a deep slumber in my bed. When she woke up this morning, she seemed her usual self. Maybe I misunderstood her quiet, and she was only tired. It's not inconceivable. What we did would take a lot out of anyone, especially someone as inexperienced as her. I'll keep an eye out the next couple of days to make sure she doesn't show signs of sub drop.

No matter. I've made the decision to tell her my greatest sins. Depending on how that goes, I may confess the information I've been keeping from her.

And if she runs scared when I tell her the things I've done?

Adapt and overcome.

That was the greatest lesson the military ever taught me, and it's exactly what I'll do. Because I'm not letting her go.

We spent the day in bed, having all our meals brought to us, then shortly before the sun began to set, I forced Rapsody out of bed and told her to get dressed. She joins me in the bedroom wearing a green romper with short sleeves that shows off her long, lean legs. The color is a close match to the green of her eyes.

"So what are we doing?" she asks.

I shove down my nerves, the same way I used to do before going on a mission, and take her hand. "I have a surprise I think you'll like."

Her face lights up as it always does at the prospect of experiencing something new.

I lead her out of the manor and onto the grounds. The sun has almost set now, but there's enough light for us to make our way. A low-hanging fog swirls at our feet as we step over the grass.

Eventually we reach the pond. The lone light by the small dock has been turned off at my request. There's also a rowboat in the water, tied to the dock.

Seeing the boat reminds me of my mother, and as always when I think of her, my mind flashes to the last time I saw her—gardening shears lodged in her chest and her dead eyes staring toward the sky.

I blink a few times to clear my mind of the image.

The boat isn't often kept in the pond anymore since there's no use for it, but I specifically asked Marcel to have Mr. Potter, who is in charge of the lands of the manor, make sure it was waiting for us tonight.

"Are we going in the boat?" Rapsody asks. "I've never been in a boat before."

I nod as we step onto the wooden dock. "We are. I'll help you in first."

"Okay!"

Her childlike excitement removes some of the sting of the memories of my mother, though it's impossible to remove it entirely given what tonight is.

Once Rapsody is in the rowboat, I untie the boat from the dock and get in, sitting opposite her, and pick up the oars. Mist swirls over the water with every row of the oars, and the sound of water dripping off them back into the pond is the only sound besides the chirping insects.

When we reach the middle of the pond, I set down the oars. The show should start any minute now.

"What's that?" Rapsody asks, pointing over my head.

I turn and look over my shoulder to see the orange glow floating up through the sky. Perfect timing. "That's what we're here for. Just watch."

A minute later, a few more lights dot the sky.

"It's beautiful." Her voice is full of awe.

"It's something the people in town do every year. This is the day the town was founded. The founder used to send lanterns up in the sky so that his star-crossed lover a few miles away would know he was thinking of her."

"That's so romantic." Rapsody's attention is still pointed skyward, but all I see is her.

"My mom thought so. She'd come out here on the pond every year to watch them float by. Sometimes she'd bring us boys."

"Your mom…" Her voice trails off as though she's just putting something together in her mind.

We watch in silence as the number of floating lanterns grows until it looks as if the sky is full of stars, and we're within arm's reach of them. Then they trail off until the last one disappears in the distance, out of view.

"I have a confession," she says.

It isn't Rapsody's soft voice that makes me stiffen but her words.

"A confession?" I tilt my head, and she meets my gaze, nodding.

"I've seen something like those lanterns before." She seems nervous, chewing her bottom lip.

My forehead wrinkles. How is that even possible? "Where did you see them?"

I watch her throat contract as she swallows hard. "In the manor."

Her words float into the night like the lanterns, but instead of floating away, they hang between us. "I don't understand."

"The night I escaped from the tower and found you sitting by the shore"—she motions with her hand to the edge of the pond —"I woke up to a warm glow under the door, and when I tried the handle, the door was unlocked. I followed the light, and it led me to you. That's why I didn't just run away when I could have."

"You followed a light?" I'm still trying to wrap my head around what she's saying.

She nods. "It looked just like those lights we saw in the sky. And then the night I found you on the patio by the pool, drinking and upset about something... the same thing happened. It led me to you."

I glance away from her at the reminder of what I've been struggling with lately and whether I should reveal it to her.

When I don't say anything for a beat, Rapsody says, "You think I'm crazy, don't you?"

"No, no." I take her hand. Lord knows I've seen some strange shit in my time living in the manor. I am curious about something though. "How did you know you should follow it? What if it was leading you somewhere bad?"

Her gaze flicks up to the sky as though she's pondering my question. "I don't really know. It just felt... right. It felt friendly, as if it was trying to help. That sounds stupid, I know."

"No, no, it doesn't."

Was it my... mother? Is that even possible?

"What do you think it means?" she asks.

"I honestly don't know." I squeeze her hands. "But I don't think it's a bad thing."

Maybe my mother was trying to help me from beyond the grave.

We're quiet for a moment, both deep in our own thoughts. My stomach tightens until it's painful, and I know it's time. This is a moment that will either bring us closer together or tear us apart. And if she chooses to leave me after I tell her everything, I won't even be able to blame her.

"Speaking of confessions, there are things I need to tell you. Confess... about myself."

She frowns and pulls her hands away, straightening up. "What is it?"

*It's already started. She's already pulling away from me.*

"I must confess to you the kind of man who sits across from you. I'm not deserving of you. Not even close. But I'm selfish enough to want to keep you anyway."

"I don't understand." Her emerald eyes are wide. She's probably imagining the worst things possible, and I'm about to prove her right.

"It's difficult for me to tell you. But the closer we get, the more it only feels fair that you know me completely." I think of how she ran off when her mother told her I had been accused of killing my father.

"You're scaring me, Kol."

"You should be scared. I'm not a good man, Rapsody." I rub my hands over my face.

Why can't I just forget all this shit from my past? Why do I have to ruin a good thing between us?

But I know the answer. It's because I love this woman. And she deserves to know that I'm in no way good enough for her.

"That's not true. You are a good person." She shakes her head, almost begging for it to be true.

"After I kidnapped you." The confession locks in my throat, but I push the words out. "I came up with a plan to make you fall in love with me, and then I would break your heart as revenge for you leaving me at the altar."

There. That's out. She glances to the sky, her chest rising and falling with deep breaths.

"It was stupid. I should have known how stupid it was because…"

"Because what?" she asks, her eyes searching mine.

"Because it's you. Rapsody… you're everything to me. You always have been."

Her lips tip, and her eyes fill with unshed tears. "Kol, but you changed your mind?"

"God, yes. I'd kill any fucker who hurt you, even if that means myself."

She rushes to me, wrapping her arms around my neck.

I place my hand on her hips, pushing her back. "I have another confession."

She sits back down, and her eyes crinkle with worry. I'm not sure how I thought she would be when I told her my original plan, but this next one is different. She knew I was mad when I kidnapped her, she knew I wanted revenge, but my next confession speaks to how horrible of a person I am.

"What?" she asks.

"I've killed people."

She relaxes once the words have left my mouth, which is the exact opposite reaction I expected. "Of course you have. You were in the special forces."

"I was. And some of what I had to do there will always haunt me. But it's more than that."

The corners of her lips tip down. "More?"

"Not only that, I've applied... pressure... when needed as a part of my duties at Voss Enterprises."

"What does that mean?" Her gaze doesn't stray from my face.

I blow out a breath. "It means if someone needs convincing in one way or another, I pay them a visit until they see things our way."

Her forehead scrunches. "So you beat them up?"

I nod. "Sometimes. Often it doesn't get that far. I can usually be fairly convincing with my words and demeanor alone."

She thinks about that for a moment. "All right, well, you're protecting your family's interests. That's not so terrible."

God, this woman just doesn't want to see what's right in front of her.

A caustic laugh leaves my lips. "I should've known you'd find some way to make what I've done unselfish. You're too naïve for your own good."

Her head rocks back as though I've slapped her. "I just don't think it's that big of a deal. I'm not naïve, I—"

"There's more."

"Okay..."

"I didn't just kill people while I was in the military. I've killed people since I've been out as well."

She stiffens. "Your father…"

"I won't speak about that night. That's not what I'm referring to anyway." My brothers and I made a pact that we would never speak with anyone about what went down the night my father died, and I'll go to my grave to stay true to that pact.

"Who then?"

"Three different people."

Her hands fly up to her face, and her emerald eyes glisten with unshed tears. "Why?"

I explain the circumstances that Asher and Anabelle found themselves in last summer and what I did to ensure they'd be okay and that no trouble would come their way.

"I don't know what to say. What did you do with the bodies of those two men from the airport?"

I rub the back of my neck with my hand. Fuck. She's going to think I'm a monster. "Returned home with their bodies on the private plane, then piloted my smaller plane out over the Gulf, weighed them down, and pushed their bodies out the door."

She gasps. "The same plane you brought me here in?"

I shake my head, then look away from her, not wanting to see what she thinks of me.

After a beat, she asks, "Do you regret it?"

This is an easy enough answer. "No. Those men threatened people I care about. I'd do it again if I had to."

They may have deserved it, but it's still not easy to look at a man while the life drains out of his eyes, knowing you're the reason why. But it not being easy doesn't mean I wouldn't do it again in a heartbeat.

Rapsody doesn't say anything. At all. For what feels like five long minutes, I sit there wondering if I've torched the best thing to ever happen to me.

When she finally does speak, her words make my guts twist.

"I think I'd like to go back to the manor now," she says.

"Rapsody, I—"

She raises her hand. "Can we just go back please?"

I nod solemnly and take the oars in hand again, rowing us back to the dock. Once we're off the boat and walking back through the mist toward the manor, Rapsody keeps a good distance between us. Of course she can't stand the idea of being near a predator like me.

We don't speak the entire walk back to the manor, and when the ethereal glow of the outside lights are first visible in the fog that's now set in over the property, Rapsody says in a quiet voice, "I think I'm going to sleep in my room tonight."

I swallow down my disappointment. Her words hurt more than the blows my father used to inflict on me when I was growing up. "Of course."

When we reach her bedroom, she doesn't say anything to me before entering and closing the door.

She's as good as gone. I should have expected it, I suppose.

Everyone I love always leaves me. First my mother, then Asher when he skipped off to boarding school and left us to deal with our father, and now Rapsody—twice.

# 32



I barely slept at all after Kol's confessions last night. It's hard to reconcile the man I know Kol to be with the one he described last night. Sure, I've witnessed what he's like when he's bent on revenge—the man kidnapped me from my own wedding. But a killer? That's something else entirely.

Of course, isn't that exactly why I ran from him after my mother showed me article after article about his father?

I don't know what went down with his father, but from his reaction last night, that's not something he'll ever discuss. Unlike the other three people he killed.

The idea of carting around those men's bodies and dumping them in the middle of the Gulf makes me nauseous. What about their families? They'll always wonder what happened to their loved one.

But then I think of what Kol said happened and how if he hadn't acted, there's a good chance that maybe Asher or Anabelle might not be here today. Then the Voss family would be the ones mourning. I try to put myself in Kol's position and consider what I might do if I found myself in the same circumstance. Would I make myself a monster to protect someone I love?

I think I would.

I know for certain that if it came down to Kol or someone else, I would choose Kol and deal with the fallout from my actions after the fact. Given that, how can I possibly pass judgment on him?

Last night, I got the impression that Kol was set on pushing me away by telling me all the worst parts of himself. But I've seen the good parts of him as well. I know there's more beneath the surface, even if I'm the only one who gets to see it. I don't care.

I fully expected Kol to come see me at some point today, but he must be leaving it up to me to come to him when I'm ready. And I'm ready.

It's evening by the time I shower, dress, and put on some light makeup to head next door to his room. I knock, and when he doesn't answer, I poke my head in. "Kol?"

When I get no reply, I enter the room to make sure he's not in the bathroom showering or getting changed in the closet. He's nowhere to be found, though he's been here recently —his scent still lingers, along with the smell of alcohol. I suppose I'll wait for him to return. I don't want to leave this any longer than I already have. He needs to hear what I have to say.

A quick sweep of the place tells me he's been drinking—there's a bottle spilled over on the floor near his desk. I bend down to pick up the bottle and notice his phone is on the floor too. He must have been pretty drunk when he left his room then. I straighten and set both on his desk.

When I do, my name on a piece of paper catches my attention. Frowning, I set the bottle aside and pick up the sheet.

What the...

Utter shock ricochets through my body, loosening my grip, and the paper floats to the floor, landing in the puddle of whiskey near my feet. My breathing picks up and my chest constricts, then I hear my name in a rushed whisper.

I whirl around to see my mother dressed in one of the same uniforms the housekeepers wear, standing in the doorway. My throat closes in on itself.

"Rapsody, come on. We have to get out of here." She urges me with her hand, then looks over her shoulder. When I don't go to her, she gets a frustrated glare and rushes to me, grabbing my arm.

"What's happening?" I can't get my thoughts together after what I've just seen. After the secret I know Kol has been keeping from me.

*I can't breathe. I can't breathe.*

My mother leads me out of the bedroom, and I can't do or say anything. I can only concentrate on my breathing and try to squeeze any tiny amount of air into my lungs that I'm able. My chest is so tight, I fear a panic attack is coming.

When I stop and bend over, gasping for air, my mother reprimands me and drags me forward.

*No, no, no.* I want to scream, but I can't. I can't!

I need to get control of this, or I'll pass out and who knows what will happen then. I'm already tripping over my feet from the brute strength my mother pulls me along with, one I wasn't aware she possessed. She pulls me outside, and I trip, stumbling on the patio, going down and skinning my hands and knees.

"Jesus, get up. We don't have much time!" my mother snaps, yanking my arm to get me to stand.

I ignore her as best I can and concentrate on slowing my breathing. My chest loosens—just a bit, but I'll take it. I count in my head, matching my breathing to the numbers until I can breathe well enough to look at my mother.

Her attention flickers from me to the manor and back, eyes wide. "Get up. Let's go."

I yank my hand from her grip and stand on my own, the patches of destroyed skin stinging with my movements. "What are you doing here?"

"I'm here to take you home, away from this evil man. Surely by now you know who he really is."

"You're right. He did tell me." I glance around quickly. There's no one within sight.

"Then let's go." She reaches for my hand, but I step back from her, and her hand falls through the air. "What are you doing?"

"What are *you* doing? I'm not going any-where with you." I scowl.

She blinks rapidly, clearly surprised by my reaction. "After everything I've done for you your entire life? I've only ever tried to protect you." Tears prick her dark eyes.

She's laying it on thick and doing a good job of it, I have to admit. If I hadn't already seen what I did, I might even let her guilt me into leaving with her.

Instead, I fist my hands at my sides. "I already told you, I'm not going anywhere with you."

She frowns. "I thought it might come to this. This is for your own good, remember that." She brandishes a knife from somewhere in her uniform and holds it out in front of her.

Unlike when Kol was holding a knife in front of me, the sight of this one fills me with terror.

I don't even think, I just run. As fast as I can and to the first thing I see, which is the opening to the hedge maze, the most terrifying place on earth to Kol. But at this moment, it will be my refuge.

I need to get away from this woman—because from the papers in Kol's office, I know that the woman chasing me is not my mother.

# 33



*KOL*

*THREE HOURS EARLIER...*

I take another swig from the bottle and stare at the papers I removed from the safe in my room as a result of the phone call I just received. The same papers that have been plaguing me lately.

Maybe I'd have been better off to have left it alone rather than listening to my instincts when they kept telling me something was amiss.

It dawned on me that for Rapsody's mom to disappear so quickly after she confronted her daughter about our engagement, she had to have already been somewhat prepared to leave at the drop of a hat. Why? What average citizen has the resources and the ability to change their identity unless they thought they might need to at some point? You don't get fake IDs that will pass inspection at your local corner store.

That, coupled with her mom's story of having no pictures of her pregnancy and the first eighteen months of Rapsody's life, didn't sit right with me. How does a woman like Rapsody's mother—one who is so hyper focused on her daughter's life and so controlling—not have photos of her daughter as an infant? Even if she was sexually assaulted, and it resulted in a pregnancy, how did she swing so far from one extreme—not wanting any pictures at all of the child and not connecting with the baby—to the other, becoming overbearing, heaping on the guilt to control her daughter?

Something felt off. I always trusted my instincts when I was in the military, and I wasn't about to ignore them now.

So after Rapsody's accident when I patched up her forehead in my bathroom, I took some of her blood from the cloth and had it tested. My private investigator who located Rapsody and her mother in the first place followed her mom around for a few days until he could get a sample to test against Rapsody's.

And then the results came back, proving that the woman I love is not the biological daughter of the woman who raised her. And I've been struggling with what to do about that since.

But there's no way I can keep the truth from Rapsody anymore. After last night, it might be the final nail in the proverbial coffin for us, but she deserves the truth. I was just afraid that if I told her, she'd take off in search of her birth parents, leaving me, which is a selfish fear.

I bring the bottle to my lips again, taking a hefty swig. I want to dull the edges of my emotions right now. Telling her is the right thing, but the idea of losing her is like a black festering pit in my chest.

She'll leave me now. Because I found her birth parents. And I know Rapsody—she's going to want to know them and the siblings she didn't know she had. And by confessing the truth last night, I made it even easier for her to walk away from me.

My phone rings beside the papers I'm still staring at, but I ignore it. I don't want to talk to anyone, unless it's Rapsody.

She's made no effort to come talk to me to-day. I swore to myself that I'd give her time to consider everything I said last night without pressuring her. She deserves that much at least.

The phone stops ringing, but seconds later, it rings again.

"What the fuck?" I grumble and pick it up without looking to see who it is. "What?" I bark into the phone.

"Sir, it's Darren, the head of security. There's been a breach."

I set the bottle of booze on my desk. "What do you mean there's been a breach?"

But I don't hear his next words. There's a prick in my neck, then everything goes black.

When I come to, it takes me a few minutes to become aware of my surroundings and the fact that I'm in a chair and can't move. I'm still groggy when I open my eyes. Whoever has me obviously dosed me with something to knock me out and I'm still under its effects because I can barely keep my eyes open.

My head lolls to the side as I drift off, and a set of shoes comes into view in front of me. I force myself to open my eyes and see who it is.

There are two of them. The men look like they could be twins, but one isn't as big as the other, so maybe they're brothers. Either way, they're definitely related. I commit each face to memory because these motherfuckers will pay. If not today, one day soon.

They're wearing the same groundskeeper outfits, which gives me some clue as to how they got onto the property, but not who these fuckers are.

My head lolls forward again, whatever drug they gave me is probably mixing with the alcohol I already had in my system.

"Why isn't he waking up? He should be awake already," one of the guys says.

"I dunno. Get the camera set up. We need to get this going and then split," the other says.

Then I'm out again. I'm not sure how much time passes, but I'm awoken by a stinging slap across the face.

I grit my teeth, feeling a little less groggy now. When I raise my head, there's a phone set up on a tripod in the corner of the room. What the fuck is this all about?

Another look around the room, and I know exactly where we are. We're still on Midnight Manor property in an old caretaker's shed. It used to store extra supplies when the crew had to do work far from the main house, back before special utility vehicles were used to move things around the grounds. It's probably sat empty for a decade or more at this point. Which means no one will come upon us by chance.

"Should we get started?" the guy with the slightly bigger nose says.

The other one grins, rubbing his hands together. "Let's."

"Are you going to tell me what Dumb and Dumber are doing on my property?" I say.

The one closest to me backhands me, and I spit out the blood filling my mouth. "You'd be wise to keep your fucking mouth shut unless we tell you to open it."

"Bet that's what his dad used to say to his mom before she got offed," the guy standing farther away says.

My jaw tics, and my hands fists at the mention of my mother.

"The more you piss us off, the more it's going to hurt until we decide to put you out of your misery." This asshole looks so smug. I can't wait until I get my hands on him.

The other one says, "Wonder if that sweet thing of his has a good mouth. I can imagine it wrapped around my dick. Maybe when we're done here, you and I should go track her down and find out, Louie."

*Louie* whips his head toward the camera. "You said my name, asshole."

These idiots clearly don't understand who they're fucking with. I was about to get myself out of here, but at the mention of Rapsody, I need to know what's going on. I have to figure out who's behind this and make sure there's not a threat against her even after I off these two pieces of shit.

"What do you want?" I ask, wanting to get on with this so I can track down Rapsody and make sure with my own eyes that she's safe.

"We were sent by a friend of yours to exact some justice. Seems you finally fucked with the wrong person," Louie says with a sadistic smile.

"Jessie Wallace," the other one says.

Fuck. The father of one of the men I killed in order to save Anabelle last year. This is about revenge.

"So you're that old fuck's errand boys? Figured he could afford someone better than you two idiots."

That comment earns me another punch across the jaw. This one makes Louie shake out his hand.

"You think we don't know how to make a man beg us to end his life? We're mafioso, it's what we do," Louie says in anger, giving me another piece of his identity.

"So why didn't you just end me back at the manor when you had the chance?"

The other guy scoffs. "Because we're being paid to make you suffer. And he wants to watch every minute of it. Seems it's about time to get started."

"I think you're right, brother," Louie says.

I try not to roll my eyes, not enjoying my face being their punching bag, but shit, these two are complete idiots. They've already given me enough information to figure out who they are, and they don't even realize it.

"Jessie sends his regards," Louie says and punches me on the other side of my face.

I temper my reaction as blood drips down onto my pants, and pretend to pass out.

"Shit, is he already out?" the other guy says.

"'Course he is. That's how strong my punches are."

Louie's breath hits my face, and I know he's leaning in to check whether I'm still breathing or not. I use the opportunity to headbutt him. He stumbles back, holding his head.

The first mistake these fuckers made was taking me in the first place. The second was tying my wrists to the chair with duct tape. All it takes is me yanking my arms toward my chest, and the tape splits apart.

It takes me two seconds to snap Louie's neck. He's barely made it to the floor before I'm lunging for his brother.

The only problem is that my ankles are still taped to the chair legs, so I twist my ankle as I move forward. Ignoring the pain, I go after the brother and bring him to the floor as he pulls a gun from his waistband.

The gun is wedged between us, and despite my adrenaline, the drugs they gave me are still affecting my actions. I don't have my usual strength, and we wrestle for the gun. I need to get it out from between us before one of us accidentally pulls the trigger, and it's just a crap shoot as to who's taking the bullet.

Adapt and overcome.

I might not have my usual strength, but I have years of military training to pull from. So I let him get the upper hand and roll me off of him so that he straddles me. As I expected, he adjusts the gun in his hand and points it at me, but before he can pull the trigger, I disarm him, the way I've done thousands of times during various training exercises.

I waste no time pulling the trigger on him and pushing him off of me. Next, I get my feet loose from the chair that's still attached, painfully twisting my right ankle because of the angle. Once that's done, I stumble over to the tripod and pull the phone off, ending the recording.

I know very few people's numbers by heart, but I know Sid's, so I call him, hoping he's somewhere at the manor.

"You finally coming up for air from between Rapsody's legs?" He laughs.

"Obsidian, I need your help."

"What is it?" His mood changes from humor to determined.

"I'm in the old caretaker's shed, and my leg is fucked up. I need you to grab one of the vehicles and pick me up."

"What the hell is going on?" I can hear him moving, probably running through the manor.

"I'll explain when you get here. I'm going to start back toward the house, but it will take me too long to walk on this ankle. I need you to get Asher or Nero to check on Rapsody and make sure she's okay. Tell them not to let her out of their sight. She could be in danger."

"Fuck. I'm on it." He hangs up without another word.

I trek back toward the manor, hobbling along, desperate to get back to Rapsody and make sure she's okay. I don't like that those guys mentioned her. There has to be a reason. Rapsody and I haven't left the property together in weeks. Have they been surveilling me that long, or do they have someone on the inside?

My ankle screams to stop, but I push the pain out of my mind the same way I had to on missions when things went wrong. There will be time to deal with my injury, but not until I have my hands on Rapsody.

The sound of an engine meets my ears before I spot one of the utility vehicles headed straight for me. Sid pulls to a stop in front of me while I slide in beside him.

He gives me the once-over before punching the gas again. "What the fuck happened to you? You look like you've been worked over."

I fill him in on what went down in the shed.

He shakes his head. "Jessie Wallace is a dead man."

I agree, but I ignore his comment for now. "Did anyone find Rapsody?"

His knuckles go white on the steering wheel, and that's answer enough for me. "She wasn't in her room. Everyone is searching. I told Nero to get with security and see what they can find out."

"Drive faster." I slam my hand on the small dash in front of me.

"I'm driving as fast as this fucking thing goes."

"Faster!"

Sid looks at me as though I'm losing it but doesn't say anything else.

It takes longer than I'd like to reach the manor, but when we do, Sid's phone rings.

"Yeah?" he answers. "Who was the woman?"

"What? Tell me!" I practically roar, desperate for any information.

"Nero says security footage caught Rapsody running into the maze away from another woman."

My stomach plummets. "What did the woman look like?"

He asks the question and waits for the answer, then looks at me as he relays the information. "Dark-brown curly hair, older."

"Her mother." I slam my hand on the dash. "Get over to the maze now."

That's how those fuckers in the shed knew about her. The three of them must be working together. But how?

Sid ends the call and hits the gas. I have to hang on so I don't fly out of the vehicle.

"I can go in if you want. You know, if you don't want to," he says. "I'll gladly take care of whoever's threatening your woman."

Sid might look like a gentleman in his ten-thousand-dollar suit straight from a trip to Saville Row, but he's the epitome of a wolf in sheep's clothing.

"No one's going in but me. Too many people, and it might spook her. Just wait at the exit in case I send Rapsody out ahead of me. If I do, keep her safe. Do not take your eyes off her until I know if anyone else poses a threat."

He nods, but I see the way his eyes question whether I'll be able to do this since the maze is involved.

But there's no question. Because there's not a chance I'll let my dad take away the woman I love. And if I don't go in that maze and get her because of what he did, that's exactly what will happen.

# 34

*RAPSODY*

I rush through the maze, having no idea where I'm going. The sun is beginning to set and there are no lights here. I can see fine now, but I worry about a half hour from now. Will the woman I thought was my mother pop out of one of the hedges and attack me? Am I even running away from her or am I running closer?

In the midst of my crisis, I think of Kol being trapped in here as a young boy and not knowing how to escape in the middle of the night.

Tears stream down my face as I run, unsure of which direction to go. Eventually I reach a large courtyard. There's a flourishing red rose bush in the center and four concrete benches on each side of the square. This must be the middle of the maze.

I stop, listening for my mother, but I don't hear anything. Four gaps in the hedges lead out of here and back into the maze. If I pick the right one, maybe I can find my way back out of the maze and into the manor to find help.

I nibble my bottom lip, unsure which one to choose. But I don't have time to sit here waiting for my mother, or whoever that woman is, to show up. So I rush forward and pick the exit to my left, but just as I'm about to step over the threshold, my mother rounds the corner.

She still has the knife in her grip, and she lunges for me, grabbing my wrist. I yelp, now crying uncontrollably. I'm incapable of holding back my tears at the sight of this woman who raised me, knowing she's lied to me my entire life, and now seems poised to hurt me.

"Why are you running away from me?" She bends my wrist at an unnatural angle, and I cry out in pain, dropping to the ground to prevent it from snapping.

"Why are you doing this?" Sobs heave out of me. She finally drops my arm, and I cradle it to my chest, crying into the ground.

"I'm saving you from yourself. I've already had to save you from this evil man once."

"He's not evil! You're the one who's evil!" I look up at her with tear-stained cheeks. "You're the one who's lied to me my entire life. You're not even my real mother!"

She moves so fast that it doesn't register that she's hit me across the face for a few seconds until the stinging sensation settles in my flesh.

"You ungrateful brat! After everything I've done for you, everything I protected you from your whole life, this is how you repay me?"

"So it's true? You're not my mother?"

Her dark eyes widen then narrow on me, growing cold. "Did your liar of a boyfriend tell you that?"

How ironic that the man she's calling a liar is the same person who bared all his sins to me, showing me exactly who he is. And the woman accusing him of being a liar has been pretending to be a good person her entire life, but she's anything but.

"Is it true?" I don't know why this matters so much right now, but it does. I need to know. I need to know if the woman I trusted, lived under the same roof with, always believed had my best interests at heart, is not who I thought she was.

"In all the ways that matter, I am your mother."

My face crumples, and more tears come. "What does that mean? What happened to my real parents? Was I adopted?"

I feel like a baby bird in a nest with its mouth open, looking to its mother for sustenance. Give me what I need. Tell me that I'm adopted.

Her face morphs from anger to pity, and she nods. "I never wanted you to find out. To me, you were just my daughter."

My tears dry up. "What about everything you said about being assaulted?"

She frowns. "I'm not proud of it, but I wanted to give you some of the truth. That's your biological mother's story. She tried to raise you, which is why I don't have any pictures of you as a baby. She found it too hard. It was too much of a reminder to her of what had happened."

I guess that makes sense. Looking up at her from below, she looks so much like the mother I knew growing up. The one who loved and nurtured me and protected me at all costs.

"I knew as soon as I saw you that I could love you like you deserved to be loved. That you were meant to be mine."

"You could have told me," I whisper.

"That was my mistake. All I ever wanted was to protect you." She bends at the waist and cups my cheek with her free hand. "Now why don't we get out of here? You may not see it now, but this place will destroy you, Rapsody. That man will destroy you."

I lean away from her touch. "Kol would never hurt me." I know those words to be true. He may be a dangerous man, but I have nothing to fear from him.

"He will. He already has. You think I don't know that he stole you from your own wedding?"

I look away from her.

"A man like him is used to getting what he wants. How do you think I knew where to find you? I knew he'd never rest until he'd taken what he thought was his. He was the only explanation as to why you disappeared the day of your wedding."

At her words, something dawns on me. I frown. "Mother, why didn't you call the police when I went missing that day?"

She opens her mouth, then closes it before she speaks. "Because I knew it had to be him. You had no money, you wouldn't have been able to survive. With all the money and influence this family has, involving the police would have no effect. All they have to do is to pay off the right people to make it all go away. I figured it was better to find you myself so that they wouldn't know what I was up to and couldn't be tipped off when I was close to getting you back."

That makes sense, I guess... sort of.

"She didn't call the police because she was worried she'd be identified as the woman who kidnapped a child two decades ago."

I whip my head around at the sound of Kol's voice. He's standing at one of the other entrances into the courtyard in blood-soaked clothes. His face looks like someone used it as target practice for their fists.

"Hello, Margaret," Kol says in a menacing voice.

I turn to look back at my mother. Who the hell is Margaret?

# 35

*KOL*

As soon as I step into the maze, it feels as though the walls are pressing in on me, hovering over me like a grim reaper with a scythe in hand. But I force myself to push on. Who knows what Rapsody's mother is capable of? Certainly more than I ever thought, given the information that came my way via phone call this morning.

Her mother kidnapped Rapsody from her parents when she was almost eighteen months old and has kept her in hiding all this time. As soon as I got the phone call confirming who Rapsody's birth parents are and I looked them up and saw that their child had been abducted by her nanny, all the dots connected.

The years of keeping Rapsody sequestered away from the world, why her mother was ready to leave at the drop of a hat, why she didn't call the police when Rapsody went missing. All of it was for selfish reasons, not because she loved Rapsody.

The darkness falling feels like an ominous cloud bearing down on me. I swear to God, if Rapsody is hurt, I will murder that bitch without a second thought.

I keep pushing myself to move forward despite the flashes of memory that assault my brain. The past attempts to derail me, but I refuse to let it. I am not a small boy any longer. I refuse to let my father win in this regard.

As I turn the corner, I come to a stop, seeing the warm glow of a floating light ahead. I suck in a breath. It's at the end of the section I'm in, and it takes a left, disappearing from view.

I rush after it, remembering what Rapsody told me about the lights she followed to find me on those nights when I needed her. It leads me up and down rows, and I feel as though I'm getting nowhere until I hear Rapsody crying. I move as fast as I can on this shitty ankle until I turn a corner, and the light is gone. But I see an opening to the courtyard, and I know that they're in there from how close their voices are.

"Thank you, Mom," I whisper into the night air, then make my way to the opening.

"Mother, why didn't you call the police when I went missing that day?" Rapsody asks her mother. She's on the ground, clutching her wrist, and one of her cheeks is bright red as though she's been smacked.

I grind my teeth together.

"Because I knew it had to be him and that involving the police would have no effect. With all the money and influence the Voss family has? All they have to do is to pay off the right people to make it all go away. I figured it was better to find you myself so that they wouldn't know what I was up to and couldn't be tipped off when I was close to getting you back." Such a good liar, that woman.

Enough of this bullshit. Time to bring the truth to light.

"She didn't call the police because she was worried she would be identified as the woman who kidnapped a child two decades ago," I say, stepping over the threshold and into the courtyard.

Rapsody's head whips around, and there's relief in her eyes when she sees me.

"Hello, Margaret," I say with venom.

Rapsody's attention returns to her mother, who scowls at me.

I limp a few steps closer to them. "Isn't that right? You worried that reporting Rapsody missing might set off a few red flags if anyone delved too hard into your past. What if her disappearance garnered international attention? The media and all the internet sleuths would have a field day breaking down every single detail of your lives."

When I take another step closer, Margaret yanks Rapsody up onto her knees by her hair. She brings the knife to Rapsody's neck. "Don't come any closer, or I swear to God I'll slice her!"

My hands fist at my side. Margaret is obviously panicked, eyes darting to find all the possible ways out of here. But there are none. At least not for her. I can't risk Rapsody, but this woman is leaving here either in a body bag or in handcuffs. The choice is hers.

"No, you won't. She means too much to you." I hope. I take a tentative step forward.

She points the knife at me, still gripping Rapsody's hair. "Stay back!"

"Let me go!" Rapsody flinches when Margaret tugs on her hair harder and brings the knife back to her neck. "You're telling me he's evil when really, you're the one who has been pretending to be someone else. You may look like a good person on the outside, but inside you're evil. Kol wears his skin inside out, showing the world all the damage and terrible things he's had to endure, but inside he's a good man. He cares deeply."

"I can barely listen to this nonsense," her mom says with a sneer.

I don't know how Rapsody will feel about me if she watches me kill her mother, but if things escalate any further, I'm going to use the goon's gun that's tucked into the back of my pants. I will not risk Rapsody's life to save this woman's.

"Did your boyfriend here tell you about how he killed Preston Wallace and his driver? How he's a murderer?" She spits the accusation at me, and it's clear from the gleam in her eye that she thinks she's gotten one over on me.

"Yes, yes, he did."

Margaret stills, eyes widening. Clearly, she wasn't expecting Rapsody to know.

"Why don't you let her go? We both know you don't want to hurt her," I say.

She gets a vile look on her face. "You've poisoned her against me. After everything, you turned her against me, and now it can never be the same. Never! I'll be alone, all alone while you two..."

I see her intent before Rapsody does. Margaret pulls the knife away from Rapsody's neck, and everything happens in slow motion. For a split second, Rapsody appears relieved, as though her mother is releasing her. But when Margaret adjusts her grip on the knife and yanks Rapsody's hair farther back, I see it register on Rapsody's face that the woman who raised her is about to stab her in the chest.

I slide my hand back to the metal of the gun and allow my instincts and training to kick in. I fire the gun, hitting Margaret in the upper chest as far away from Rapsody as possible. The bullet strikes, and Margaret screams, releasing Rapsody's hair and stumbling backward.

I rush to Rapsody. She's heaped over, crying on the ground. I ignore the searing pain in my ankle and collapse between her and her mother.

"Sweetheart, are you okay?" I pull her up by under her arms, and she winds herself around me, sobbing into my neck. My hands rub up and down her back, trying to give her comfort, but knowing it's not enough. "It's okay. You're okay now."

After a minute or two, she pulls back enough to look me in the eyes. "I was so scared."

God, the devastation in her eyes kills me.

"I know. You're okay now, though. No one is going to hurt you."

She starts to give me a hesitant smile, then her eyes widen and a look of horror transforms her face.

It takes a moment for the pain in my lower back to register, and when it does, I blink and collapse to the side.

Rapsody screams, then there are sounds of a struggle. I try to get up, but I can't. Then more shouting, and Sid is hovering over me along with Rapsody, tears streaming down her face.

Though I try to keep looking at her, my eyes drift closed and darkness consumes me.

# 36



I lie in Kol's bed, clutching his hand and waiting for him to wake up. It's mid-morning the day after my mother...er, the woman who claimed she was my mother broke onto the property.

I've only left his side for ten minutes since he was brought here and that was only to shower because I was covered in blood.

The panic I felt when I realized Kol had been stabbed will stay with me until the day I die. The doctor who was called to the property insists that nothing vital was hit, but I still can't force myself to leave his side.

When the doctor was here earlier to check on Kol, I finally relented and let him check my wrist, which he determined had been badly sprained. He wrapped it up.

When Kol's hand twitches in mine, I sit up and look down at him. His eyes flutter open slowly, and it takes him a moment to focus.

"Kol, are you okay? How do you feel?" The words rush from my mouth.

He blinks several times. His shoulders lose some of the tension that was there moments ago. "You're okay."

"I'm fine. Don't worry about me. How do you feel? I should get the doctor." I start to shift away, but he grips my hand harder.

"No doctor."

"Asher said you'd say that. That's why he insisted you be allowed to recuperate here rather than at the hospital."

He gives me a wan smile and tries to shift his body, but winces.

"Your ankle is wrapped up because you have a bad sprain, and you have stitches for the stab wound in your lower back. The cuts on your face just had to be cleaned." I run my hand lightly over his head.

"What happened after I passed out?"

I suck in a breath. I knew I'd have to tell him at some point, but I thought it could wait. I don't even know why I'm so nervous. "Let's not worry about that right now."

Kol narrows his eyes and bares his teeth at me. "I need to make sure you're safe. If you think that—"

"Relax, I don't want you getting agitated. Obviously, you're feeling like yourself." I swallow and continue. "I stabbed my mother —I mean, I stabbed her in the chest, and she bled out."

How long will it take my mind to wrap around the fact that the woman was not my mother?

"Fuck." He reaches for me, trying to disguise the pain it causes him. I take his hand and set it back down. "I'm so sorry you had to do that."

I meet his gaze and hold it, wanting him to understand what I'm saying. "I'd do anything to protect the people I love. Just like you."

"But with my training I should have made sure she was dead and taken the knife. I was so scared, I had to get to you, hold you and know that you were okay. All my training didn't even register. I'm sorry, sweetheart."

"You don't have to be sorry about anything. We're safe now."

He's quiet for a moment while tears build in his eyes, then he nods at me. I think if he tried to speak right now, he might start crying and that wouldn't go with the tough guy image he likes to project to the world. But he understands what I'm telling him—that I don't hold what he did in the past against him.

There's a soft knock on the door, and a few seconds later, Asher steps through. "You've rejoined the land of the living. Good." He steps up to the side of the bed, and I think the expression on his face is relief.

"Sorry to disappoint," Kol says, trying to muster a smirk.

I get the impression that this is their default as far as communication goes.

"Rapsody was just filling me in on what happened after I passed out." Kol looks at me with concern.

"I haven't gotten a chance to tell him all of it yet. Well, what I know," I say to Asher.

Kol frowns. "What am I missing?"

"Sid showed up and called the hospital, who sent the air ambulance to pick you up. Then he called Anabelle to find us so she could lead us the fastest way out of the maze. Thank God she knows it so well. Asher was the one who insisted on bringing you home to recover, against doctor's orders."

Asher shrugs. "Figured it was what you'd want."

"Thanks. Any lead on the two goons who drugged me?" Kol asks.

Asher's mouth draws into a straight line, and he glances at me for a beat, almost judging whether he can say what he wants in front of me. "They were Marcello Costa's men from the northwest. I've been in contact. He assures me that they went rogue and were not working on behalf of the Costa family."

Kol seems to mull it over for a moment. "You believe him?"

Asher nods. "Yeah. He was pissed when I told him. Told us to chop the bodies up into bits and feed them to the fish."

"What'd you do?"

"Just that." Asher smirks.

I feel the color drain from my face, and Kol must notice it because he changes the subject. "What about Rapsody's... what about the woman?" He squeezes my hand.

"We called the police for that one. Seemed easier since you were going to the hospital."

I stiffen. I didn't realize that—didn't think about it, if I'm honest. I've only been concerned that Kol will be okay.

"Will Kol or I be in trouble because of what happened?" I nibble on my bottom lip.

"It's fine. Asher will take care of it." Kol squeezes my hand again.

Asher confirms by nodding. "Already did."

I guess when you have as much money and influence as them, it's that easy.

"You figure out how they made it onto the property yet?" Kol asks.

"While I was dealing with the cops, Sid and Nero figured it out. They came in on the weekly food delivery truck. The bodies of the two drivers were found ten miles away, tossed into the woods at the side of the road. The police have no leads on them, but security shows Marcello's goons driving the truck through security. Rapsody's mom must have been hiding in the back."

"She's not my mother." The words fall from my lips without me thinking about them.

"Of course. Apologies," Asher says.

"They must've been watching the house for

some time if they knew the weekly food delivery schedule."

"Agreed." Asher's voice is ice cold.

"Unfortunate that the families of the two drivers will never know how or why they died."

"Again, agreed." For some reason, Asher seems to grow uncomfortable. He shifts where he stands and shoves his hands in his pockets.

"What is it?" Kol asks, obviously able to read his brother.

Asher clears his throat. "It occurred to me when I thought we might lose you that I never had the chance to say something to you that's long overdue."

I look between them. "Maybe I should give you guys some privacy." I begin to get up from the bed, but Kol snatches my hand, cringing in pain from the fast movement.

"Whatever Asher wants to say, he can say in front of you. I don't want you out of my sight."

I look at Asher, and he nods, so I settle back down on the mattress.

"I'm sorry," Asher says.

Kol arches an eyebrow. "For?"

"I should never have enrolled in boarding school and left you to take the brunt of Dad's abuse."

It feels as if all the air is sucked out of the room. I look at Kol, who's looking up at his big brother with amber eyes full of an emotion I can't quite place.

"I understood why you did it, Ash. You don't need to apologize."

"I do." Asher swallows hard. "It was my job to protect you all, and I bailed on it."

Kol frowns. "You always thought it was, but it wasn't."

Asher pushes a hand through his perfectly coiffed hair. "At any rate, you should know that if I could do it over, I would."

"I appreciate that," Kol says.

"I'll let you rest. The doctor said you need it. He'll be back tonight to change your dressing." Then Asher turns to me. "If you get sick of this one's bedside manner, Anabelle has been asking about you."

"Okay. I'll be sure to touch base with her later today." There's a warm feeling in my chest that for the first time in my life, I have a friend who's concerned for me. Once Asher has left, I lie down next to Kol again, taking his hand. "Do you want anything to eat, drink?"

"I just want you."

Turning my head, I kiss his shoulder. "You came after me into the maze."

He stiffens for a moment before he relaxes. "I wasn't about to let her take you away from me. I'd face all my worst nightmares to prevent that from happening."

"Still... I know that wasn't easy for you." Tears well in my eyes, but I suck them back. The skin on my cheeks feels raw from all the crying I've been doing in the past twenty-four hours.

"It was easy when I considered the alternative." He squeezes my hand. "How are you? Are you okay after what happened with Margaret?"

"I will be. I'm still trying to wrap my head around the fact that she's not my real mother. I wish I hadn't had to do what I did." I squeeze my eyes shut as the image of me plunging the knife into her chest resurfaces. "I would do it again though to save you. I know now why you did what you did for your brother and Anabelle. I'm sorry I doubted you." A tear slips free, and I swipe it away.

"Look at me," Kol says.

I let go of his hand and turn onto my side, resting on my elbow so I can look down at him.

"I would have questioned your sanity if you hadn't doubted me at all."

A small smile tilts my lips. "How did you find my biological parents?" It's something I've been wondering about while I was lying here with Kol, waiting for him to wake up and going over everything in my mind.

He blows out a breath. "When I couldn't find any adoption records for you, I figured that you were either bought on the black market or kidnapped when you were a baby. I had a hunch, and I was right. If my child was stolen, the first thing I'd do is upload my DNA into one of those public genealogy databases so that if my child or their descendants ever uploaded theirs, I'd know about it. After you were hurt during that thunderstorm, I sent your blood in to be tested. I paid the company handsomely to keep the results from being public, but I wanted to see if anyone matching your DNA would be a close enough relation to track down your parents. Turns out they were both in the database. I'm sorry I didn't tell you about Margaret right away. It was selfish. I thought you might leave me to go find your real family."

I lightly place my hand on his chest. "You are my family, Kol."

His amber eyes glisten as he looks at me. "And you're mine. I'm never going to be separated from you again, sweetheart. I'm sorry it took so long for me to get my head out of my ass, but I promise that if you'll let me, I'll work the rest of our lives to make you happier than you were the day before. You're everything to me."

"I love you, Kol Voss."

"I love you more, sweetheart. Believe me. You can't even fathom how much."

Careful not to put any weight on his chest, I lean in and kiss him. Just a chaste kiss, but it's the seal of our promise to each other.

"I'm so glad all of this is behind us," I say when I pull away.

He frowns. "There's one loose end to tie up, but I'll take care of it in time." Before I can ask what he means, he asks me another question. "Do you want to know about your birth parents?"

I shake my head. "Not yet. I'm still trying to sort out how I feel about everything. But I think I'll eventually want to meet them."

He nods.

"Will you come with me if I do?"

He smiles at me. "Is that even a question? I'm going to be worse than Nero."

My forehead wrinkles. "What does that mean?"

Kol shakes his head. "Never mind, just get back here and kiss me again."

So I do.

# EPILOGUE

*KOL*

*FOUR MONTHS LATER...*

Jessie Wallace died on a Monday morning on the golf course. It was reported as a heart attack, but what the autopsy didn't show was the untraceable poison that somehow made it into his drink courtesy of the cart girl, a member of the Costa crime family.

I told Marcello Costa we're even now.

We're still not one hundred percent sure how Margaret got hooked up with Marcello's goons, but the best guess is that she too was surveilling the manor, and they stumbled upon each other, and she had something to offer them. Information maybe, or possibly just getting Rapsody out of the way so she wasn't a problem when they took me. We'll never really know.

There was no chance I was going to let Jessie keep breathing when he still posed a threat to Rapsody. She's been finding it hard enough to get over everything Margaret did to her and lied to her about.

A couple of months ago, Rapsody decided that she wanted to reach out to her birth parents. They were skeptical at first, since more than twenty years had passed since she'd gone missing, but we told them that Rapsody had decided to do a genealogy report, and I sent them the findings.

The story we went with was that Rapsody confronted Margaret, and she stabbed herself in the chest.

Rapsody and her birth family talked over the phone at first, and a month later when Rapsody was ready, we took the private plane to Ohio where they live. Turns out Rapsody is the big sister to another sister and brother. They're an extra bonus to having her parents that she's thrilled about.

We even flew in again last week right before Christmas so that she could drop off some gifts to all the family members.

Things are still a little awkward between them, but that's to be expected. I'm sure in time it will get easier. We have plans to go visit again in the new year.

But tonight, it's New Year's Eve, and I have something special planned. Something I've been forcing myself to put off since I woke up with that stab wound and Rapsody lying beside me.

The only reason I put it off was because I didn't think she was ready. I knew she was still processing all the shit that went down. It wasn't the time to ask her to be my wife—again. But I've waited long enough, and tonight is the night. I refuse to start the year without solidifying our union.

Originally, I was going to plan some elaborate setup, but decided against it. That's not who she is. She enjoys adding people and experiences to her life. So I figured why not give her something else to love as part of the proposal?

I step into one of the many living spaces in the communal part of the house to find Marcel where I left him with the newest member of our household.

"He peed on the rug," Marcel says as he sees me approach.

"I'm sure it won't be the last time."

"It's the Pearl Carpet of Baroda, sir."

I shrug and bend to pick up the yellow Labrador puppy sniffing around the area rug. "Come here, big guy." I hold him out to Marcel. "Here, hold him so I can put his collar on."

Marcel takes the dog, albeit with a pained look on his face. I pull the collar from my pocket and slide the giant pear-shaped engagement ring onto the leash ring at the front, then I secure it around the puppy's neck.

"Perfect. I'll take it from here." I pull the puppy from his arms.

"Thank God," Marcel mumbles.

"Better get used to him. You'll be seeing a lot more of him." Laughing at Marcel's expense, I turn and make my way back to the conservatory.

Rapsody wanted to get some painting in before the festivities tonight. She's been doing more and more painting and experimenting with erotic art regularly now. I haven't told her, but I reached out to an art dealer in New York with some pictures of her paintings and they're interested in seeing more and talking to her.

The puppy wiggles in my arms as I make my way through the manor, whining to get down, but I keep a firm grip on him.

We finally reach the conservatory, and I poke my head around the doorframe. "Mind if we join you?"

Rapsody looks over her shoulder at me with a smile. "Of course. But who's we?" I step fully into the doorway, and she gasps, her paintbrush falling to the floor. "Oh my god, who is this?"

She crouches down, and I set the dog on the floor. He races over to her.

Smart dog.

"This is your new dog. Happy new year."

She looks from me to the puppy, clearly at a loss for words. When he leaps up on her to lick her face, she giggles, and it's the best fucking sound in the world.

"What's his name?" she asks between licks.

"Why don't you see for yourself? It's written on the gold bone on his collar."

She looks at the name tag. "Max. What a perfect name for a perfect boy."

The moment she sees the ring, she stills and looks up at me with wide eyes. I step over to them and take her hand, helping her stand. Then I bend to pick up the dog.

"Hold him while I get this?"

She takes him in her arms while I work the ring off the collar. All the while, she watches my every move with glistening emerald eyes.

Then I get down on bended knee. "Rapsody, this may not have started in the best way, but what it's grown into certainly is the best. I want to show you the world. I want to give you all the experiences you can handle, and I want to prove to you every day that we're meant to be together. I never thought much about love until you came along. And I'm thankful every day that I'm a jealous, prideful, angry man, because if I wasn't, you might be married to the wrong man right now. I love you more than I ever thought I could love anybody, and somehow, you've found it in yourself to love me too, flaws and all. Will you do me the privilege of becoming my wife and my partner for the remainder of our days?"

Big fat tears roll down her cheeks, and she nods. Vigorously. "Yes, yes, I'll be your wife. Yes!" She shifts the puppy to hold him with one hand and holds out her left one to me.

I slide the oversized ring on her finger. I don't want any asshole to miss the fact that she's taken.

"Wow. Kol, this is… just wow."

I chuckle and stand. "I'm glad you like it. Now give your fiancé a kiss."

She leans forward and places her lips to mine, kissing me briefly while Max wiggles between us.

"I promise I'll show up to our wedding day this time." She laughs.

I scowl at her. "That's not even funny."

I lean in again to kiss her, and this time Max stretches his head up and his slobbery tongue joins in.

"What the hell? You'd better not be a little cockblocker, Max." I wipe my mouth with the back of my hand while Rapsody laughs hysterically.

Why do I get the sense that this is going to be a theme in our lives now?

As long as Rapsody is mine, everything is right in the world. At least in my world.

~

LATER THAT NIGHT, we head to the dining room to enjoy a New Year's Eve feast with my brothers and Anabelle, Max in tow. I'm already regretting getting Max because he *is* going to be a little cockblocker.

But I don't mind—much—since Rapsody's face lights up whenever she sees him. I've never once in my life wanted to have, or even thought about having, kids, but now I find myself thinking about them and what Rapsody would be like as a mother.

"Oh my god, who is this?" Anabelle springs from her seat at the table and rushes over to us.

"This is Max. Isn't he the cutest? Kol gave him to me today." Rapsody looks up at me, and I swear there are fucking hearts in her eyes.

I'm getting laid so good tonight. That is, if that little ball of fur in her arms lets me.

I scowl at him because I know he won't. Rapsody sets him down.

"Wait." Anabelle yanks Rapsody's left hand forward. Her attention goes from the sizable diamond ring to Rapsody's face and over to me. "Are you guys engaged?"

Rapsody presses her lips together and nods, emerald eyes glistening.

"Oh my god, congratulations!" Anabelle wraps Rapsody in her arms.

Asher and Sid get up from the table, walking over to us.

"Congratulations." Asher sticks out his hand, and we shake. When our gazes connect, I see what he's not saying—that he's happy that after all the fucked-up shit we went through, I was able to find my piece of happiness.

"Another one bites the dust." Sid shakes his head. "Jesus." He pulls me in for a hug and claps me on the back.

"Don't knock it until you try it," I say to him.

He guffaws and clamps my shoulder. "Yeah, no thanks."

I look around the room while they give their congratulations to Rapsody and realize that Nero's not here.

"Where's Nero?" I ask.

Sid frowns. "No idea. He should be here already."

We shoot the shit, but when the staff brings the food in, we make our way to our seats around the table.

Max spends the first half of dinner running around and whining for food, which of course the women give him, until he finally conks out in the corner.

Our champagne glasses are in the air, and we're about to toast when Nero walks in.

"Finally! Where the hell have you been?" Asher asks.

"Sorry, I'm late. I, uh... had something that came up."

A blonde with big boobs, the bartender at Black Magic Bar, steps around him.

"Guys, this is Cinder," Nero says.

My eyes narrow on Nero, as do my other brothers', because she isn't just the bartender at the local dive bar. She's also the woman Nero's been stalking for the past six months.

But I'd bet my bank account she doesn't know that.

The End

~

Don't miss the next book in our Midnight Manor series, *Midnight Whispers*.

# Acknowledgments

We hope you enjoyed your time at Midnight Manor! If this was your first visit, welcome! And if you've already read Moonlit Thorns (Midnight Manor #1) then welcome back!

We'll be honest, Moonlit Thorns was so well received by readers (thank you!) that it piled on the pressure to do the same with Shattered Vows. But that's almost impossible to do because each brother has their own story to tell and they're not the same people. So whether Asher or Kol is your favorite, or maybe one of the other brothers, we hope that you still enjoyed the story and all the elements of the world that remained the same—the gothic vibes, the sex club, the anti-hero MMC, etc.

Poor Kol, we knew the whole time we were writing Moonlit Thorns why he was so abrasive and distant. His pride and his obsession with Rapsody were festering under his skin and this man would not rest until he found her. And because that had been his sole focus for so long, once he did, he was kind of like... what now? He hadn't thought that far ahead and hadn't realized how it would feel to be around her again.

When we were plotting this one out, we knew we wanted the when/where that he snatched her to be dramatic. Her wedding day to someone else fit perfectly because we LOVE a jealous hero and what a better way to bring out that side of Kol.

We have to give much thanks to everyone who helped bring this book to market...

A big shout to Regina Wamba for the gorgeous cover. Her work on the entire Midnight Manor series is breathtaking.

Thanks as always to Cassie at Joy editing for the line edits and for My Brother's Editor for the proofread. You both helped make this story what it is today.

The Valentine PR crew always keeps us in check and follows up to make sure we're hitting those deadlines. Not only do we need it, but we appreciate it!

A HUGE hug to every blogger, influencer and reader who read the first book in the series and was excited about this story. We weren't sure how Moonlit Thorns was going to be received but you all opened your arms as wide as possible to welcome it into your life. Thank you is too small a word, but it's all we've got. Word of mouth is so hard to come by in this marketplace and we appreciate everyone's hard work, efforts and enthusiasm to spread the word about this series! We see you and are so, so grateful! <3

And of course a massive thanks to YOU for taking your precious time to read our story and to escape into the world of Midnight Manor for a while.

Have you figured out what fairy tale we're tackling next in the series?

If you go back and look through Moonlit Thorns and Shattered Vows you'll see that the brothers refer to Nero as *Prince Charming* a few times. We were dropping hints all along! Midnight Whispers will be Nero and Cinder's book and it's a reimagining of the classic fairy tale, Cinderella.

There is SO much more to Nero than meets the eye, just you wait!

Until then!

xo,

Piper & Rayne

# ABOUT P. RAYNE

P. Rayne is the pseudonym for the darker side of the USA Today Bestselling Author duo, Piper Rayne. Under P. Rayne you'll find dark, forbidden and sexy romances.

# ALSO BY P. RAYNE

**Mafia Academy**

Vow of Revenge

Corrupting the Innocent

Corrupting the Mafia King's Sister

Craving My Rival

**Standalones**

Beautifully Scarred

**Midnight Manor**

Moonlit Thorns

Shattered Vows

Midnight Whispers